The Pyramid of Askia Burtune

Aminu Hamajoda

1

They say it takes a great event to silence an African market. When the rock splinted into two and the loose boulder thundered down the Tibesti Mountain with a fury and a rumble never heard before, people were very frightened. It was a rumble that shook every part of Barduvai that Friday. It was a market day, but even when the thunderous rumble stopped and the birds and the crickets resumed chirping, the citizens stood stupefied in silence as if they were suddenly reminded of a difficult test ahead.

They stood gazing at the mountain unable to return to their trades. Decades after that event, surviving old men who were asked about it shook their heads sighing. It was no use any way being inquisitive or asking too many questions in Barduvai those days without sounding foolish.

Asking someone where he came from was regarded as taboo in Barduvai and had caused many fights with strangers. If one was daringly insistent about knowing the origin of a person, a herder among the Barduvai citizens would have answered by saying,

`My friend the cattle egret say follow those bigger than you to the pasture and you will eat and grow fat'.

If it was a trader that was pestered with such a question, he would have said, `Worldly businesses are conducted with living people, isn't it so?', But mostly an elderly person might have said, `My son upon this wide expanse of God, a world widely spread, why should you ask me such a mean question?' He might have shaken his head walking away from you.

To one who was prone to imagination, it must have appeared to him as if the Tibesti Mountain beckoned people to come and when they came, cast a spell on them to stay. They must have arrived in groups and as individuals or so and must have found comfort under the imposing mountain. For instance at the foot of the mountain lived an ancient warrior called Damolishi, a graveyard guard. No one knew why he chose guarding a cemetery as an occupation or when he exactly came to Barduvai. His age as well was a mystery to the citizens. Some said he was ninety years old, but many others believed some years must be added to that figure.

He was a strong warrior, as tall as he was lanky. Having firm features, he walked with long gangling strides, his eyes looking straight and unflinching. With his bow and quiver strapped on his shoulders he appeared as if he was going to a war each day as he walked across the city of Barduvai to the graveyard at dusk. He didn't speak to citizens yet citizens had so many stories about him and his awesome exploits. He spent most of the day sitting on a rock that was shaped like the gizzard of a hen. Whenever he sat on the rock gazing on the rooftops of the city he appeared like a warrior mounted on a horse ready for a battle. Few people could ever recall seeing the rock without Damolishi mounted on it.

He rarely ventured into the city except on market days to buy foodstuff. On the last Fridays of every month, he also stood guard as citizens cleaned the cemetery, plugging holes dug by foxes and hyenas in graves. The main intention of the exercise was to make men achieve sobriety.

The Pyramid of Askia Burtune

Whenever they were repairing the graves, Hajji Buruji a bearded dervish sang the Horrifier, an old song written by a Zamfara reformer. He told people that the ultimate aim of life is the avoidance of the fire of Gehenna.

I have been shown a horror so mighty
I dread the lord my summoning creator
Whoever is blessed and ungrateful is lost
I thank thee oh terrifier owner of horror
Gatherer of mortals on a judgement field

Hearken to prepare for everyone he will expire
From Adam none of the rulers was spared
No single mortal can escape this sweep
Unsparing of friends and enemies alike
Everyone should dread this assembly of terrors

This bringer of men into the enriching world
Addicting them to pleasures for a while
Stalking them shortly and tearing them away
Taking them to addictive, engrossing settlements
Such involuntary sojourns to distant alien lands

Then illness would set in the body failing
Mother and father and acquaintances cry

One mortal isn't enough as it snatches away
Families, friends, even strangers gather
To witness a creature in dins and thunder

He secured the world for us to be engrossed
Admonishing us to revere him for life
As he has screened us from the nature of death
Our mortality blunted for his serene adoration
Dying a believer is auspicious, heretics go to hell

Find them in the world deep in indulgence
Quick in forsaking striving and preparation

It was a traditional expectation for people to cry while repairing the graves and listening to the song. Those who couldn't cry were regarded as the worldlings who have not achieved sobriety. As Friday was a market day in Barduvai, this gathering of mortals drew a large number of people, coming from neighbouring settlements and far places to buy salt and other goods. Those on transit purposely arrive Barduvai early to participate in this exercise of sobriety.

The commanding voice of Buruji rang across their heads, as they shed tears and plugged holes and repair damaged graves.

What is difficult in divorcing this world you cry!
Fear this world the transposer of happiness!
Fear day in day out the hastener of chastisement!

Fear the pang of death that arrive with battles
This noisy carrier of abundant pains

Strangulation and yanking of body veins
Tethering, tying and bottomless sighing
The exit of breathe with incessant grunts
Those whips, spears and heavenly snakes
This journey of souls to a serious lord!

Buruji appeared in Barduvai during the period of Al-Waliya when speculations reigned of who and who were saints. Every evening as the sun disappeared behind the Tibesti Mountain, he was seen dancing and whirling the rotary in front of a cave. This made people to suspect at first that he was living in the cave, but nobody ever asked him where he came from, as it was a taboo to do so in Barduvai then. This city of salt, cattle and scholars. This city that links the North and the South, the East and the West.

Buruji spent most of the time in the day singing his Horrifier in an emphatic voice over grain sellers, butchers, and milkmaids who chuckled at the images he used in the song. The traders especially who were used to his voice would say,

`Please don't hasten the day of judgement! Hajji Buruji singer of Gehenna'. They usually burst out laughing as he approached them. His permanent abode however was the Barduvai Central Mosque, where he cleaned the oil lamps daily and swept the mosque clean, lining up ablution jars for people to wash their limps.

It was here that quite often one can meet Hajji Buruji, but if you hadn't met him there you must have met him close to any event happening that day or at the Daula orchard washing his only gown. People claimed nobody planted the orchard, believing it predated the city. Whenever people wanted some fruits they walked in and plucked some few mangoes, bananas or guavas and generally ate to their satisfaction. It was forbidden to carry some fruits home. Doing so was considered as a sign of ingratitude and greed. Who wanted to be greedy in Barduvai those days?

Visitors coming to the city on market days or otherwise, also walked into the orchard to eat some fruits and refresh themselves before getting into the city to accomplish their businesses. Visitors must have often remembered the orchard for one other thing- the fresh water pond in its middle. One could hardly stop drinking it when one tastes its water for the first time. The water had a kind of taste that made strangers drink continuously using the small calabashes stationed at the bank of the pond. On such occasions, people of Barduvai stand aside laughing at the oblivious visitors whose thirst would be quenched, but who couldn't stop drinking from the pond.

The orchard was also the centre for many schools in the past and the recent history of Barduvai. It was said that, a certain Sheikh Marduka was the first person to use the orchard for the education of the Barduvai children. He was a renowned scholar who had fled from Timbuktu when its university was being purged of radical scholars. He was labelled a heretic by other scholars for writing a famous pamphlet to the king of Timbuktu, which later became a popular pamphlet known as *The Timbuktu Testimonial*.

In the pamphlet, he suggested the reversion to a method he called *Hime* to stop what he called the trap of history - the rise and fall of societies. The Hime method, he believed, was the best way of moving forward in a society. He denied ever inventing the method. The pamphlet was written concisely and economically even from the first sentences:

The eminent scholars said last Friday that teachers and judges were laxed in reviving the hearts of men to good conduct through religion. I beg to say that the decision reached by the eminent persons are not new and I'm sure the Askia gathered such an assembly perchance a new way could be found to arrest the present decay in the society. Throughout history, after reaffirmation of truth by prophets, philosophers and divines, the light of that truth gradually faded into two realms that are not synchronous. The realm of belief and the realm of social action. To solve this problem, it is wrong to concentrate on education, sermons and propaganda. The path of the heart is not sufficient, *unless the path of conduct is vigorously pursued and the path of conduct lies at the collective level, not at the individual level. If over the decades people have been taught and sermons have been propagated and yet society is degenerating, then I'm sure our eminent persons must have realised that a new way must be sought after. Igniting the desire to do well in the hearts of men through education and exhortation through lectures and sermons cannot solve our present decay. We need to understand that two realms now exist that are not synchronous in our existence. The realm of beliefs and dogmas and the realm of action and the products of those actions. People in misunderstanding religion wrongfully believe that the judgement of conduct should be left to posterity or the day of judgement. The scale is always closer to us than to posterity. Unfortunately such a problem cannot be solved at the individual level, it must be solved at the collective level. What were labelled as concern and discussions about the declining goodwill among men are mere lamentations and nothing else. The Hime method is a reversion back to the primordial mutual consultation and the urgent action on resolutions. `If mankind was one but later divided' then it is worthy to strive back to the original state. People are not ready for truth. All efforts should be geared towards solving existential problems to make condition suitable for the acceptance of truth or worship as it was preferred to be termed. Citizens must first get prepared for truth by repairing the way they exist and use their senses, especially the emphasis on the collective intelligence, `Mankind was one but later divided'. This is a lost faculty of the human race. Without repairing the way he exist collectively, man can't be ready for truth. The creation of a happy society is not the sole* *confine of religious practice. People must change the way they do things. In that way a greater part of the missing link between dogmatic precepts and the preoccupation of people in life may be restored....*

The pamphlet was banned after a meeting of scholars who regarded Marduka as craving after distinction, especially as he avoids arguments, which he said, is the weapon of the hypocrites. 'If our theme is truly the making of a happy society, then what is the need for argument if we bear that theme in mind in speech and action'?

The king, Sonni Alli, who hated scholars anyway, stripped him of his position and title on charges of 'invention' a term coined for him by surrogate scholars hostile to Marduka. When he realised his life was in danger he migrated to Barduvai where he heard Askia Ba'ashi had made some favourable comments on the pamphlet.

When he arrived in Barduvai, Askia Ba'ashi appointed him the *Son of Knowledge* and a personal spiritual guide. In Barduvai the Hime method started in earnest much to the chagrin of the conservative scholars. It was the beginning of the period of al-Waliya when every scholar wanted to be seen as a saint who was capable of many feats and a solver of any human problem. Daily people flocked to their reception huts presenting their problems in life ranging from love to cattle hustling, hoping for solutions. The scholars saw the Hime method with its emphasis on the collective intelligence as a usurpation of their privileges.

The method employs what Marduka called the kernel of existence; *that mankind was one and the scale was closer to us than to posterity.*

'Religion is a Standard', he told gatherings 'so the judgement has been passed!' If we are truthful then we know the judgement has been passed. We are dealing with standards!' Marduka smiled as he explained to gatherings.

'Conduct eloquently speaks more than sermons. Will you partake in what is said or what is done?' he asks the crowd, 'Do you suppose the average citizen can venture into setting his desires on anything except he sees the elite do so? It follows therefore that if society is corrupt, then the elite are to be blamed'.

If there was any problem perceived, it was reported to the palace, the Askia then summoned the representatives of the various occupations in the city. These groups decided on the thema to hold the Hime. If a thema is agreed upon then it was decided if the Hime was to be a general one or to be held by a specific group. The Hime sessions done by people sitting in a circle were immediately followed by actions.

Most scholars loathed the sessions especially as argument didn't formed part of the method. They had wanted to show how much learned they were by quoting books and traditions and since that was absent in Hime sessions, they hated the gathering. Sheikh Marduka had said the Hime was `the flasher of the hypocrites!'

In addition, he set up a school to teach youth at the orchard, where he said they could develop their minds and bodies at the same time. In his spare time he was reported to be an avid reader of Abu Sienna's books, practising medicine and helping people with free medical care. He was frank to them, telling them the combination of herbs he was using and making no promises regarding cure.

This was not to be impressive with many people, especially nomadic herders who supposed a man of his calibre should be able to communicate with djinns and cure people with amulets and invocations. Marduka wanted his son Lamiri to practice medicine, but as Lamiri underwent training under his father, he developed a different personality and failed to understand why his father was not charging any fee for the medicine he dispensed just like the other learned persons who were by then building some fortunes and privileges around them.

Marduka's house must have been in dire poverty. Even when gifts of rams were sent to the house by nomadic clan leaders or by the Askia, Marduka would give out all the meat in charity and retain only the offal, legs and the heads of the rams which he mostly ask Lamiri to roast outside the house.

While roasting the parts, Lamiri squinted his eyes from the irritating smoke and cursed and swore never to be like his father. Sometimes in anger, Lamiri when taking food to his father would sprinkle salt and more pepper wishing the 'old man would wheeze to death!'

One of the pioneer students of Sheikh Marduka was Tugga Bukele, then, a young energetic son of the leader of blacksmiths in Barduvai. Tugga was a diligent student who respected Sheikh's Marduka's ideas about life. Like his mentor, he was averse to hypocrisy and was greatly disappointed when he found the trait in Marduka's son, Lamiri, who he noticed was prone to cheating and taunting of other students while they were studying.

The Hime was practised in earnest in Barduvai. Specific group sessions and general sessions were held. It got so that visitors started calling Barduvai 'the naked city' where nothing is left hanging.

Lamiri succeeded his father as the son of knowledge of Barduvai, as Burtune succeeded his father Ba'ashi as the new Askia of Barduvai. Tugga grew to be a short and heavily built person who had a long moustache and looked like an ox. They called him 'master of metals' in the city because of his obsession with metal works. Unless he was in his workshop making hoes and ploughs, he was usually seen walking around picking pieces of metals and abandoned tins. He had promised that metals were never to be wasted in Barduvai.

His workshop was situated immediately after the

orchard on the way to the city from the East. A stranger might have supposed the workshop was the hut of a spy for the Askia or a shoer of birds. As one approached the workshop, the heavy slams of Tugga's sledgehammer could be heard amidst his grunts. Outside the workshop he display hoes, tins, trinkets and various household wares. Citizens passing by would shout, `Ahoy master of metals!' and he, mostly recognising their voices, answer them by calling their names.

He was best at fabricating missing parts and solving technical problems in the city. He was remembered most for the creation of an indigenous script to write the history of Barduvai. The late Askia Ba'ashi, who gave him the assignment in recognition of his inventiveness in the city, assigned the project to him. Also to his credit were the inventions of the sowing hoe and gravity method of irrigation, which he developed after experimenting at the orchard. He also made the plough lighter thereby increasing the performances of oxen in Barduvai.

To create the Kalfuuje Script, Tugga formed a circle of people interested in the history of Barduvai. Everyone was free to participate. A prospective member needed only to carve a wooden slate and a gourd of charcoal ink and a quill. He ardently observed the Hime method in the project. Sitting in circle, Habarana Choodal, the griot of Barduvai who memorised the oral history of the Hubaluba people, recited a stanza, which every member was obliged to memorise. Then they tried to write each word in the stanza individually.

Afterwards, the scripts and ideograms were collected and a consensus ideogram was agreed upon for each word. Members at first complained the process was tedious, but Tugga begged them to be patient until they finish writing their history. He told them the oral history of their people provided the most authentic oral corpus for starting the project. Later he said their activities would get more exciting as they create more scripts.

Many citizens joined the Kalfuuje circle and for some years the Hime method came to be associated with the Kalfuuje project because they had met more often as a group than any other. In addition, Tugga introduced the Kalfuuje scripts into the *Nafobe* School, which he took over after the death of Sheikh Marduka. This school grew popular in the city, especially as children were learning to farm as early as possible. Sheikh Marduka has said that children must be taught to develop both their minds and their bodies. 'Education for what?' was such central theme, which the children, despite their age were able to fashion.

2

The palace of the Askia was built by Durugu master mason of Barduvai who was reputed to have caught all the mud balls thrown to him by his numerous assistants.

He was in his prime when he built the palace. One Barduvai tradition says that crowd of people used to gather at the site marvelling at Durugu's display of dexterity in building as he caught the mud balls thrown to him by assistants while he was mounted on the tall wall.

The whole palace was plastered with clay mixed with groundnut husk that gave it a shiny appearance. Inside, the Askia's court was draped with beautifully tanned leather and floor cushions made of selected quills. Various drapes representing gifts from different kings adorned the inner chambers of the palace.

That fateful Friday, Burtune was inside his court reclining on a cushion and negotiating the price of a horse, which he wanted to buy from Danjanjo, a renowned buffalo hunter.

'How wide a stream can it jump?' Burtune asked the hunter.

Danjanjo said, 'my lord it is the famous horse that was reputed to have jumped over streams during the Sariam Wars. I'm sure you must have heard about it my lord. It was used during the war and it can jump across most small streams without any difficulty.'

Danjanjo knowing the Askia's obsession with collecting rare horses, demanded for forty bulls to make the most of the Askia's passion.

`Are you planning to open a ranch Danjanjo?'

`I swear my lord I also bought the horse from a nomad who was unwilling to part with it. It is because I know you value such horses that I brought it to you'

`The horse is not even fully tested and you are demanding for forty bulls. Didn't Barmaki say the stallion had difficulty jumping over a ditch near the orchard?'

`My lord, assess the weight of Barmaki. Not many horses can carry him and jump at once'

It was at that moment that the rumble at the mountain was heard in the palace. Barmaki, the palace guard rushed in and announced that something must have occurred at the mountain. Askia Burtune ordered him to prepare the horses.

It was a full court in session with judge Akilu and Lamiri the son of knowledge. Judge Akilu was some years older than Burtune. He was tall, slender and very alert. Most of his statements seemed to be weighed before being uttered. Most people found conversation with him to be difficult because he was liable to be cynical by picking holes in people's statements and he was not keen on accepting a dialogue just to banish silence. He combined the portfolios of the judge, the minister and the treasurer of Barduvai.

Askia Burtune couldn't bring himself to separate the portfolios despite persistent recommendation by Lamiri. Burtune found it difficult essentially because Akilu was the only survivor among those who had surrounded his father. Lamiri knew Burtune had never learned to construct themes like Ba'ashi did, and therefore had found sessions tedious, especially as Buruji was always present to scorn him. Yet he couldn't accept Lamiri's insistence to reduce the portfolios held by Akilu at his court. Although Lamiri was a close friend even before he succeeded his father, he was wary of Lamiri's strange views about life.

Many times Lamiri had confessed to him when they were young that he felt like tripping his father whenever he walked behind him to the mosque carrying a pot of burning incest on Fridays. He also knew that on market days, Lamiri stole bottles of medicines from his father's room and gave them to traders with whom he made secret deals to sell or while grazing cattle in the bush he sold them to unwary nomads who were keen to get portions for everything in life, from love affairs to cattle rearing.

It was the arranged marriage forced on him by his father that made Lamiri to part with Marduka finally. In their house he grew up with a girl called Kumbo. His father adopted her from a deceased kolanut trader called Ambosel who considered him as his spiritual guardian. When Ambosel died of a mysterious fever, the sheikh took pity on his family especially little Kumbo who had nowhere to go after Ladi her cousin married another man and left the city.

Kumbo attended the Nafobe School with Lamiri who

led a group of children in taunting her for her fatness. They called her `senior cassava' for her plumpness. Kumbo always felt bitter but she never reported to Sheikh Marduka. In the night, she cried and wondered who her parents were.

The day when Lamiri was summoned and informed by Marduka that he was going to tie a knot of marriage between them, that day Lamiri couldn't bear it any longer.

`Why should we continue to be simpletons in this city? Here we are fools then, always holding the wrong end of the stick!'

`Come here Lamiri', Marduka summoned him.

Lamiri came and squatted aside, he was in no mood for politeness. He knew one day such an outburst was inevitable. He felt his father had turned the family into a laughing stock. When other scholars were gathering people and building large compounds, Marduka could hardly boast a single person visiting him on a day except when the Askia called him to the palace for Hime sessions. Other scholars had visitors from Agades and Timbuktu, receiving them with feasts and crowds of followers.

`If you have sense enough, you should know that what people say is not to be the basis for your actions. Unless you set your sight on nothing else but to strengthen your service to your creator you cannot be called successful'.

`Sheikh I'm not going to marry that girl!'

With that statement, Lamiri walked out of his father's

house and was not seen until after three years. But Marduka went ahead and tied the knot of marriage as if with the full knowledge that wherever Lamiri went, he was to come back. Indeed he did returned one evening when it was just about to rain. The Eastern sky was pregnant with rain and a furious wind was blowing. Lamiri came in as if he was blown by the wind. He was lean and had grown a beard.

Sheikh Marduka didn't ask questions and Lamiri who returned with some books written in a strange language moved in with Kumbo. People began to notice that Lamiri became shameless and chuckled a lot when people were engaged in some activities. He told people he was an alchemist, a strange term to most people at that time. He also talked a lot about a distant land called Kudulantis.

He was cold to Kumbo but she didn't mind because she didn't know what marriage was or what other men were like. The first night she cried silently thinking it was not becoming of girl to cry. Lamiri who returned with some bottles and tubes mostly spent his time either gathering roots and leaves in the bush or reading his book and mixing herbs in his room. Lamiri re-established his old contacts and opened a new market for his medicine. He made an exihilir he called *sharaba* which became a popular tonic among citizens especially the nomadic herders some of who couldn't graze their cattle without carrying a bottle of the tonic with them.

Lamiri talked a lot about Kudulantis. Whatever citizens did, he told them it was done differently in Kudulantis. They listened to his strange stories amazed about the existence of such a land, its people and its traditions

So when Askia Ba'ashi and Sheikh Marduka were killed in a mysterious ambush on their way from a meeting with the King at Timbuktu, Burtune and Lamiri ascended the throne as the new Askia and the Son of knowledge respectively. Lamiri moved all his books to a room and locked them. He demolished the round hut used by his father as a reception room and in its place he built a clinic. Soon he started making more tonics that were popular among citizens. For a fee, he provided medicine to people for any problem they may have. The people of Barduvai soon started to call him 'Son of Sheikh detester of ascetics, a ram with a wolf-tail son of the venerable sheikh! Master of Kudulantic knowledge, the alchemist of one-thousand-minus-one medicine!'

Lamiri mostly smiled, saying, 'The divine has agreed, even the remaining one medicine is not beyond knowledge we assure you'. He also started a school to teach children the forty-eight alphabets of Kudulect, but few pupils attended as most parents had preferred to send their children to Tugga's Nafobe orchard school. Lamiri also introduced new plants he called laradish and catabeans, which were also not popular with citizens who purged after eating the plants. Only the wealthy salt trader Babbadajaka, grew the crops, which Lamiri promised, was to fetch huge fortunes from Kudulantis.

3

Barmaki walked in and announced the horses were ready. The court rose in a hurry, Burtune walked ahead followed by Lamiri and Akilu. As they rode through the market on their way to the mountain, people followed them behind talking excitedly. Almost the whole market trooped behind the royal entourage eager to see the rock that had fallen. As they approached, they saw the rock resting at the foot of the mountain. Damolishi was sitting on the gizzard rock but no one paid any attention to him.

When they reached the rock they saw the splinter surface was facing the East and looking up the mountain they saw the path the fallen rock created on its thunderous journey down the mountain. On the face of the splinter rock appeared a circular mosaic of patterns that were strange in the sense that they appeared differently to many people. The patterns inside the circle were like an intelligent inscription, a plan, a drawing, it was the ultimate teaser for configuration. The citizens stood watching in wonderment. The patterns were strange but attractive.

`Is there anything understood from this?' Burtune asked completely absorbed in the figure. There was silence as people looked at the figure. People were to confess later that they felt as if they were shortly about to decipher the figure while they were looking at it. Many afterwards swore they felt they knew the figure, but what it was and where they learned about it, none of them could say with certainty. They all stood sighing. As they stood watching the rock, Tugga Bukele, in his usual leather apron and holding his large sledgehammer, walked to the rock to have a closer look. At that Lamiri shouted at him, `You have started your meddling again!'

`Oh you Lamiri, isn't this supposed to be studied?'

`Is this writing or what?' Burtune asked again.

`Just a moment sir', Lamiri brought out a piece of leather and a bottle of ink and started to copy the figure. Members of the Kalfuuje circle also brought out their slates and started copying the figure. Burtune looked at Lamiri expecting some kind of explanation.

`My lord I hate to say in a haste but it looks like the graffiti of the magog'.

`What are they saying?'

`It behoves me not to translate the statement my lord' Lamiri said, `but according to historians, they start this kind of insults when they are ready to make an invasion'

People started to mummer, some even chuckling, Burtune asked what was been discussed. Habarana Choodal said, `My lord Tugga said there is no need trying to read meaning from the figure, the city should regard it as a divinely sent ideograms for the development of the Kalfuuje script. So said Tugga, master of metals my lord'

People broke in to laughter because Habarana Choodal, the griot had in recent months stopped going around villages on market days to chant the history of the Hubaluba people, preferring to spend most of time at the Askia's palace. People said he started to change after Askia Burtune bought a mule for him. A tall, fat and a cheerful griot, Habarana rarely got angry. He had strangely stopped carrying his Kora around and instead had fashioned out from a zebu cattle horn, a trumpet-like instrument.

This horn he usually hanged over his shoulders. People frequently got angry with him when the horn jabbed them whenever he mingled with a crowd. But those days he was seen more often at Lamiri's clinic in the afternoons or at the palace during meal times. It was rumoured Lamiri bought sandals for him after every three months.

Hajji Buruji arrived holding his staff. He looked at the figure intently for a while, then stomped his feet and started the rotary dance singing the Horrifier. People started to laugh, some saying, 'Hajji Buruji singer of Gehenna', but Buruji was not bothered as he sang;

The signs of ruination have arrived

Bewilderment has veered souls to the world
Corrupt leaders arise as wicked men
Wisdom and insight have become worldly bound
Idiots exceed the people of knowledge
These are the signs foretold before
Where is there a sanctuary for the worshipful one!
Where is there a sanctuary for those that know!

After singing for a while he started his usual scorn waving his staff wildly regardless of the royal presence, `If you do not understand your hapless journey, how then can you understand a simple anagram like this one, you heedless ones! Today you see it clearly, what has Burtune to say to this? A man who refused knowledge, full of desires and lacking in wisdom. You are lost to the wolves, oh people, perdition awaits you in the hands of the worldlings!'

Askia Burtune turned away in fury walking to his tethered horse, followed by the royal entourage. Akilu walked after them with a smile on his face, he knew how Lamiri and Burtune felt about the dervish who had no respect for the court in Barduvai. Buruji always insisted that a leader must be learned, to the extent preferably, being a spiritual leader. But if he couldn't be an Imam then at least he should be above average spiritually.

The dervish's resentment increased however when Burtune snubbed his suggestion that the Askia receive tutorials from him. That refusal Buruji regarded as a sign of arrogance, the stamp of sinners.

'My son your father had spent most of his time reading and learning to increase his knowledge. You need it if the Hime is to continue', Buruji told Burtune, who later confessed to Lamiri that whenever the bearded dervish appeared, his heart missed a beat, and Buruji never failed to appear in the court of Burtune daily to say a word or two, mostly when the court was full.

He kept coming irregularly to make it difficult for the court to prepare for his arrival. He came when not expected and left when he desired to. The court usually kept silent until he finished his barrage of sermons or scolding. During such moments, Burtune usually kept his head down and the others looked away until the bearded dervish left the court.

4

People returned to the market trying to figure out what the thema for this strange rock appearance shall be. Members of the Kalfuuje group couldn't understand why their copies differed. Each person seemed to have copied a different pattern, as if they have not copied from the same figure. Tugga called their attentions to the advantage of the differing patterns, 'Don't you see, this is a divine providence for the development of the Kalfuuje script!' The members brought out their slates and started to study the inner patterns of the rock figure. The Kalfuuje group had already developed up to eight hundred ideograms before the appearance of the rock figure and one hundred and fifty stanzas of the history of Barduvai and the people of Hubaluba were transcribed.

`This is what I call a permanent reference, my dear dedicated ones. Now we have a permanent reservoir of patterns for developing our scripts. Not only us but our children as well can depend on this permanent inscription for perfecting the Kalfuuje in the future'.

They saw Habarana coming on his mule, frequently adjusting his dangling zebu horn on his shoulders. Many citizens thought his mule was too small and short for his size.

`Come over Habarana, we just said we have a divine reservoir of patterns for our project on the fallen rock. We wonder what the thema could be today.'

`Hmm, hmm, hmm,' Habarana grunted, `my dear Tugga, you heard what the son of knowledge said about the rock being ominous, or so'

`What will happened?' Bango asked

`I'm not sure but the son of knowledge was telling our Askia to take the figure serious. He said according to Kudulantic knowledge such occurrences prophesy some ominous calamities'

`Calamities?'

`So he said, excuse me I will have to go'

`It is time for our meeting, where are you going?'

`My dear Tugga, I have an urgent message to deliver for the palace'

`Who will narrate for us if you are absent? You are the only one who has memorised our history.'

Members of the Kalfuuje group were worried about Habarana's declining interest in the Kalfuuje project and in chanting the history of Barduvai on market days. They noticed he preferred hanging around the palace of Burtune carrying out some duties for the Askia. Prominent members like Jari Daniro, Halabutu Jalo and Bango Toudo tried in vain to persuade him to change.

`Habarana you must know that you are a griot not a palace messenger or town crier. You have even stopped using the Kora. We feel...'

`Wait, wait Bango. Are you the one who appointed me a griot?'

`The responsibility is entrusted on you by your father as I suppose you would later on entrust on either your son or someone you train'

`Silly of you, inheritance... I say weren't your father a herder?'

`He was but...'

`But what? Why aren't you a herder now, or was Tugga's grandfather a blacksmith? What I want to say is that since none of you appointed me a griot and never knew if I was sustaining my family or not, Then leave me alone. If the Kora was a blessed instrument why didn't it buy me this?' Habarana asked riding his mule and spurring it. The group stood silent as they watch the huge torso of Habarana waddle on the trotting mule as it disappeared from their sight.

Later some members mooted the replacement of Habarana with Gaulojo the market poet, but other members pointed out that although Gaulojo was an ardent Kalfuuje Member, his oral poems are mostly praise songs and are therefore too narrow in scope for the project.

5

Burtune stormed into his palace slumping on his seat, and keeping quiet for a while.

`If it was the king of Timbuktu he would have the dervish beheaded' Lamiri uttered before taking a seat near the Askia. He wanted the Askia to brood for sometimes on the persistent embarrassment caused to him by Buruji.

`Stop this kind of comment Lamiri', Akilu interrupted, `it behoves you to remain silent if you don't have anything constructive to say. My lord let's proceed with forming a thema in preparation for a Hime on this incident.'

Lamiri turned to the Askia disregarding Akilu, `I feel soon my lord you will have find a way of putting a boundary between your honour and the expectations of this community'.

Burtune shook his head sighing, `I can't keep having this old man disgrace me before my subjects at will. I can't just do anything, without him scolding me. If all rulers are like the one in Barduvai....'

`Change the way you react to him my lord, he is like a father to us' Akilu said quickly, `He doesn't intend ill my lord. We grew up before him. Once you see him as a father, his utterances wouldn't sound like insults'.

`He hates me. That is the truth'.

`How can you say that my lord! Overlook his comments; he spares no one in the city in any case. He can't mean anything ill my lord. Even to your father he was not cordial. You know it"

During the rule of Askia Ba'ashi, Buruji had insisted that Ba'ashi memorise _Liya Al-Hukum_, a book about leadership obligations written by a renowned scholar from Gobir. Ba'ashi at first insisted on only reading the book but Buruji insisted that every useful piece of knowledge must be memorised. Ba'ashi had found Buruji's tutorials tedious at the beginning, especially as he had to accommodate the dervish's harshness with obedient smiles during lessons.

Although he thought the dervish was not a particularly talented teacher, he confessed to Sheikh Marduka that knowledge of the book helped him in Hime sessions.

Habarana arrived in the court and told the Askia about the intention of the Kalfuuje group to use the rock figure as the reservoir for inventing scripts.

'My lord do you think a Hime can decipher this phenomena?' Lamiri asked, 'I advise we contact the Seers of Bazahu instead of meddling with something beyond the comprehension of this city'.

Akilu began to realise the difficult relation that lies ahead of him and Burtune. The Askia and Lamiri he knew were no lovers of the Hime method. After the death of Askia Ba'ashi he had thought of retiring to his cassava farm, which he bought with his first salary. But he had felt at that time that it was akin to betraying the trust bestowed on him by Ba'ashi who had acted as a father to him and had always talked about his role after his death.

Tugga Bukele, Jari Daniro, and Bango Toudo, members of the Kalfuuje group came into the palace.

'Have you decided on the thema? I still see it as a blessed gift to us my lord to develop our Kalfuuje script. Please my lord assist this project, it is the best for us, to finish this Kalfuuje script'.

'I don't know much about that'

'My lord what time do we have for people who are trying to take us back to hieroglyphics', Lamiri said.

'Well I tell you Lamiri!' shouted Tugga, 'It is better than turning us into illiterates overnight. At this stage we don't need any foreign language to conduct our affairs. We must develop our language first my lord'.

Lamiri sought for an audience with Burtune inside the inner chamber. There he told him not to hold a Hime on the matter. 'This affair is becoming unhealthy for your leadership. Understand me, you will soon lose your throne. Your power is being decentralised. This Hime is no good for leadership; it strips you of your powers. Soon you will be a mere figurehead. I am sorry to say but your father was nothing more than a hermit!' Lamiri looked at the Askia's face to see if he had gone far by making such a remark.

'What I dislike most is this old man who always insist I begin school afresh. At my age how could I do that Lamiri? I'm really neck up with the vicissitudes of this old man.'

'Not only you, am I also searching my head to find out a way to spear the old fool! But our best bet is stopping the Hime'.

When they returned to the main chamber, they met Barmaki who announced that people had gathered outside waiting for a thema for the Hime. Burtune afraid to venture out in case Buruji was hanging around called Lamiri into the inner chamber

'Well what do I tell them?'

'Instruct Habarana to announce to the people that whenever an explanation is in hand, they would be informed.'

When Habarana made the announcement outside, people were amazed and began to talk about declining institutions as they dispersed. A rumour began to spread that Tugga said Burtune had reduced the citizens of

Barduvai to lepers. `This is the beginning of leprosy in our society', he was quoted as saying.

Habarana's new role as a palace announcer was curious to the people who couldn't understand how a griot could become the link voice between the community and the Askia.

Buruji as was to be expected stormed into the palace unexpectedly, `Burtune what has bewildered you? What has bewildered you I asked?' He came to a halt in front of the Askia. Burtune lowered his head. `This is exactly what I have been warning you about, increase your knowledge Burtune, don't be arrogant and lax, the burden of leadership is not a sack of luxury! Don't invite disaster on Barduvai!' Buruji stormed out of the palace his forehead glistening with sweat.

`Now this what I hate most', said Lamiri.

`His only licence is that he was my father's teacher', Burtune said with a sigh.

Akilu turned to Burtune, smiling encouragingly, `be glad you have someone blunt enough to tell you his perception. *The scale is nearer to us than to posterity. Remember the maxim, the scale is closer to us than to posterity.* They appreciate the kernel of existence more than we do my lord'

`I'm fed up with the torments of this old man. Can't he leave me alone? He should have followed his generation and passed away!'

There was silence in the court. Even Lamiri was not expecting such an outburst from the Askia. Akilu felt embarrassed, `that is not proper talking my lord. I again advise that the dervish means no personal slight. Stop seeing it as a personal hatred'

`I told you he hates me because I refuse his tutorials!' Burtune retorted angrily. Lamiri turned his face and smiled delightfully.

Realising the Askia was in no mood for counselling; Akilu took his leave and left the court. On his way out he met Babbadajaka coming into the palace.

Lamiri felt happy the Askia was finally neck up with the Hime method and the dervish. When Babbadajaka arrived, he proposed the building of a temple of contemplation near the fallen rock. `This is how it is done in other places. I suggest everyone should start playing his role as it is known in life. If I'm the son of knowledge of this city, then let me perform my duty. My lord build this temple so that I can spend my time figuring out what the incident is all about.

'I know it will be all over that I refuse to hold a Hime!' Burtune said uncertain of his new standpoint.

'My lord you are the Askia of Barduvai. Suggest everyone to stick to his role'.

6

When the Kalfuuje group left the palace in disappointment, they went to the fallen rock and were clearing its surroundings when they saw Habarana on his mule galloping towards them in a hurry. He stopped, dismounted his horse and unstrapped his zebu horn. It became clear to the members that he was going to make an important announcement:

`To tell you oh people
That a study of this strange phenomenon is already commissioned. So citizens are advised to keep calm until the results are out. Meanwhile Askia Burtune has ordered that no one should come close to the rock until the investigation is over. Those who depend on rumours do so at their own peril. So said Askia Burtune the son of Ba'ashi, the torso of an elephant'.

The zebu horn, in amplifying his baritone voice, made a menacing sound that leaves a tormenting presence in the minds of the listeners.

'Who will ever have believed that a griot will turn into a palace announcer?' Jari Daniro lamented.

'The most important question is who gave him the idea to use a zebu horn?' replied Tugga as they watched Habarana strapped back his zebu horn and rode his mule down to the market to repeat the announcement. The Kalfuuje group stopped clearing the shrubs surrounding the fallen rock. Bango watched the huge torso of Habarana on the mule as it trotted away and felt there was a treachery rearing its head out. He raised his cutlass pointing at the rock figure, 'This will be the source of our perdition in this city if we are not watchful'. As they walked towards the gizzard rock, the other members agreed with him.

'When it was announced there was to be no Hime, I knew ...my heart skipped a beat. It was unusual, because it is only premonition that makes my heart to do such' Jari said as they stood under the gizzard rock.

The Kalfuuje group stood under the gizzard rock lamenting the erosion of institutions in the city. They promised to hold a Hime the following day. As other members departed to the city, Tugga stood under the gizzard rock. He wanted to look up to Damolishi but changed his mind, as he was wont to do. He knew the old warrior posture was to be the same- a still figure gazing at the eastern horizon spread over the east of the city penetrated by spiralling smokes evaporating from the thatches of houses like the smoke coming out of the pipes of old men smoking under a canopy.

'Were you around when the rock rolled down the hill oldman? Well that is a stupid question to ask you. Well were you frightened? Eh old man were you frightened like the rest of the people?' Tugga chuckled still not turning to look at Damolishi who didn't utter a word.

'They said this figure is mysterious, enchanting, but it didn't appear so to me. How many similar patterns can one see in the wild? Sometimes old man I agree with... Do you know what the nomads call us sedentary folks? They call us 'grain eaters' and 'those who suffocate under square houses'. Who would deny them? Eh old man?

There is nothing too trivial for us to rush and see and to be astonished at. A tree cut down by lighting, an unusual bird perching on a tree. Nothing too trivial. We are suffocated.'

Tugga stood watching the city in silence as if he was helping Damolishi in gazing at the rooftops of Barduvai. He recalled Buruji's lessons before Sheikh Marduka came to Barduvai.

`Your ultimate duty is to save yourself from the fire of Gehenna, and you can only to do that by making sure you constantly remember the fire' He made potato ridges as he sang the Horrifier while washing his gown or sitting on a meditative posture. Buruji told him, `No man can obey religious laws unless he is sober. You can't be sober unless you are face to face with the dreadful fire. Then saving yourself will be the urgent thing to do. Indeed Buruji was an urgent person. His forehead was always glistening with sweat as he did whatever he was doing vigorously.

7

In the afternoon of the following day when the market was full, Habarana arrived to make another announcement with his zebu horn. The zebu horn blared that the Askia had given Lamiri the full responsibility to come out with an explanation of the rock pattern. Habarana's new announcement techniques and the sound of his zebu horn drew the attention of children who followed behind him laughing and clapping as he stopped at various spots in the city to make the announcement

The Barduvai Court was a square structure with two large windows on either side of the judge's seat. The windows were purposely made large and low so that people can stand and watch any court session they were interested in. During some court sessions, people would fill all the windows so much so that Judge Akilu ordered the people to give some space for air to ventilate the courtroom. Quite often, he worked late in the night recording details of court cases he held during the day or counting the cowries in the treasury of Barduvai. He became concerned with the attitude of Burtune to the Hime and the Kalfuuje project. He had yearned for a day when he will write court proceedings in Kalfuuje.

That day Burtune ordered him to give one hundred thousand cowries to Lamiri to build a temple and to travel to Bazahu to contact the Consolidated Seers. He had to prepare some documents for Lamiri to sign. It was getting dark by then and he wanted Lamiri to count the cowries quickly and sign the documents pertaining his receiving the cowries.

While Lamiri was signing the documents under the oil lamp, he felt bitter, because he knew Akilu was preserving records for posterity. The clinical way he was going about giving him the cowries told Lamiri that the judge knew he was influential on trying to prevent the Hime method. Like Burtune, he really felt inadequate whenever the Hime was carried out because he couldn't express his ideas in Barduvailect very well. Both he and Burtune felt really inadequate and awkward after Hime sessions.

After signing the documents, Lamiri hissed as he walked out of the courtroom with the cowries he collected from the treasury. He felt Akilu regarded him as a scoundrel and had never expected to achieve any dignity in his presence. Upon arriving at his clinic, he was disappointed, Jabbi the milkmaid has not brought yoghurt for his lunch, something she did on a daily basis. She frequently came with a horde of other chattering milkmaids. They giggled, screamed and gossiped to the delight of Lamiri. They buy ointments, syrups and charms.

As Babbadajaka had not arrived for their meeting as well, Lamiri walked inside his house to eat lunch, something he rarely did. The sight of his wife Kumbo depressed him a lot and the whole atmosphere in the house tormented him. He was not sure if it was the presence of Kumbo or the reminder of his father that tormented him that much. It was a dull sensation that mounted up to his upper thorax, blinding his common sense and filling him with rage. Part of the rage could be because Kumbo, being plumy and sweaty never got angry or complained because Lamiri was the only man she knew. He spoke to her harshly and never uttered a word of love to her except to ask for food or his other daily conveniences.

Lamiri ate a portion of the food swallowing hard and cursing Jabbi for not bringing some yoghurt for him. Afterward he drank a sour gruel before walking back to the clinic. By that time Babbadajaka had arrived and was sitting aside waiting for him.

`You have arrived'

`By the grace of God' said Babbadajaka adjusting his gown, and smiling widely to reveal his kolanut-tainted teeth.

`I want to give you the contract for the construction of the temple. We want to show our enemies something'

`That is it sir, that is right. You should tell the Askia to ignore those nonentities. What business has he with paupers, unblessed paupers'

`Where is it apart from Barduvai that you find a king downgrading himself and making himself a carpet for his subjects. Hime, Buruji and that unblessed ironmonger'

`Tugga, he is nothing more than an ex-slave. If I meet him on the way I always turn my face away'. Babbadajaka laughed, `If you let paupers close to you, they disrespect you. Keep a distance. I don't joke with ordinary citizens'.

Lamiri shook his head saying, `my plan is to stay apart from such people. In Kudulantis, Kings stay in castles, away from their Subjects. Whenever they come down to the cities, their Subjects receive them with drums and cymbals. Figure it out. Unless there is a dividing line between the ruler and the ruled, then where is respect'.

'So, indeed' nodded Babbadajaka

'I tell you' continued Lamiri 'There is no going back to the Hime; there must be a boundary on this affair. I mean didn't you see the Askia was happy when I suggested he stops the Hime. You saw him. The King is not happy he is vulnerable.'

'An Askia so vulnerable. Where on earth but Barduvai. Please sir work hard at stopping this nonsense. How can the Askia continue to rub shoulders with his subjects?'

Lamiri gave Babbadajaka fifty thousand cowries, 'Mobilise your donkeys and the workforce and start immediately. There is no going back'.

Jabbi entered the clinic together with a friend. Lamiri's face lit up, 'you should have brought the yoghurt earlier. You made me eat the undelicious'. The sight of Jabbi increased his heartbeat and filled him with a possessive desire. He wanted to possess Jabbi desperately but her uncouth and wild personality made it difficult for him to establish any meaningful and mature relationship with her. Jabbi giggled as she placed her milk gourd aside, 'we were wondering in the city', she said, 'Here is Nedi my friend, she wants the ointment too'. Lamiri walked to one of the counters and picked up a bottle, which she gave to Jabbi. The milkmaids giggled. Nedi was shy.

`Don't be shy, smear it on your body morning and evening'

The girls paid up and left the clinic giggling.

`You see that Jabbi', Lamiri drew the attention of Babbadajaka, `She reminds me of a Kudulantic poem where a mermaid sings for her demon lover on a hanging garden'.

`Wonder. Hanging Garden'

`What do you know; they are not slaves to any archaic tradition. What benefits them is what they pursue. I will set for Bazahu tomorrow to consult the Consolidated Seers. They will decipher the anagram there. Wait and see'

`Are they sages? I believe they must be like wise oldmen, looking like our Buruji' Babbadajaka asked.

`They are like us Babbadajaka. Just like us but they are not handcuffed like us. No mystery has remained unresolved by the Consolidated Seers of Bazahu. When they set their minds on to something, kalas! It is torn to pieces'.

Babbadajaka raised up his hand in agreement, `I suppose so. At the foot of the mountain I thought, here was a big one. A splintered rock thundering from the top of the mountain down to the plains. First time in the history of Tibesti'.

`I knew it was to come to that one day. A day when

the method will come face to face with a big one! A real big one! Then what will a pauper a real peasant has to say to something beyond his knowledge. Hear what Tugga said, a reservoir of ideograms!'

Babbadajaka broke into laughter

'Such infantile perception!' Lamiri drew the calabash gourd of yoghurt urging Babbadajaka to draw closer as he dipped a wooden spoon to drink from the gourd of Jabbi, the gazelle of Barduvai.

8

The following day at noon, the Kalfuuje class had a Hime on the thema *proceeding on the right road*' where they discussed the prospect of the circle under the prevailing circumstances. They sat in a circle as Tugga opened the session: *how do we proceed on the right road? A rock splintered and rolled down the mountain. An enigmatic pattern appeared on the surface of the fallen rock. A Hime was not held on this incidence. Habarana Choodal, the only one who memorised our history has quitted this group, 'how do we proceed on the right road?'* Tugga asked as members set to contemplation.

Bango was the first to make an input, 'is the project still important to us? What is the relationship between the fallen rock and our project? 'How do we proceed on the right road?' I feel since the project pertains to developing a writing system to record our history and express ourselves. The Kalfuuje project is important'.

Members nodded grunting in approval. Tugga spoke again, 'the project is important, we can't articulate our experience without our language? The project is important. *'How do we proceed on the right road?'* Habarana has quitted our project. *'How do we proceed on the right road?'* Jari sighed as he contemplated.

`Do we need a corpus for our project? I feel an authentic corpus is important in developing our scripts. 'How do we proceed on the right road?'      `Remember our folktales! Remember our folktales, they are as well authentic oral corpus. Let us use our folktales in place of oral history'.

The Hime proceeded thus, and after some more contributions, Tugga cleared his throat and read the summaries, ` so today we proceed our session on the theme *`you articulate your experience through the language. Self-realisation is not possible without language'*.

As people passed by the workshop, they frequently walked in to contribute to the session. Very soon the session transcended the Kalfuuje circle as the thema *`Proceeding on the right road'* attracted many citizens who trooped into Tugga's workshop to contribute to the Hime. It was during that time that Delu the daughter of Barmaki came. She walked in haughtily and looked at the assemblage with disdain.

`Are the trinkets ready?' she asked Tugga rudely.

`Have you brought the fee?' Asked Tugga.

`Just give me the trinkets. You can come for your

cowries at the palace'.

`Listen my dear lady I'm no slave to the palace. If you want the trinkets go and bring some cowries'

`Is that your message?'

Tugga nodded. Delu walked out of the workshop wriggling her bottom provocatively.

Tugga sent a boy to collect a calabash of yoghurt from Tataraktu his wife at the market. She was the most successful millet ball seller in Barduvai market. Her millet finished first before that of any other lady at the milk market. Whenever the Kalfuuje group was meeting, she usually sent in a huge gourd of sour milk mixed with millet balls for the members to take as lunch.

It was while they were taking a lunch break that Barmaki the palace guard and some guards stormed into the workshop. Barmaki was wearing the red turban, a sign that he was officially empowered to arrest and search anybody or place. The Kalfuuje slates were confiscated, and the members were told to come to the palace if they want to know the reason for the action. Furthermore he told the gathering that no more Hime session is allowed to hold, as it had not received any permission from the Askia. At that Tugga protested vehemently shouting,

`Hime is not by the permission of the Askia. Don't believe him my people. The teacher had never said Hime is to be held by the permission of a King!'

`I'm not here to argue about that. Like I said, anyone aggrieved could come to the palace for explanations. Tugga you are not the son of knowledge of this city. You have no right to enlighten people. After all you heard the announcement that Lamiri is going to Bazahu to get an explanation'.

News spread in the city about the confiscation of the Kalfuuje slates. They said strange things were happening in Barduvai, such ominous events. In small groups people gathered talking about the new role of Habarana Choodal as the palace announcer, Lamiri's trip to Bazahu and what the rock anagram could be. Some said it was the stamp of the magog creatures, a prelude to their invasion. Others however said the pattern was Amharic predicting the rise of a redeemer who was going to take Barduvai to heights never experienced before. The citizens who were not used to gathering in such small groups savoured rumour mongering and speculations as newly found habits.

Tugga was in a different state, sensing a treachery, he went around that day telling citizens that whenever a problem is left 'Hanging' it was wont to result in rumours and lamentations. Carrying his huge hammer and wearing his leather apparel, he kept urging people to gather for a Hime at the market square. 'This is the beginning of leprosy in Barduvai, cut it short my people! Cut it before we are reduced to lepers! The Hime is not a palace affair, don't get confused. The sheikh had never said the Hime should be initiated from the palace', he walked around Barduvai urging people to converge at the market square. But it was to no avail as the citizens savoured their newly found habits. Some citizens claimed they heard from Habarana that Burtune has sent for 500 seers from Egypt to meditate on the event. This infuriated Tugga and some of the key Kalfuuje disciples. But their campaign to draw the attention of the citizens to a Hime session was to no avail.

Barmaki and some guards arrested Tugga while he was campaigning and took him before Askia Burtune, who asked him why he was undermining his throne. Tugga denied undermining his rule, `we are losing our collective responsibility. How can I undermine what is ours.'

`You have no responsibility in the affair of Hime; Lamiri is our son of knowledge. My father listened to his father, now I'm listening to him. Do you want to usurp his position?'

`God forbid!' Tugga picked his hammer and left the palace, feeling it was a big error that Hime sessions were held in the palace of Askia so much that citizens came to associate it with the palace. It was regrettable he felt that the sessions were not held in the market square.

Tugga knew Lamiri in addition to preventing the Hime also desired to stall the Kalfuuje project because of the unpopularity of his Kudumaria, a school he opened when he returned from his adventures and wanted every Barduvai child to attend in order to learn the Kudulect language. At first parents were willing to experiment, but later on farmers started to complain that their children were abhorring hoes and not knowing how to use sickles.

'We are tired of our children coming home with sticks and singing strange songs. We can't eat sticks!'

Others complained of the long whip used by Lamiri to discipline the children. When he heard they were planning to return their children to Tugga's Nafobe School where they learn the Kalfuuje and tendered the Daula orchard, Lamiri introduced the farming of catabeans and larradish, two exotic plants from Kudulantis.

The crops grew in two weeks and were considered a wonder then but when the children took the harvest home, their parents had stomach troubles and swore to their children never to bring catabeans and larradish to their homes again. They said anything that grows so fast is not healthy.

Since then Lamiri took the exodus of the pupils to Tugga' school personally. He called Tugga an unmitigated hieroglyphician who was taking Barduvai back to primitivism.

Many people came from neighbouring settlements to see the rock. It was then that citizens realised the real reason for fencing the rock. A guard stood by the fence collecting a cowry each from anyone who wanted to see the rock. They noticed also that Babbadajaka was moving stones and loads of clay to the site of the fallen rock. The building of the temple started at a furious pace. The traffic of the horses and donkeys carrying building materials raised a lot of dust at the foot of the mountain. Damolishi as usual sat on the gizzard rock unnoticed and unperturbed by the flow of traffic and noise. Only his hair and moustache was covered by dust, as he sat staring over the horizon. As citizens didn't know the reason for the building, rumours increased about a temple being built to house seven Wazuli spirits who were to ultimately roll back the rock to its former position on top of the mountain.

9

By the time Lamiri returned from his trip to Kudulantis, the Temple of Light was completed and it was rumoured Babbadajaka collected a huge sum of cowries as a contract sum. It was a shiny marbled building with a huge parlour and two side rooms on the left. The parlour was heavily carpeted with quill pillows thrown all around for visitors to recline.

Throughout the period of building, citizens had imagined Damolishi after getting fed up with the dust raised by Babbadajaka's horses, donkeys and his entire work force as they carted stones and soil would have descended on the project with a warrior wrath. Nothing even nearest to that happened. The project went ahead and was completed.

A wide window on the left of the parlour was built directly opposite the rock anagram. When the temple was completed, many citizens flocked to the parlour in the mornings and evenings. As they sat looking at the anagram, they noticed that it appeared differently in the morning, noon and at sunset. That phenomenon drew a large crowd of citizens in the mornings and sunset as they didn't mind to pay a fee to witness the changing mosaic pattern of the anagram.

As they did, the citizens argued about the shapes the anagram resembled and the significance of those shapes. In the morning when the rising sun shone on it, the anagram appeared like a hastily jumbled calligraphy, of what language it was not certain. When the sun is setting, it appeared like a swooping figure, as others see it. Some even swore it resembled a mighty primordial eagle swooping. Some said it didn't appear to them like a bird but like a flying mammal. Configurations were inexhaustible as citizens argued and discussed the shapes the anagram took during the day but it was at noon that the anagram appeared mysterious of all. At exactly noon, it becomes a glowing and receding mosaic that left citizens only sighing as it happened on that fateful Friday when the figure appeared.

Later it dawn on citizens that the Kalfuuje disciples could have been right in calling for a study of the anagram. There was a strong feeling in the city that the refusal of Burtune to allow the Kalfuuje group to copy the anagram on their slates was not right.

When Lamiri returned from Kudulantis and was briefed by Babbadajaka he immediately ordered the veiling of the large window facing the anagram to stop citizens from gazing at it. Habarana went all over the city that day galloping on his mule and announcing in his baritone voice, the return of Lamiri from Kudulantis. He informed citizens that whoever wanted to know the meaning of the anagram could do so at the temple by paying a cowry. Hundreds of curious citizens rushed to the Temple of Light paying a cowry each to hear Lamiri explain the mystery of the Tibesti rock. Lamiri sat on a raised cushion gesticulating, as Babbadajaka sat close to him chewing kolanuts and smiling.

People sat apprehensively waiting to hear what the Son of Knowledge had to say. The parlour was filled to capacity. Fargarjaji and Dabalo Ceddo, two promising persons in Barduvai walked up to the window overlooking the anagram to open it.

'Stop!' shouted Lamiri, 'who asked you to do that!' Citizens were surprised, as they had thought the window was veiled to provide a dramatic moment when Lamiri will unveil the window in the course of whatever explanation he might give about the rock anagram.

'What appeared is a warning my dear people. It is not clear what is going to happen. Lamiri brought out a leather patch and spread it out; 'the exact interpretation of what appeared according to the Consolidated Seers of Bazahu is: *when the glitter passes over the elevation few will be saved*'. We discussed this with the Askia but couldn't agree on the meaning exactly of such words as the glitter and elevation, but we believe it would be known soon'.

'How can you give an explanation that refers to only the written aspect of this phenomenon?' Bango asked as he stood up angrily.

'It appeared like writing only at sunrise. So how was a statement derived from the anagram?' Jari Daniro also stood up to support Bango.   Lamiri sighed, 'you see them again worrying about the unimportant! Why worry about terms, a disaster is coming soon, why don't we figure out what to do instead of arguing about terms'?

There were murmuring by People after this statement. Barmaki ordered all citizens to leave, as Lamiri was to rest from a tedious and useful journey, another surprising decision the crowd felt. They dispersed contemplating the statement read by Lamiri. They speculated on what the glitter could be and when it would come to pass. What is the elevation? They wondered what wrong was done to merit a calamity in Barduvai.

People walked out to the gizzard rock to continue discussing Lamiri's statements. Babbadajaka walked out of the temple closely followed by Fargarjaji who was lamenting Babbadajaka's inordinate support for Lamiri. 'Even if he is the son of knowledge of this city, we shouldn't just keep mute and accept whatever he says!'

Arguments continued, people unaware of the

presence of Damolishi, only Tugga looked up and saw the dust-covered face of Damolishi. Some citizens said the glitter must be some lighting and therefore the event must be in the rainy season, while others thought it would be a bird, the kind never seen before in Barduvai. Was it going to be an earthquake, a volcanic eruption or what?

The Kalfuuje group refused to accept the interpretation brought by Lamiri, insisting on the belief that a plot was being hatched to kill the Hime method and the Kalfuuje project. Tugga who was surrounded by people tried to draw their attention to the incompleteness of Lamiri's statements,

'Don't listen to his assertion about the completeness of knowledge. Complete knowledge is beyond human capacity. The Hime is based on complete senses and the pivot of action stems from the perception of the whole city. If he brought some new knowledge, then we must examine it in a circle. I was the one who said leprosy has started in the city. What is the best way to explain what is happening now but that way? Since the rock thundered down the mountain, how were the actions taken on it based on our collective intelligence'.

Lamiri at noon ordered the gate of the Temple to be closed for consultation. It was at that time that Jabbi, the pretty milkmaid came in.

'Sit down here, come close to me. You won't?'

Jabbi giggled sitting away from Lamiri after placing the gourd of yoghurt in front of him. She loved to see the veins of his neck bulge out of the violent desire he had for her.

'If you know your assets Jabbi', Lamiri said in a hoarse voice, 'in Kudulantis you will be a queen'

Jabbi giggled, 'Oh I, God protect me. I don't care about that. I am happy singing and dancing when I want. What else do I want?'

'Remember that poem I told you about?' Lamiri asked her.

'God protect me, the one you recited about a girl wailing of her demon lover?'

'That is Hasnamouss' most famous poem. The one he composed for King Atamin. You always remind me of this poem. If you were in Kudulantis someone would have built a castle with a hanging garden and have you sing the Careless Girl in your mermaid voice'

Jabbi giggled at that.

'You don't know the asset you have. With your voice and beauty, there is no limit for you. You could sing on bridges, or in canoes traversing the canals of Bazahu, and people will pay you for that'.

'What will take me there sir' Jabbi raised her arms, 'I love to sing and dance at Poli. And be happy and eat millet fritters with my friends, Delu and all'

'Bring them here in the Temple and sing the *Careless Girl* for me. Come here in private. I will slaughter turkeys and let us have a feast tomorrow'.

'You city folks are amazing, if you feel shy to dance in public then how can you enjoy life'. She laughed at such suggestions repeating the nomads' derisive term about 'City folks suffocating in their settlements'.

While he was drinking the yoghurt she brought, she asked him what the meaning of the impending disaster was, that she heard people talking all over the city.

'I don't know presently because some of the words are not easily understood, but I'm sure my dear Jabbi, everything would be clear very soon'

'Who are those to be saved?' she asked

'This is something you have to decide yourself. What do you want in life?'

'Charm. It is charm I want. What is a lady without charm? A lady who has charm speaks with her heart.'

'So you want to be a charming lady until the disaster comes?'

'What do you think sir? What are your plans? Any way you must be among those who would be saved I'm sure'

'Like I told you, one has to find what he wants to do for the rest of his life before the disaster falls. Few would be saved it said; not knowing how the disaster would be how could you know how to save yourself then. Everything is possible Princess'

10

'*When the glitter passes over the elevation few would be saved*' Babbadajaka was fond of rising in the early hours of the morning to check his chicken pen and to ensure his troublesome goats have not broken out loitering and eating the laradish nursery he planted in his large compound. Three weeks have passed since Lamiri returned from Kudulantis. A bright object in the sky caught Babbadajaka's attention. His heartbeat increased and involuntarily he screamed `the glitter has appeared! The glitter has appeared!' His wife and children came out and stood beside him watching the bright object in the sky.

`That is all!' he shouted in excitement, `the dissenters are finished. Oh son of sheikh you are vindicated!' Babbadajaka instead of feeling any dread was feeling excited, as if the vindication of Lamiri was a boon to him.

Babbadajaka wore his sandals, broke a kolanut and chewed it savagely as he walked to Habarana's house where he woke him up, `The glitter has appeared!' he told the sleepy griot, who rubbed his eyes and looked up the sky before he rushed into his room to bring out the zebu horn. The zebu horn re-echoed across the streets of Barduvai as Habarana followed by Babbadajaka awake citizens. Oldmen could only liken the situation to the war drums of Askia Tengele when the Almoravids were invading Barduvai. Before down all citizens were gazing at the object which most agreed appeared like an unusually big comet in a strange shape.

Babbadajaka went around purposely close to the workshop of Tugga shouting 'Where are the dissenters, yours have finished today'. Babbadajaka was always inpatient with Tugga and the Kalfuuje group because he thought they should be concerned about making more cowries than forging a writing system. He saw them as pretentious fools seeking for glory. People gathered first at the Temple of light. They had thought it was the Magog creatures that were coming to invade them and they were wondering if the comet was their warship. Lamiri intentionally refused to come out in order to increase their horror. People throughout the night run around the city, as if the voice of Habarana was not enough, hollering, 'the glitter has appeared! The glitter has appeared!' It was dreadful. In the morning it was difficult to see the object clearly but people strained their eyes trying hard to see the figure in the sky.

People trooped to Burtune's Palace and sat in dread waiting for him to come out. Lamiri, followed closely by Habarana and Babbadajaka arrived with a group of anxious citizens. He looked serious and walked with a new air of dignity and power, saying; 'I told you, I told you' as he walked into the court of Burtune.

From a far people saw Hajji Buruji coming in a haste holding his staff and muttering furiously. Upon seeing him Barmaki walked to the entrance of the palace and positioned himself in readiness to prevent the dervish from entering the court of Burtune.

'Is this more frightening than the fire you heedless lot?' Buruji shouted at the gathering upon his arrival. He then started chanting the Horrifier and dancing the rotary

Where can you stand or sit in a fiery scourge?
Where can you sleep in a blazing inferno?
The incinerator leaves people only hollering
These are combined with tornadoes and darkness
The rumblings of heavens are ceaseless clamours

Movements are impossible in eternal darkness
These endless nights of ceaseless chastisements!
The inmates of fire wailing in damnation!
The fire will roast them with a fiery blast
The doors of the inferno are the most blistering.

Later Burtune came out after they had a short meeting with Lamiri but upon seeing Buruji he rushed back into the palace. Lamiri in turn accompanied by Babbadajaka and Habarana, walked hurriedly to the Temple of Light without saying a word to the gathered citizens. By then the sun has appeared and the traces of the comet had disappeared. That day the sun appeared like a ray of doom to the citizens, it only reminded them the dreadful comet they saw the previous night.

In desperation people followed Lamiri to the Temple of Light, shouting 'is that the glitter? Is that the glitter?' Lamiri intentionally kept quiet as if he was in a state of meditation. Later when he spoke, he told the apprehensive crowd that the glitter must have been referring to this comet that has appeared and from further analysis it is apparent that the elevation referred to in the writing must have been referring to the Tibesti Mountain. So it means when the comet moves over the mountain a great disaster shall befell people.

`What are we going to do? What are we going to do? People began to shout, amazed Lamiri was looking less perturbed than the impending calamity he implied.

`Increase your knowledge!' Lamiri shouted at them `If you had any knowledge other than the Hime you wouldn't have asked me this stupid question!' Lamiri was harsher on the bewildered citizens who as they dispersed started to feel the kind of alienation you feel when you are overwhelmed. That day Tugga went around secretly summoning members of the Kalfuuje group telling them that they must hold a Hime in the night. They assembled at Tugga's workshop at night.

Tugga told them it is urgent to get another opinion to the one popularly held about the disaster. Members although apparently committed were not sure if Tugga was right in condemning Lamiri whose esteem by then had increased with the appearance of the comet. He suggested they walked outside to study the glittering object before reaching any conclusion.

`Let us stand on nothing, let us forget about the announcement, and let us concentrate on the object in the sky'.

Outside, people were discussing excitedly about the

comet especially about Lamiri impeccable assessment. They said apart from him, who could have unravelled the mystery of the rock. They said if the comet has a tail like a rodent, then the disaster would come in the form of a plague, if the comet has a tail like a sword, then a war was imminent as a disaster.

When the Kalfuuje group returned to the workshop,

`It looked like a comet, it looks like a comet'

`But do comets flicker intermittently?' asked Tugga.

Bango agreed, `Yes I saw it flicker too'

`Are there comets that flicker intermittently'?

Some of the members confessed they know nothing about comets. Tugga sensed most members were getting discouraged, he therefore urged them not accept the label comet for what the members should regard as an object until they could agree to what it was. But it was too late; most members had caught on the fallacy of the incompleteness of knowledge in Barduvai.

Lamiri grew popular if not revered, many parents returned their children to the Kudumaria and in turn started to attend the Kudras evening classes, which became jam-packed with people. It was a school he designed to teach citizens to write and speak the Kudulect, study the history and philosophy of Kudulantis and to rewrite the history of Barduvai. Quite often during classes, the large window overlooking the anagram was unveiled He raised the school fees from ten to thirty cowries. In the days following the appearance of the comet, in packed sessions, he used to explain the phenomena and justify himself;

`When I told you to study the Kudulect, you thought it was a plan to alienate you, but I knew even then that one day you will come to realise the fallacy of developing the Kalfuuje script. What has the Kalfuuje to say to this phenomenon, but to see the phenomenon as a reservoir of scripts and ideograms? So naive, so simple. That is what I want to warn you about. There are certain aspects of knowledge that we don't know and we would always be left behind if we are arrogant enough to feel that we need not look outside for their solutions'.

Citizens asked him persistently what nature the disaster was going to take and how they could save Barduvai.

`You are worried because you have no knowledge but that of the Kalfuuje. There is Habarana sitting down at that corner, for years his only role was the recital of the ancient history of Barduvai playing his Kora. What else does he know?'

`Sir' Dabalo Ceddo rose, `How do we then save the city from the imminent disaster?'

`This is another sign of lack of knowledge I told you. Dabalo you have memorised the incantation of Bazadi. You pride yourself in being the only one in the city who has memorised it. Now tell me the solution to the impending disaster'

Dabalo smiled and the rest of the class chuckled, `For

a solution, I could call on the whole city to recite the Bazadi incantation.'

`Bazadi is dead and gone but the glitter is around and moving to the Tibesti. You see the discrepancy of your thinking!'

`But his prayers is still alive!' said Dabalo

`In your mind Dabalo, in your mind'

`Let us go back to the Hime method!' Fargarjaji shouted.

The class became silent. A flash of anger crossed the face of Lamiri, but he turned his face away from the class. Everyone knew the Kudras was not the place to mention the Hime method, the instrument of the Kalfuuje group. When Lamiri finally turned, he said calmly, `Fargarjaji if it is the Hime method you want you know where to go please this is not a forum to show your rascality'

`I said it in truth. We haven't tried the Hime on the appearance of the comet. We are talking about solutions aren't we?'

Lamiri couldn't suppress his anger any more, `I know more about the Hime than that illiterate hieroglaphician! My father developed the method. I know my father more than Tugga knew him, if there was any good in that system, I would have been the first to adopt it! The solution lies in acquiring knowledge because ultimately the choice is individual. When people act together, think of solving a problem together that stems from fear of the unknown. Primordial methods to compensate for lack of encompassing knowledge. If you have knowledge you are free!

Rando Cartoza the master philosopher of Kudulantis spent years contemplating alone. Then he found out the truth. He rushed out naked in the streets of Bazahu shouting `I'm! I'm! People followed him in amazement thinking he had gone mad. He was running and people were following him, then sitting close to one of the Bazahu canals he told them the beginning of wisdom. It was the beginning of his principle, which says he believe therefore he was; therefore "the self come first is the beginning of wisdom". Some citizens brought some clothes for him to put on, but he refused saying it would be a total defeat of his philosophy. Here you sit doing nothing but memorising the inventions of a mad hieroglaphician!'

Many members of the class laughed.

`According to Rando Cartoza what is imprisoning people is the lack of a consistent realisation of the `I'. When you are, then you are free. When you are not then other forces take control.'

Lamiri went further to tell them how the Rando Cartoza's principle influenced Kudulantic kings like Atamin `the king of the first night' and Warum Kudulix the audacious warrior who couldn't sleep unless he had speared 50 buffaloes during the day. Members of the Kudras School wrote on skin leather instead of the wooden slates as a mark of difference with the Kalfuuje class. They started by learning the forty-eight alphabets of the Kudulect. Dabalo Ceddo and Fargarjaji quickly established themselves as the brightest students in the class. They were the ones asking tougher questions and the ones learning hard.

In one of the classes, Lamiri introduced them to the new calendar.

'The most memorable part of our history is the appearance of the comet. This has vindicated our earlier opinion about the backwardness of the Hime method.'

He told them the new calendar would make them remember the impending disaster. In the new calendar, days are counted as before the appearance of the comet (B.A.C) and after the appearance of the comet (A.A.C). He told them that this calendar combined with the knowledge they would acquire was all they needed to close the gaps in their 'I' so that they can be. Lamiri told his disciples that enormous power and resources await those who could acquire knowledge, practice Rando Cartoza's principle and hence realise themselves. The citizens couldn't understand how knowledge could shield them from a real thing like a disaster. In excitement, Habarana during the class, vowed to use the new calendar in making further announcements.

After the class, members in groups tried to figure out their dates of marriage, birth, and other important dates in their lives. They kept wondering at the knowledge of Kudulantis and how they were oblivious that such a learned teacher like Lamiri was residing among.

After some weeks, some prominent Kudras disciples like Babbadajaka, Seibu and Habarana Choodal went as a special delegation to the Askia requesting him to formally turban Lamiri as the Son of Knowledge of Barduvai. A ceremony was organised for the turbaning ceremony of Lamiri as the `The son of knowledge' of Barduvai. People thought it was amazing that there should be anything like a formal occasion for such a duty. Everyone in the city they said knew Lamiri was the Son of Knowledge of Barduvai, as his late father was. What is the turbaning ceremony for they asked?

It was a lavish ceremony, which cost the city a huge sum of cowries. On that day Babbadajaka presented a horse as a gift on the day of turbaning yelling, `knowledge is not the business of slaves' probably trying to slight the members of the Kalfuuje group.

In the evening of the day of turbaning, Lamiri rode on the horse waving at people with Habarana trotting behind on his mule shouting, `*Cometic calendar A.A.C.1, Son of Marduka master of Kudulantic knowledge, seer into the intestine, the alchemist of a thousand -minus-one medicine, son of the venerable masters of knowledge from all directions!'*

With great excitement citizens discussed about whether the Hime was a blessing or a draw back in the history of Barduvai. Babbadajaka and Habarana went around proposing that matters of knowledge should be left to the knowledgeable ones just as matters of metals should be left to a blacksmith,

'Take for example Tugga', Babbadajaka said, 'we have not known him for knowledge, or his family ...imagine the darkness we shall have been in if we had insisted on the Hime. In essence we would have been heading to a disaster in darkness'

Matters small and big were quickly referred to Lamiri. In a day Burtune seeking his counsel on the affairs of Barduvai would summon him more than five times. The Temple of Light and the clinic became the centre of activities in Barduvai. Hundreds of people came, some from neighbouring settlements. Nomads especially were Lamiri's foremost customers. They came seeking for help on various matters. Milkmaids patronised the clinic more than any other group. Lamiri placed a large mirror in the clinic asking the ladies to spend a long time seeing themselves, asking themselves what they want in life and trying his ointments. He called such sessions (SRL) Special Rando Cartoza for Ladies. He kept mirrors of different sizes and different distortions. Each mirror gave a lady a different perspective to her looks. Some of the mirrors were handheld, some, standing, while others were hanging on the wall.

Lamiri told them that in Kudulantis most ladies when they close their gaps felt that adornment and beautification is the essence of a lady's life. They love his ideas, especially the battle they needed to face with age. He told them age was the enemy of ladies, and a lady's duty is the maintenance of her beauty and the battle against age. They often recalled the Nomadic *togu* concept, which said a charming lady, speaks with the heart. He told them that was an archaic philosophy, that artificial beauty is better than natural ugliness. After they left his clinic, it would smell a mixture of different perfumes and creams that he prepared.

Babbadajaka and Habarana spent most times in the day urging people to 'leave the affairs of Barduvai to the learned.'

11

In the past four weeks Tugga Bukele was greatly disturbed because the morale among the Kalfuuje group after the appearance of the comet was very low and he knew it was out of shame that many of them didn't go to the Temple of Light to receive lessons. He might be right or he might be wrong he thought as he stood under the gizzard rock waiting for the other members to arrive. He wondered how many of them would come, because for the past two weeks he had been trying to hold a Hime to no avail. He looked up the gizzard rock and as usual saw Damolishi seated on it facing the east.

As he tapped his hammer on his palms he watched the rooftops of Barduvai and felt the city was being engulf by a narcotic breeze and wondered what would be the ultimate destiny of its citizens. He knew he was keener on the Hime method than anyone else in the city, but he thought there was a way he understood the method, which no other person did. He thought the mistake made by Sheikh Marduka was to allow the palace as a venue for sessions. This has resulted unnecessarily into the association of the method with the palace for Hime sessions. It was difficult to change this fixation especially citizens have now come to associate the office of the son of knowledge as solely responsible for thinking about the existence of the community.

One by one he received messages from the other members that they were not opportune to come due to some engagements. He knew they were not sincere. Tugga walked down to the city trying to figure out how he could convince the people of Barduvai that accepting the verdict of Lamiri was not the right thing to do.

As he passed through the market, Habarana who was drinking from a gourd of yoghurt called him with his unmistakable baritone voice. Habarana smiled when Tugga approached the stall.

`Ahoy Tugga master of metals, join me to drink a special preparation from your wife'.

`God be praised, I'm fine. Habarana you have done a terrible thing by leaving our circle and that is abandoning your responsibility.'

`Master of metals, I can't be a griot forever. These

days the Kora can't retouch a roof. I have five mouths to feed, master of metal'

`Listen Habarana, I know Lamiri more than you. He is a self-centred person. I knew him when he was a kid. I was a student of his father. He used to skip pages when he was assigned to read a book. He is a charlatan and an eternal liar. We could make a big mistake by accepting what he said about the object that appeared.'

`What did he say that didn't come right?'

`It can be a hoax'

` What do you think the object is, a hawk? Tugga it is said that light is the medicine for darkness. Don't be tenacious, if things are beyond your comprehension, don't be stubborn, accept the verdict of those who know.'

`If we do that we are surrendering an important aspect of our life, the ability to make sense of what surrounds us. Why should a single brain decide what is right for us.'

`For me Tugga, to cut it short, I'm a griot but what I hear and see is what I believe in. If the son of knowledge says everyone should know what he wants and what he thinks. Then be it. Keep your thoughts they are yours Tugga, why bother yourself.'

Tugga undauntedly stacked to the last Hime thema `*Proceeding on the right road*'. He reached a resolution by himself to start plotting the path of the comet to the west. Using the tall baobab tree in the market as a permanent mark, he plotted the movement of the comet in relation to the tree by illustrating it as a clear pictogram on a large slate, which he pinned on the baobab tree.

In the year of the comet, children spent most of their time at the Kudumaria learning the Kudulect alphabets. Holding a long whip, Lamiri whipped any of the children who wrote in Kalfuuje the script they were already familiar with and which they were used to writing with their forefingers. Lamiri who forced them to write with sticks stopped this.

Kudumaria classes were held under a cotton silk tree on which he pinned a large board containing the Kudulect alphabets. In the morning he normally checked their progress, punished the boys still writing in Kalfuuje and leave them to sing while he left for the palace of Askia Burtune. Parents became obsessed with their children learning the Kudulect. The Kudras Classes were always full. People were obsessed with the impending disaster. Anxious citizens were always seeking for help and advice from Lamiri either at his clinic or at the Temple of Light where they are mostly barred from entering by guards.

When Tugga's first almanac of the comet appeared, it was a simple pictogram of the comet in relation to the baobab tree in the market. Using charcoal, he plotted the course of the comet on two slates. One he pinned on the baobab tree in the market and the other at the entrance of the Barduvai central mosque. The first day he pinned the almanac, citizens crowded around the baobab tree laughing and making various comments on the drawing.

Lamiri continued to denounce him as a mad hieroglaphysician who was taking people back to primitive pictogramization.

'What is the use of plotting the course of a comet instead of preparing for its disaster?'

'How many degrees longitude is not specified. You can't use the baobab tree as a reference mark for a cosmic phenomenon!'

Hajji Buruji was banned from entering the court of Askia Burtune but it didn't bother the old dervish who continued to sing his Horrifier in public places and at the orchard. He sang over the butchers, salt traders, milkmaids and grain sellers. At the central mosque, he would stand over abluting citizens saying; 'The prayers of hypocrites are in vain'. Or at the market, he hovered over salt sellers exhorting, 'weight correctly when you weigh'. Being used to his voice, they would laugh and say Hajji Buruji singer of Gehenna. Then Buruji waving his dervish staff would stomp his feet dancing and whirling and singing the Horrifier,

She was given thousands of sinners but fain satisfied
She consumed them in a flicker what is there to be said
She sunk them by dragging their wilting legs
She yanks at flesh and break some bones
Intestines boiling and putrefying in stomach
Thousands thrown in different cauldrons
Burning above, burning below
Every sinner shall wear seventy sheets of flames

Everlasting punishment is consolidated
Everlasting bodily pains are worsen
Baked to finished the poisons of hearts revealed

The year of the comet was coming to a close. Many opinions were held regarding the manner of the day of disaster and who among people would be saved. Some said it was those who could speak the Kudulect language; others believed the answer lied in studying the history of Kudulantic kings. They said the language and the history of Kudulantis are the requirements to eliminate the notorious gap between the 'Is'. Habarana Choodal in his baritone voice continued to praise the emulation of those advanced in Rando Cartoza's principle. He cited examples of Babbadajaka and Seibu Albasa as the best companions for those who want to master the principle. Others like Fargarjaji emphasised the study of both Kudulantic history and the history of Barduvai. Fargarjaji enraged Lamiri by modifying the recitation of Barduvai's history. Fargarjaji argued that it was not right to eliminate the history of Barduvai prior to the appearance of the comet as Lamiri liked to do.

'Your hatred of Tugga Bukele and the Hime method will not erase them from our history. They are facts. What of the achievements of Ba'ashi and the Kalfuuje circle?'

'Enough!' Lamiri shouted, 'you can keep your views

but I am warning the others not to meddle into a dark period in search of ways to eliminate the gap. Many of the younger disciples of the Kudras saw Fargarjaji as an audacious intellectual, especially his convincing arguments.

During one of the classes, Lamiri told them the story of the Kudulantic King Atamin `The king of the first night' who was able to eliminate his gaps remarkably. He read to them from a spread skin patch that he called <u>The Confessions of King Atamin</u>,

`King Atamin was the son of Warum Kudulix, the audacious warrior with the horned helmet, the one who couldn't sleep until he had speared fifty buffaloes. Atamin had an uncontrollable desire to lay the wives of his Subjects. When he got tired of scheming and hiding, especially lying to his Subjects, he called the citizens of Bazahu and brought out the sword of war. People were amazed. He also called Slaughery the executioner whom people despised because he was fiendish-looking and seemed to look persistently into the crowd like a werewolf seeking for its next victim. Then Atamin addressed them,

`Oh citizens of Bazahu, I stand today your king as well as a plaintiff. Today you are my Subjects as well as a jury. Today my life would be fulfilled or be terminated like wise. All is the same, all is potential for Atamin. On my right is Slaughery the executioner and on the left is Analog my scribe. I come to you oh citizens of Bazahu with a perennial soul under the garb of a king sitting on the seat of your forefathers.

I say today you are my Subjects and jury at the same time. I tell you I have a perennial soul. I lay your wives in secret and *eat only imported food. I spend weeks away from my palace seeking comfort in castles of other kings thinking they were the types I should own. I tell you I have a perennial soul.*

I go for weeks with your wives to castles seas away seeking for pleasure and that unfathomable pleasure I experienced once in a dream. I vowed to find that pleasure. I dared not disclosed all the creatures that I lay seeking to recapture that dream. I was duped several times; I was humiliated several times in search of that pleasure. I tell you I have a perennial soul.

I visited Bero Koron that dreadful friend of my late father Warum Kudulix. Destiny took me to his castle. Fate pulled me to the Julmire, his castle. There I found the extreme test for Rando Cartoza's philosophy. There the rape of virgins was the pass time of Koron and his guests. A peasant girl was brought to me and I hesitated when I saw her eyes. I was divided in mind and body. I felt I should not go ahead, but I remembered I was and therefore should be. I decided to be because I was. Those eyes of hers I remembered my people. It was a mixture of sorrow tingled with pleasure and since then my body trembled for a repeat to capture that test of Rando Cartoza's philosophy. Oh my perennial soul!

Since then I swore to capture that experience again. So I started laying your wives. I say today I'm a king and a plaintiff and you are a jury and a subject. On the right is Slaughery the executioner and on the left is Analog my scribe. I tell you I have a perennial soul. If you find me guilty then here is Slaughery, put a rest to my perennial soul. If you believe I am, then I make a request. Build me a castle so that I can be. Give me the right to the first night of all newly wedded brides in the kingdom. The seeker must find. I lay my case to you oh my Subjects.'

After the speech, Lamiri told the class, people of Bazahu openly wept saying that since the death of Rando Cartoza they have never seen a person who has successfully closed his gaps. They said Atamin has realised himself. They said in history they knew kings came who doubled up as saints, Atamin must be one of them they said. They granted the king his request and that day escorted him back to his palace with drums and cymbals. That day Hasnamouss the poet wrote the most memorable poem in commemoration of the event.

That day some even offered their wives, but Atamin said the newly-wedded sufficed, *'The first night is the night of consolidation', he said, 'If I pass my seeds unto them. These would be the seeds of commitment, for if I see any boy in Bazahu, how can I then hate him? When he cries how can I then close my ears, or my eyes to his miseries? I tell you citizens of Bazahu, my seeds are the seeds of commitment'. Ladies ululated. That day he rode his chariot crossing all the bridges traversing the canals of Bazahu thanking people for granting his request and saving him from the tyranny of his perennial soul, 'I feel free my people, I feel free, I am, therefore I am my people' he kept on saying. Spinsters feeling overwhelmed opened windows and waved their braziers at him, 'Hail Atamin, take us with you!' they shrieked as he passed under their windows followed by a huge crowd of excited citizens witnessing the epitome of Rando Cartoza's principle.*

Every night, newly wedded girls were brought to his chambers of consolidation to receive the seeds of commitment from king Atamin son of Warum Kudulix `The king who was'.

`Yes he really was indeed' Babbadajaka broke into laughter and soon the whole class was laughing

`Rascal, real rascal. How was he able to persuade his people like that'.

`Once you are advanced in Rando Cartoza's philosophy then you realise you are; and that sets you free because you have closed all the gaps'

He told them the dread they felt about the comet stems out of their inabilities to be closing the gaps between the 'Is'. With every level of understanding of the Rando Cartoza's philosophy the question of the nature of the disaster and who are going to be saved will be clear to each of them according to his degree of advancement in the philosophy.

Citizens after the lessons stood in groups speculating the nature of the disaster prophesied. Some said a great fire was going to consume all those who couldn't speak the Kudulect. Others said the comet was going to collide with the Tibesti and burst killing many people on earth. Others also contemplated an earthquake.

By that time a number of people could speak basic Kudulect, especially abled students like Labaran Fargarjaji, Dabalo Ceddo, Jonkal Awembi and

Babbadajaka. A crowd of students normally gathered under the gizzard rock to discuss further on topics. The warrior Damolishi was normally unnoticed by the crowd.

'Sometimes', Seibu confessed to the gathering 'When I want to tell a customer the price of tomatoes, I feel pity. Some can't afford the price. So I asked them to give whatever they have. But now as I am closing the gaps, I recall Rando Cartoza principle and then stick to the price regardless.

'See!' Babbadajaka pointed his long finger in appreciation. 'That is it. You are closing the gap Seibu. Very soon you gap will be closed. You sell tomatoes to make profit, therefore you fix a price. As time goes on when profit always remain on your mind, then you are. When you are not then primitive feelings will sway your mind.'

'You see that is what I don't understand! Is that right for us? If profit remains the only idea in his mind is it the best? For me I know I am not learned yet, but I know many too don't know the implications of what they are learning. Really in our Barduvai terms this Atamin is just a shameless evil character. Then everyone was clapping and amused about his story. This type of person is not worth even talking about. Absurd. Oh this Rando Cartoza principle is really difficult', Sumanguru lamented.

Babbadajaka spat kolanuts and said, 'Sumanguru it will take you a long time to learn the principle. What is absurd to you today will be your desire after you learn much.'

12

Under the baobab tree as usual on Friday citizens stood reading Tugga's almanac and making comments about their destiny under the comet.

The year 1 A.A.C was a year of changes and speculations. Many people were torn apart by conflicting feelings. The strange philosophy of Rando Cartoza was debated and the stories of the kings of Kudulantis as told by Lamiri were re-narrated and discussed over and over by citizens. Discussions and stories of how Kudulantic people conducted their affairs generated tremendous interest among citizens. After most discussions some citizens felt relief and thereby attribute the relief to knowledge. The gaps are truly closing they said. Others however felt more despondent.

It was in the afternoon when the market was full that a stranger arrived on a chariot driven by two horses. White linen covered his whole body; only his eyes and mouth were visible. He appeared as if he was from a cemetery. People fled upon seeing such a strange person until he approached the baobab tree where he stood reading Tugga's almanac. After reading for a while he chuckled and chuckled again

People approached him cautiously. He asked them

the direction to the temple. They were surprised he spoke to them in Kudulect without even asking if they could speak it. Some citizens ran inside the city and returned with Dabalo Ceddo, whom they believed was the best student of the Kudulect. Dabalo arrived sweating with excitement. Lamiri had told them that one day they will meet a person from Kudulantis, and for those who could speak Kudulect fluently, a great reward awaits them.

'What is your name?' Dabalo asked

'Sharok Waladus' he chuckled.

People wondered why he chuckled intermittently. Sharok dismounted his chariot, tied the horses and brought out some roller skates, which he wore. Dabalo Ceddo led him to the temple. On the way Dabalo saw Sharok quickly sidetracked the gizzard rock. He skated behind Damolishi who unusually cleared his throat loudly. Sharok trembled on his skates and increased his speed towards the temple. They met Lamiri was eating a roasted turkey and Jabbi and some milkmaids were giggling in front of a large mirror. Dabalo noticed a flash of fear on Lamiri's face when he saw the visitor. Sharok started talking angrily in advanced Kudulect and Lamiri seemed to be pleading.

Dabalo was astonished at the way Lamiri was belittling himself. Lamiri asked Dabalo and the milkmaids to leave the temple, but Dabalo hid behind a window and peeped in. He saw Lamiri washing the feet of the visitor and he felt disgusted and the reverence he had for Lamiri suddenly dwindled.

Barduvai was gripped in tension and fear. Nothing

could be too trivial to divert the attention of people from the foreboding bewilderment. News spread that a stranger from Kudulantis had arrived at the Temple of Light. People learnt that the stranger was dressed like a corpse and didn't walk but floated on the air. Almost the whole city including Burtune and his courtiers turned up at the clinic, where they found the visitor sitting on a skin mat and chuckling intermittently.

Burtune arriving with dignity was introduced to the stranger who refused to shake hands with him. People wondered at his superior airs although they restrained their anger considering he was a foreigner who probably was already advanced in Rando Cartoza's philosophy.

'Why is it that he chuckles so often? Amazing. It is unsettling Lamiri' Burtune said looking at Sharok intently.

Lamiri told the Askia not to worry because people from Kudulantis are already advanced in Rando Cartoza's philosophy.

People muttered about how the philosophy really changes a person. 'What have you seen yet', Lamiri said, 'It changes more than the manner of speech and dressings'.

A lot of food was brought from Babbadajaka's house. It was a specially prepared laradish and catabeans dishes. When others brought some food for him they were told

Kudulantic people eat only catabeans and larradish. It was with fascination they sat watching Sharok eat the food with two long thorns held in both hands. They noticed he swallowed without chewing and after he finished eating, he picked his teeth with both thorns. As he did that it appeared as if he was smiling mirthlessly at the people.

Burtune seeing the fascination on people's faces asked Lamiri to ask the visitor to address them regarding the comet. Lamiri stood up saying to the assembly;

` Today the advantage of learning the Kudulect will become clear. Those of you who can understand Kudulect can drink from the spring of Kudulantic wisdom'. He turned to Sharok conveying the request of Burtune in a respectable manner. Sharok chuckled,

`Oh the people of Barduvai you asked me to address you but I must go back to Bazahu. There are many things I want to tell you but how can I tell you when you are not. I came prematurely you unrealised ones! Years ahead my proper visit lies'. He chuckled.

People started to murmur some regretting not having learned Kudulect while those who understood felt that his manner of speech rang familiar but they failed to agree whether it was a poet or a prophet who spoke like Sharok did that day.

`Gabriel!' one citizen hazarded a guess.

`Oh prophet Jibrin, was it?'

`There wasn't any prophet called Jibrin'

`Was it an angel or a poet who spoke like that?' One trader asked to be sure.

Sharok chuckled, 'I said I came but you are not ready for me. Your gaps have not been closed the wedge has not been removed. So I must go back to Bazahu. Be diligent in closing the gaps and trust the learned ones. The bees come to the blooming flower, the birds chirp around it, and only it stands brightly among trees. I say people of Barduvai follow those who are so that you can be'. He chuckled.

'We shall follow, we shall follow' people replied, assuming he was referring to Babbadajaka and Lamiri

Dabalo said, 'Please tell us about Kudulantis'

Sharok chuckled, 'How can I tell you about Kudulantis when you are prone to estrangement because you are not. You bewildered lot, Kudulantis is light years away. There we don't till the land, because the curse of Adam was lifted on us. You saw me eating with thorns and you giggled months after the comet has appeared in your city. How do I describe Kudulantis to you unless you know the meaning of freedom?'

'Then tell us at least about this dreadful comet' Said Dabalo. People clapped in admiration of Dabalo's ability to use advance Kudulect vocabulary.

Sharok chuckled and shook his head, 'Oh people of Barduvai the expanse of the universe is wide and you ask me questions of the bewildered ones. What is seen is seen what is unseen is hidden. If you use only your eyes, then you are deaf ones, if you use only your ears then you are blind ones. Don't you understand you heedless flock that to understand the universe you must use all your senses at once! To use all your senses at once you must be. If you are not, then you don't use your senses at once. If you use only one sense then you are a cripple, and cripples know only infinite dangers. Use your senses at once and know the freedom of the liberated ones. You must be, to be free, unless you are, you cannot be free' He chuckled.

'Do you have griots in Kudulantis?' Habarana's baritone voice rang across giving his Kudulect a unique accent that made people to laugh.

'Rot learning is for the dumb and the deaf', said Sharok, 'When Hasnamouss composed the *Castle Poem*, it came not from his memory but from active soul. He was, therefore the poem flowed from a heart that was, so that those who will read the poem shall be'.

Habarana grunted, grumbling about how he wasted his time over the years memorising the history of Barduvai and playing the ancient Kora.

'What is the nature of the disaster?' Babbadajaka asked, turning his face sweepingly to see if his question could represent the most important question that day.

Sharok shook his head and chuckled, 'the condemned prisoner examined the list of death options. What does it matter you tethered ones, whether it is fire, flood or brimstones. I say to you oh descendants of Hubaluba my visit is premature'

'Don't go without advising us since we are the ignorant ones'

`When you close the gaps, fear crumbles away, you must be to be free'.

It was at that time that Buruji came and started singing the Horrifier loudly. For the first time, people rose in anger against the dervish. Askia Burtune shouted and Barmaki and a number of guards descended on the dervish, gagging his mouth and tying his hands and legs from behind. Buruji continued singing the Horrifier nevertheless, his beard pitifully twitching as grunts and moans came out of his gagged mouth.

Judge Akilu bearing the atmosphere no longer asked Burtune, `my lord what is his crime?' Burtune turned his face away and Akilu walked out of the temple. People were too involved in listening to Sharok to have paid any attention to the exit of Akilu.

When he was leaving, Sharok gave Burtune his roller skates, thousands of people trooped behind him singing the song prepared specially by Lamiri and chanted by Gaulojo the market poet:

That day Buruji became very hyperactive. He sang the Horrifier as it was never sang before. He walked up and down the city singing, his head glistening with sweat. He must have stepped on a sharp object, for his right foot was bleeding, the red blood mixed with sand to present an awful sight that filled the citizens with pity. But agitated Buruji was totally unconcerned as he danced the rotary dance singing the Horrifier:

> *Know that the world is only a witness*
> *Know all we can gather in it can't salvage us*
> *Know that what we see in it forever will hook us*
> *Where is the pharaoh the lord of towers?*
> *Where is Hamana his master schemer?*
> *Where is Kora of the wealth that staggered camels?*

When people dispersed from the temple, it became clear that those who couldn't speak Kudulect were disadvantaged. Dabalo, Habarana, Jonkal, and many students of the Kudras were pestered with questions regarding Sharok's address. That day many vowed to be attending Lamiri's tutorials, vowing to study the history and language of Kudulantis diligently.

So many things were said about the people of Kudulantis. That they don't go to toilets, but sweat out their excrements. Others argued about their eyes, that they could see through a person's intestine. That Lamiri had learned the secrets of doing that.

Burtune was fascinated by the roller skates given to him by Sharok. Inside the palace he expressed his desire to practice riding them, but he was shy of doing so. Lamiri urged him to remove his regal attire and not to be afraid of riding the skates outside the palace.

`This is the right moment for you to understand the Rando Cartoza philosophy, my lord. I have always prayed for a time when you will be torn between such considerations.'

Akilu sensing Burtune was getting overwhelmed, told him not to forced himself into doing something he would regret, `My lord this no mount for you' he told the Askia when Lamiri started to urge the Askia to remove his turban and gown.

`You are right Akilu, I also thought it is unbecoming for me to remove my regalia. This affair must have a boundary Lamiri. I have many horses of different calibre...'

`Don't you want to ride the skates my lord?'

`Yes I do'

`Then ride my lord, ride! This is an important moment for you my lord. Don't hesitate. Remember the words of Atamin the king of the first night'

`I can never get the wits of that rascal!'

`Why, it is all in the mind, my lord! These are the times to practice the real essence of Rando Cartoza's philosophy, and Buruji is not outside, I know how...'

`Really?' asked the apprehensive Askia.

Burtune heaved a sigh and removed his regalia, Akilu protesting and finally walking out when he saw the determination of the Askia not to fail in the eyes of Lamiri. He strapped the leather wraps on his feet and breathed deeply before rolling out of the palace. Soon news spread that the Askia was riding skates given to him by Sharok Waladus.

Hundreds of citizens trooped to the palace to watch their Askia. They giggled each time he fell down and was helped by Lamiri who kept encouraging him to continue each time Burtune said it was enough. Burtune kept saying, `Oh I have disgraced myself today!' until they walked back to the court, Lamiri holding the dusty skates, the citizens laughing in amusement and wondering where in the world was Hajji Buruji singer of gehenna.

`What I did is it right Lamiri?' Burtune asked as he reclined on his throne for the first time without the royal regalia.

`My lord I told you about changing the way you perceive yourself, you are!'

`Yes I'm'

`Therefore you are! You are closing the gaps!'

`Even then, I felt as if I have disgraced myself. They must have seen my bulging stomach. It is a shame Lamiri. This your Rando Cartoza philosophy is not for Askias!'

`It is your thoughts my lord, I don't know how to make you understand'.

13

The following day citizens gathered under the gizzard rock discussing the events of the period especially the riding of the roller skates by their Askia. They said Burtune must have reached the stage of freedom that Atamin reached in his fight against his perennial soul.

Their discussion mainly centred on how closing the

gaps of 'I' can free a citizen from the dread of the imminent disaster. That day Babbadajaka was in a hilarious mood, dominating discussions as he chewed his kolanuts. His views about Rando Cartoza's principle were greatly respected because it was rumoured he memorised <u>The Confessions of King Atamin</u> and understood the story more than anyone else in the city.

'You said knowledge of Kudulantis will help us close the gaps and then when the gaps are closed one cannot feel any dread? Well I swear I still spend sleepless nights'

People laugh because they thought Sumanguru appears naive and had always been a plain unassuming person.

`Ah, ah Sumanguru, my dear Sumanguru' Babbadajaka smiled revealing his kolanut stained teeth, `It depends on how you are affected by knowledge, if you learn without doubt, you can be free but if you hesitate in swallowing, half of the morsel's benefit to your body is gone!'

`All this is too complicated for me. All these affairs ... I swear Babbadajaka I tend to feel we should go back to the Hime method. I swear I feel more comfortable'.

People laughed again.

`It is good not all people are lazy like you Sumanguru. Now that Barduvai doesn't practice the Hime, has it stopped anything? Eh has it? Ask yourselves? Has anything happened?' Babbadajaka turned around smiling and looking at the faces of the gathered citizens as he made his point, 'Like the Son of Knowledge said Hime is fear. I tell you I witnessed the conflict in the mind of our Askia before he rode the roller skate. I was there. It is not easy for one to become. It takes a lot of struggle and remembrance of self. Like Son of Knowledge said, when there are no more gabs between the 'I' then you became and all fears cease. This is the kernel of existence. As we came alone, so are we going back alone!

'But the comet is a phenomena that affects all of us' lamented Sumanguru.

'It affects all of us but each of us must find a way to cope with it, because each of us is. Are you not Sumanguru?'

'Yes I'm', answered Sumanguru reluctantly in order not to further look foolish.

'Therefore you are', said Babbadajaka 'you folks are just being naive, as Lamiri has said at the Kudras. Take for example the affair of catabeans and laradish, when these crops were brought, the whole city was against it. Now after Sharok Waladus came and went, everyone has started to eat once in a while in his house. Did we have any Hime on it? Previously didn't most people complain that catabeans gave them diarrhoea? Have their guts changed after the visit of Sharok?'

People burst out laughing.

'Babbadajaka you have gone far with the Rando Cartoza's principle but remember not all of us have gone that far...'

'Now when this disaster comes what are we going to do?'

'I heard Dabalo saying it would be lighting that would strike the Tibesti'

'Who said?'

'Dabalo'

'Dabalo didn't say that. It was Lamiri who said it not Dabalo.'

'Listen, Lamiri said a rainbow would preceded the arrival of the Magog creatures'

'But no creatures were mentioned in the sentence brought from Bazahu'

'All these arguments are useless' Babbadajaka said, 'study the Kudulect hard. Lamiri said study the Kudulect hard and understand the history of Kudulantis, then the meaning of the mandamus and what you need to do would become clear.'

'Mandamus, what is mandamus, I ask?'

Babbadajaka turned to him smiling, 'Let me give you an example, remember when Atamin said "on my left is Slaughery the executioner and on my right is Analog my scribe, you are my subjects and my jury, I tell you I have a perennial soul" do you understand the deeper meaning?'

'No'

'Truly unless you study deep the Kudulantic history and language the nuances of such would escape you'.

`This Kudulantic people are really strange. Sharok is the first visitor isn't he?'

`Who told you that?' Babbadajaka asked turning to Dabalo Ceddo, `The Son of Knowledge told me privately that the first man from Kudulantis was a man called Presto Yohah. You never heard of him in our history. There is Habarana, in all his narrations have you ever heard of Presto Yohah? No. This man Presto Yohah, Son of Knowledge said, was the first man ever from Kudulantis to come to Barduvai. He came to teach us knowledge but unfortunately he turned into a hunter of monitor lizards, for the reptile, he found out, has great medicinal substance that was valuable to his people. One day however approaching a hole he mistook a viper for a lizard and that was his end'

The citizens dispersed in twos and threes laughing and talking about how Babbadajaka was advanced in Rando Cartoza's principle and the history of Kudulantis. Owner of 30 mules, a large catabeans and laradish farm and reader of *The Confessions of King Atamin*.

14

The inner chamber of the Temple of Light was lavishly furnished. It was said in Barduvai at that time that if a person pursues the Rando Cartoza's philosophy relentlessly, a time will come when the person will desire seclusion for self-realisation sessions especially as he gets closer to closing the gaps of his `I'. Babbadajaka especially kept referring to Atamin's request for a castle as the important point in the realisation envisaged by Rando Cartoza.

So the Temple of Light was regarded as following the step of Atamin 'the king of the first night'. On a carpet beside the bed and resting their elbows on cushions, reclined Lamiri and Barmaki.

During Kudras tutorials in the day, Barmaki had beaten Sumanguru for giggling when he couldn't recite the 48 alphabets of the Kudulect. After months in the Kudras, Barmaki couldn't memorise more than 10 alphabets. He vowed to drop out of the Kudras, as Lamiri carefully reassured him.

`All this is caused by lack of promotion in your duty. In Kudulantis guards like you are graded. First from ordinary guards to *guardonel,* then after some years to *Guardodier* and then *Guardoral* and finally *Guardomarshall.* In that way you feel valued and thereafter confident. But here it was the Hime ruling and everything else was secondary. Recall deeply and figure out the great duties you performed before. Like on the day of the fallen rock when you prepared the horses very well'.

Barmaki drinking gruel from a calabash nodded.
'I will surely discuss with the Askia on how palace guards are graded and promoted. You know they even give medals to decorate their chests. Warum Kudulix alone had 50 of such medals adorning his wide chest

before he died. In truth every action deserve a medal. You see we need to get rid of the old dervish. When he disappears, then we shall introduce many changes in this city. Let him disappear first!'

`On his own he would leave the city. Why should we bear the blood of an old dervish?' Barmaki asked.

`It pains me how the Askia keeps getting nervous about this oldman. He is preventing the Askia from realising himself. He is dangerous to us!'

` Don't you worry at all! I will never allow him into the palace ever again' Barmaki said.

'Not that only. Our Askia is always afraid of doing things outside as if the oldman is a hanging sword'

Habarana arrived and sought permission to enter the parlour, his zebu horn hitting the door and making a dingy sound, `Master of knowledge!' he saluted Lamiri and smiling went straight to the bowl of gruel to help himself after hanging his zebu horn on a rafter.

`The Hasnamouss of Barduvai' Lamiri teased him.

`Who will give me the talent of Hasnamouss, my lord? This great poet who was in no need of Kora or a zebu horn'

`Gradually Habarana. Gradually, wisdom in life is a pinnacle that is to be sought not bestowed.'

`You can start by cutting the number of meals you eat. You are killing your mule, its back is already like a bow', Barmaki said jokingly.

Lamiri laughed, and Habarana smiled as usual, `Oh please stop exaggerating, Babbadajaka is heftier than I yet you don't express that. You are exaggerating on me!'

`Would you like to sing a parody Habarana?'

`What is parody?' he asked in between two gulps of gruel.

`I want you to make a mockery of Buruji's Horrifier'

`We don't have such in our oral traditions. Why do you want to mock the oldman? His anger is not particular to any person.' Habarana said swallowing some gruel.

`I want you to just mimic the Horrifier in a mocking way. This is the highest form of art in Kudulantis.'

Habarana grunted and continued drinking the gruel. Lamiri sensed he was not impressed and that if he didn't play it safely he may cause a short barrier between him and Habarana who was too valuable an asset to waste, `I have invited Gaulojo as well' he added.

`Well now you have named the right person. This is his field sir. He is good in proverbs, riddles, praise poetry, and insults. He is versed in our oral traditions' said Habarana with relieve.

When Gaulojo the market poet came, he walked in nervously as it was his first time of coming into the Temple of Light.

`Come in and sit down' urged Lamiri.

Gaulojo sat down looking avariciously at the various decorations in the chamber. There were colourful calabashes adorning the walls and a large bed at the farthest end of the chamber decorated with many pillows.

Gaulojo thought the room was anything but a meditation chamber. Several times he heard traders arguing about the need for a secluded place to fully appreciate Rando Cartoza's principle.

`I want to pay you a fee to sing a parody for me'

`Parody?' He sceptically asked turning to look at Habarana who was drinking gruel `I have never done such'.

`I also said I have never heard of it in our traditions' Habarana absolved himself, 'He said this parody is like mimicry'

`This sounds like provocation to me. You know it is forbidden in our traditions' Gaulojo said.

`I hate to hear about traditions, taboos, months after you heard about Rando Cartoza's principle. 'Answer this question Gaulojo, have you ever mimic any sound' Lamiri asked.

`Of course I did that several times when I was a child'

`So you can mimic, if you can mimic you can parody. I am suggesting to you how to make cowries. I advised Habarana to throw away his Kora and fashion the zebu horn. And now he is ahead.' For the first time Gaulojo heard how Habarana adopted the zebu horn.

'Parody the Horrifier'.

Gaulojo was silent for some moments. He looked at Barmaki and Habarana and wondered if they were not plotting to get him into trouble. `But why should they?' he thought, concluding that Habarana refused to accept the offer because it was not his field.

`I dread to earn cowries by insulting people' Gaulojo

said.

'How much would that cost?' Lamiri asked quickly to divert his attention. He knew the Horrifier had become part of the people, they may not pay any attention to it but they as well wouldn't take it kindly to anyone who would mock it. A song that had been ringing in their ears for years. But Gaulojo also realised he needed some cowries. Praise singing was not as patronised as before. He usually compose praise poems for salt traders and herders who on market days, the day they choose to enjoy themselves most, pay him heavily.

They had loved to hear his enchanting voice ringing across the market. Some said when Gaulojo sang it was as if the ancestors had sanctioned his voice. They had loved to hear him sing about how they could build houses on cattle horns or turn water into milk. But times had changed, the comet had appeared and the pastures were no more as green as before. So nomads don't patronise him as often as before. The nomads say, 'this dreadful comet stares at them mercilessly especially in the night when they was nothing between the comet and their kraals'. They therefore no longer desired to be praised, 'what are you going to be praised for under this dreadful comet!' they lamented.

If in the earlier days you could hear his voice ringing every minute on market days, after the appearance of the comet it was a good day if you heard his voice five times during any market day. Gaulojo sighed deeply knowing the enormity of the task he was to carry out. 'How much are you going to pay me son of the venerable?'

'Three hundred cowries'

'It is going to be difficult and you know I'm putting my life on danger. This one is in the same category as insult. You know I'm a praise singer, we only insult when we are forced to defend our profession, parody you said? Well this is not Kudulantis...'

'We shall protect you against any eventuality', Barmaki said waving his arm. That seemed to have comforted Gaulojo, for he knew Barmaki was the most feared guard in the city.

'Give me five hundred cowries then, I would do the job'

'I have an evening class, not to prolong our discussion; I would give you what you asked for. I want the parody sang next Friday. You get your cowries after that and not before'. Gaulojo left the house wondering why Lamiri should pay such a huge sum of cowries just to mock an old dervish who was not an enemy to any one in particular in Barduvai. Shortly after Gaulojo left, Jabbi and her friends arrived into the temple. Lamiri quickly send Habarana to tell Jengeldo to go and cancel the Kudras class.

'Please Jabbi sing for us' Lamiri said, too excited to sit down. Jabbi laughed and started to sing the *Careless Girl* in her reverberating mermaid voice with her friends. Lamiri signalled Barmaki to stand up and dance.

The Pyramid of Askia Burtune

I am forever and ever a real one
For I bath and wash
I pick eye pencil and apply
I pick lotion and smear
I pick perfume and spray
And I always pick my handbag and fumble

I am forever and ever a real one
I heard they desire an old man for me
If that is so may my ornaments be cursed!
How I wish men have breast for girls to watch too!

I am forever and ever a real one
Walakiri make men cry make men swear
Walakiri give men pebbles to grind
Don't give them grains to grind

I am forever and ever a real one
If mother -in- law beats me
And I turn my back
If father - in- law beats me
And I turn my back
If a step - mother- in - law beats
We go into a rumble
Dragging ourselves to the river bank

To drop more leaves

I am forever and ever a real one!

As Lamiri and Barmaki danced their bulging stomachs swayed and made the girls to reel back in laughter. Even Habarana chuckled saying, 'Please stop this joke, you are responsible persons you shouldn't dance like this'

'Leave them' Jabbi laughed mischievously 'we must go to Poli tomorrow and dance in the open where everyone is seen. How can you dance in a room and enjoy yourself'.

Barmaki grunted before sitting and resuming eating his roasted turkey. He was looking grim and regretting agreeing to join Lamiri in the dance. He thought they had turned themselves into a laughing stock.

Lamiri was less concern and was breathing heavily after the few dance steps. As the girls laugh at him he pointed at Habarana saying the griot must practice playing violin to accompany the song.

'I have since abandoned the Kora and you are telling me to pick a violin. This will be a disgrace to a griot'.

15

Dabalo Ceddo stopped gulping gruel; he placed the calabash spoon on the weaved cover and reclined on the wooden cloister of the stall, watching Jonkal Awembi as he continued drinking from the gourd. The whole city was obsessed with fighting the dread they felt about the impending disaster

Dabalo was less worried. After the departure of Sharok Waladus, Dabalo was greatly disappointed that he was not honoured as promised by Lamiri.

'I may stop going to the Kudras'

'Hmm' grunted Jonkal as he gulped in gruel, his beard jutting up and down. Dabalo often felt something is hidden in Jonkal Awembi's mind, but he couldn't fathom what it was. It was like Jonkal while being with the Kudras group, was having his own plans. Dabalo suspected Jonkal hated them. He couldn't know why, so he dismissed that from his mind. Jonkal Awembi talked little, spoke from the throat and generally stuck around the butchers.

'What do you thing about Rando Cartoza principle?'

'You know better Dab' Said Jonkal as he wiped his moustache.

Dabalo felt unperturbed by the impending disaster. Was it because he had read Rando Cartoza's principle, the history of Kudulantis and the Confessions of Atamin? He wondered. His most serious concern was how his respect for Lamiri has withered. Whenever people gathered around him, whenever he spoke to inquisitive citizens about Atamin and Rando Cartoza, Dabalo sense a certain dislike for him.

After the visit of Sharok things were changing very

fast in Barduvai. Most people came to accept that an imminent disaster lied ahead of them. The comet was true to them, every night they gazed wondering how many years it would take for the comet to cross the Tibesti Mountain, and the impending disaster to occur

Lamiri had said that the secret of salvation from the imminent disaster lies in knowledge of the history of Kudulantis and especially a personal actualisation of Rando Cartoza's philosophy.

People were obsessed with finding personal meaning of the impending disaster, despite, their continuous lack of agreement concerning the nature of the disaster. Kudras bright students like Fargarjaji and Dabalo Ceddo and Jonkal Awembi had gone far in studies. They memorised the story of Atamin and the philosophy of Rando Cartoza.

As their knowledge of Kudulantis increased, they grew confident and started asking tough questions during lessons. Many times, Lamiri refused to answer their questions. Babbadajaka had grown rich from his exports to Kudulantis and the contract of building the Temple of Light. He sought for a special permission to build a castle based on the design of the Temple of Light at his personal expense. The Askia gave him a huge plot near the Daula Orchard. When the castle was completed, it was celebrated with pomp. A small horse durbar was organised, and Babbadajaka was escorted to spend a night in his castle of contemplation.

`Just like Atamin! Just like Atamin!' Lamiri kept telling Babbadajaka as they escorted him to the castle amidst blaring *Algaita* and drums.

`Babbadajaka is a lucky one, he must be among those to be saved' people said, as many yearned to build a castle like that of Babbadajaka. But to do that required a huge sum of cowries. Babbadajaka imported many horses of different breed and colours from Egypt. In the evenings he rode one of them to the fascination of citizens, who stood in groups arguing about the breed of the horses and how many cowries Babbadajaka had made from exports.

`Why could you get enough cowries to build a castle unless you are an exporter of laradish or catabeans', Seibu Albasa kept telling ambitious traders.

The beginning of the second year of the comet was a period when the individual search for salvation from the day of disaster was at its peak. The *Confessions of King Atamin* became a popular narration in Barduvai, especially among youth. The sons of Babbadajaka and Burtune were the first to open a shop they called Atamin Plaza. There, charcoal drawings of a naked Atamin laying on a rug and carvings of his Julmire Castle were displayed for sale. Those who were regarded advanced in Rando Cartoza's principle adorn their parlours with it. In addition nude statuettes and drawings of what they called the *Spinsters of Kudulantis* also started appearing at that time. Soon other youth started copying the success of the Atamin Plaza by opening their own with different names. Elders in the city were annoyed but couldn't do anything, "nudity and nakedness for sale! What a shame" they can only exclaimed.

Tugga couldn't believe the amazing speed events were overtaking Barduvai. He was so worried that he started to lose weight. Day and night he tried hard to figure out how he could convince the people that the comet was a hoax and that real salvation lied in the Hime and the Kalfuuje project.

It was extremely difficult he knew because he had lost prestige and finding a superior way to restore faith was very difficult. Tataraktu at first laughed at him for taking affairs so seriously but later when she realised her husband was losing weight she started to get really concern.

`You are worrying yourself to ill health. What is your concern, if they all want it that way, who are you to say it is different'.

`My bitterness is the ease with which that rascal has overridden people'

`He is a worldly man who had travelled far. He must have learned some superior wits. Leave them to time.'

Tugga couldn't, so he set to work on a theme of finding a way to restore the faith of people. He decided on the thema: *Revealing the truth about the Object*. It was particularly difficult but he decided on the idea of developing an observatory that can reveal what the object in the sky was. He thought what Barduvai needed most was an observatory station. He realised that plotting a daily almanac alone was not sufficient for a cynical citizenry to appreciate. It was only by sufficiently revealing the object can people start to be objective. The Hime method was forgotten and he knew no citizen was ready to sit to a session of Hime.

During that period, Fargarjaji wrote a small book about the contemporary history of Barduvai in Kudulect and titled it _Barduvai since Waladus._ It was an interesting booklet because it especially traced the conflict that nearly resulted into anarchy in Barduvai.

The revival for the search of origins began after a lecture delivered by Lamiri on the essence of the Rando Cartoza's philosophy especially in regard to individual search for meaning in life. Some citizens said that it started with the mentioned by Lamiri that Tugga came from Nok, a group of what he called `bloody figurine makers'. I was present during the lecture but I didn't hear the man said that Tugga came from Nok. Some said he said it outside the class after the lecture. At that time I was not present. Whatever, thereafter the search for origins became a serious matter in Barduvai. As the kernel of existence, it was agreed that when a person closes the gaps between his 'I', according to Rando Cartoza, then his personal attributes and history becomes important- his origin, his language, his likes and dislikes, etc. Every aspect of his world is illuminated. To understand the tension that arose, we must recall that it was taboo in Barduvai to identify a person by his *origin. It normally started with a rumour about a person coming from a certain place, then that person upon hearing it vehemently denying it and subsequently trying to find the person who started the rumour. The rumour mongers were never found and in the end people just vented their anger to all citizens some accepting the labels of origins and defending it vehemently. The question of who is an aborigine arose. Some said Damolishi was the only citizen who can claim aboriginality. Opponents denied saying he came from Gudur. Even top citizens were not excluded. For instance, it was rumoured, Judge Akilu came from Agades and therefore had no right to preside as judge in Barduvai. Typical of Akilu he ordered the arrest of Habarana and refused to let him go until he told him who started the rumour. The judge said he held Habarana responsible for all rumours in Barduvai because he was the only griot he knew there. After Habarana disclosed the origin of the rumour, I heard there was a row in the palace, but it was hidden from the citizens. All citizens unanimously or so it appeared abhorred the rumour mongering but it appeared there weren't ways to stopping it. A taboo was broken and the consequences of which could never be fathomed until after some years it seems. With the demise of the Hime method, citizens gathered under the gizzard rock most evenings during sunset to argue on many topics, frequently resulting into fights...*

Many students of the Kudras copied Fargarjaji's manuscript and soon it was in wide circulation in Barduvai. Habarana undertook to read portions of the manuscript in the evenings under the gizzard rock, where citizens argued on the points mentioned there, disputing and arguing especially when Fargarjaji was around to answer charges of false narrations.

Sometimes it appeared as if the citizens were keener on aggravating his allergic conditions than forcing a debate on him. Seibu Albasa, the prominent grocer especially was a persistent critic of Fargarjaji. Citizens had always found the verbal confrontations between the two to be hilarious. Seibu had always said that Fargarjaji was an ingrate, especially when he criticised Lamiri. Seibu had believed Fargarjaji was misusing his knowledge and being unnecessarily angry when he should use his knowledge to seek for wealth.

16

One Friday towards the end of A.A.C 2 the Barduvai market was full as usual. Under the baobab tree stood some people studying Tugga's almanac and expressing how the comet was moving closer and closer to the Tibesti Mountain. Dabalo was arguing with Fargarjaji about the way to measure the movement of heavenly bodies. He said he heard Lamiri saying the baobab tree was not a suitable object for studying a heavenly body.

The market was full, herders, milkmaids, and traders from neighbouring cities and settlements. It was the early part of the day when traders had finished displaying their goods and were looking forward to a prosperous day.

Gaulojo knew Buruji only arrive the market after the Friday congregational prayers. He chose the period when it was easy for his voice to reach all nooks and corners of the market. His enchanting voice echoed across the market whenever he sang. It was said his mother fed him with crickets when he was young, which was how he got a strong voice. He cleared his voice and started the paid parody:

> Ahoy me Gaulojo singer of the wild
> Ahoy Barduvai the haven of strangers
> Land of Hubaluba the domain of Samba Tengele
> Ahoy people under the Tibesti
> Come and listen to my satanic song

People were surprised at the change in Gaulojo's pattern of singing. It didn't sound like he was going to praise any one, so people stopped whatever they were doing and listened attentively especially as he called his song, satanic. When he started the satanic song it was obvious he was mimicking Buruji.

People stood in disbelieve wondering if Gaulojo had gone mad. They couldn't believe someone could mimic the voice of Buruji let alone parody his Horrifier. No one knew who informed Buruji but he came waving his staff looking particularly violent.

Upon seeing the gleam of anger on Buruji's face, Gaulojo ran across the market kicking milk gourds and jumping over grain sellers. He first hid at the butchers but realising he had no sympathy from them and realising one of them could have easily knifed him, he ran to the Tibesti where he hid in one of the caves. Peeping from the entrance of the cave in the evening, he saw Buruji dancing his whirling dance in front of the saint cave.

They said in confinement people grow wiser, Gaulojo regretted with utmost regret his acceptance to parody the Horrifier of Buruji. He expected Lamiri to show up or to at least send some encouraging words. None of that happened, so he ate wild berries and spent a week in the cave before the figure of Barmaki appeared. He looked at Gaulojo gravely and threw a bag of cowries at him.

Gaulojo screamed, `Is that all!'

`Don't shout at me. That is your fee' he turned and started walking down the mountain.

`I don't want the cowries. You hear! Take these cowries back to the bastard!' Gaulojo threw the bag of cowries, which landed in front of Barmaki. The Guard stooped, shocked at how daring Gaulojo was. He turned and glared at him but Gaulojo looked back in defiance, `I want my life not some cowries!' he shouted, `You know very well that old dervish would kill me', he said in a frustrated voice.

`Why don't you get down to the city and sing about it!' shouted Barmaki.

`Good thing to say to a poet. Well thank you and bye', he waved at Barmaki who realised he shouldn't have approach the matter the way he did. He realised the level of frustration the poet was in.

He thought of murdering him and putting to rest once and for all the threat he might have posed to him and Lamiri but changed his mind, especially as he was not carrying a sword with him, `We have a plan if you are patient'

`What type of plan? I want to get out of here today. This is what I want and I'm tired of eating wild berries and sleeping in a cave'

`Just wait can't you, I will be back soon. Barmaki went back into the city and returned with a fake beard and a hat. He asked Gaulojo to put it on and told him that from then henceforth he was to be Paha, the dumb onion seller. That four sacks of onions were waiting for him at the grocer's corner in the market.

`I have already told Seibu Albasa the leader of the grocers that you are my uncle, under no circumstances should you talk to people. You must remain Paha the dumb onion seller. Do you understand'.

`Impossible! If you think you can silence me that way you are wrong', Gaulojo shouted.

`Well for the sake of your life, do what I told you to do' Barmaki said walking down the mountain.

Gaulojo thought deeply about Barmaki's proposal. He knew his life was in danger once Buruji knew where he was. There was no question of migration, because he knew wherever he went to, news would arrive in

Barduvai because he was popular and Buruji would seek for him until the end of the world. He was however tired of eating wild berries, and anything was better than staying in the cave.

He wore the costume brought and walked down the mountain. As he did so, he saw Buruji performing his rotary dance in front of the saint cave. Although he felt save in the Paha costume, the thought of leading a life as a dumb onion trader greatly troubled him. He turned back and looked at Buruji and felt envious of the old dervish. Now the old man had power over his life. For the first time in his life the meaning of power over life dawned on him profoundly and he began to cry as he descended down the mountain.

At the grocery section of Barduvai market, Seibu Albasa, the leader of the grocers there smiled and made some dumb signs to him welcoming him to their section. Tears started to roll down the cheeks of Paha and Seibu asked the other traders if he made a nasty sign, but they told him he was correct. Thereafter he offered Paha some gruel, which he ordered specially for him.

In tears, and watched sympathetically by the grocers, Paha drank the gruel, his first meal for over eight days. He felt a certain dry feeling in his throat, the kind that results from anger, but he was not sure if he was angry with himself for being used by Lamiri or angry for accepting to turn into a dump onion trader. More tears rolled down his cheeks.

`Why is he crying?' Seibu was worried, `Barmaki told me he was born deaf'

`Only god knows why. I swear Seibu, remove his side burns, his beard and the moustache and I will swear he resembles the wicked Gaulojo. Sorry to say'.

`No don't say that'. They turned looking at Paha.

Upon hearing this, Paha wiped his tears quickly, stopped drinking the gruel pulled his straw hat over his forehead and turned his face away from the grocers. A dump onion trader is better than a lynched Gaulojo, he thought.

17

Sumanguru is short and walk with a limp, a result of a fall from a baobab tree when he was ten. His addiction to the baobab fruit earned him a nickname 'Guru Nboye' in his youth. When the sun was setting, Sumanguru now addicted to listening to the arguments walked to the Gizzard Rock thinking how sad it was that unexpected thing as the insult of Hajji Buruji was allowed in Barduvai, all in the name of Rando Cartoza. 'How in the world had Gaulojo who is not even a disciple of the Kudras got the idea of parodying the Horrifier?' he wondered as he walked thoughtfully to the rock. Approaching, he saw Damolishi straddled on the rock as usual and he wondered if the old warrior saw Gaulojo escaped the city if he ever did that through the west.

Under the rock he saw among the assembled citizens as usual, Fargarjaji, Seibu, Babbadajaka, and Jonkal Awembi. They were arguing heatedly. He guessed they're arguing about the outrageous parody by Gaulojo. Arguments were by then carried out in Kudulect as citizens like Babbadajaka and Fargarjaji had mastered the language adequately enough to use it in any discourse. Those who were less fluent kept mute, as they felt ashamed to speak in bad Kudulect.

'No one should be surprised that Gaulojo parodied the Horrifier. Since the coming of Waladus everything is changing in Barduvai. It is a hidden agenda of the Kudulantis executed by their surrogates', shouted Fargarjaji.

'Fargarjaji you're troublesome, what is it that make the Askia and the Son of Knowledge surrogates? Gaulojo sang what he felt like singing. Everybody is becoming as if you don't know Fargarjaji' Babbadajaka said smiling

'Is that all. Notice the increase in the consumption of larradish and catabeans. These shouldn't be our stable food.'

'Ah, ah did you earnestly expect us to be eating only cornflour and Agama lizards'

'Not that only. Why should the Askia be riding roller-skates when expensive horses like Fileenge are bought for him with public cowries!' Fargarjaji was flaring up as usual.

Seibu stood up from where he was glaring at Fargarjaji, 'this is Barduvai city not a village. Our Askia should ride on the best horses and roller skates. Because you are unblessed, you want everybody to be in rags and tartars like you'.

People burst out in laughter, including Babbadajaka who bared his kolanuts tainted teeth.

'Seibu you always interrupt me when I speak, I warn you I hate this, you Kudulantic surrogate!' shouted Fargarjaji.

'Here comes Dabalo!' Sumanguru announced. Dabalo arrived with his usual heavy steps and inexplicable grunts that made people assume he was just about to speak. Sumanguru since Dabalo rescued him from the clutches of Barmaki on that terrible day he giggled when Barmaki couldn't read all the 48 alphabets of Kudulect, had loved his over-bearing presence in gatherings.

Sumanguru had since concluded that Rando Cartoza's principle means apathy and among all the Kudras students it was only Dabalo who had shown he could still be brotherly. Dabalo despite his knowledge of the Kudulect and the principles of Rando Cartoza still had remained attached to Barduvai's legends, tales and traditions. Whenever there was a heated argument regarding the relevance of Rando Cartoza's principle, he had suggested the digging into the past traditions of Barduvai and its lore to come up with fresh solutions. His favourite tradition was that of the famous Bazadi incantation. A certain Bazadi, it was reported, had used an ancient incantation to mobilise a group of youth to save ancient Barduvai from marauders.

18

Paha was resting on two sacks of onions, with his straw hat drawn over his eyes. He bought a larger straw hat, large enough to cover his face from inquisitive glares, especially when citizen kept referring to how he resembled Gaulojo. Now he kept mute and dump as he was initially commanded. He found it very hard to communicate in the sign language at the beginning but later learned enough to sell to people especially as it didn't take more than stretching the number of fingers representing the price of a heap of either onions or tomatoes.

He listened to two grocers argued with Sumanguru about the applicability of Rando Cartoza's philosophy in Barduvai. The Hime, maintained Sumanguru, still remained the best salvation for the people of Barduvai.

`How do we go back to it, something that has passed already, can you even recall how sessions were started?'

Paha has since sold the sacks he was given and had preferred to be an assistant to Seibu who spent most of his time purchasing vegetables in bulk from neighbouring settlements. After selling the two sacks of onions initially offered to him, he couldn't balance his finance and wondered admiringly how the grocers were able to manage their lives on selling vegetables.

Paha also realised it was exciting listening to the world without responding. It set him to think a lot about people's beliefs and methods of reasoning. He realised, speech robs people the power of listening and the ability to assess and understand people. Most people he realised are poor listeners and that has robbed them the ability for genuine sympathy. He began to feel pity for the grocers and other citizens who discussed Rando Cartoza's principle and the general problems in Barduvai.

They tend to talk, it appeared, as a way to understand the topic they were discussing not to find a solution. Paha found that strange, and felt people were just pitiful, bewildered creatures trying to force meaning in their existence. Much of their talks centred on rehearsing what they heard, especially the repeating of stock phrases they heard elsewhere. But each speaker appeared to be contented after others listened to what he had to say. No insight, no solution, just sheer joy of lamentation.

It was while he was sympathetically watching the grocers argue that Seibu returned in a hurry and informed them that Lamiri was going to prepare a portion from the skin mat used by Sharok during his blessed visit. That people were rushing in numbers to the clinic to drink a portion. Seibu quickly folded his mat and stacked his cowries inside his pocket.

Paha eagerly joined the grocers in a rush to the clinic. At the clinic he saw Lamiri talking and gesticulating as a group of citizens gathered to taste the blessings of

Sharok's mat.

'This is the blessed skin mat the august visitor used during his entire visit. Let this day mark the day when people will openly imbibe Rando Cartoza's principle and do away with darkness. Where are those who said they could not comprehend Rando Cartoza's principle, this is the day to cast out the doubt in your minds. Come forward and drink from the seat of an epitome. Waladus' visit was the most precious of all visits by mortals to Barduvai. Come forward and drink the dispeller of darkness and fear. Come and find cure from the blessed mat of Sharok Waladus'

Paha nearly shouted 'You bloody liar!' as Lamiri folded the mat and deep it into a barrel of boiling water. People waited in eagerness as Lamiri asked an assistant to stir the mat. He brought out a bag of small gourds, which he filled and sold at five cowries each. Soon news spread that Lamiri prepared a protection against the imminent disaster. People especially traders rushed to his clinic to buy the portion.

'By the grace of Rando Cartoza!' An old blind man guided by his son moved towards Lamiri, 'Help me my son. Help me, by the grace of Sharok Waladus'.

The Blind man drank the portion, 'I'm, and I'm by the grace of Rando Cartoza'.

'You should be, my dear old man. Believe that you

are! Cure can come only when you know you are. It is your mind that is a barrier between healing and you. Fight your minds!'

The oldman drank the portion uttering `I am. I am. By the grace of Rando Cartoza!'

It was while people were queuing and buying the portion that Buruji came in a hurry his eyes rolling as usual. From a distance Tugga saw the dervish coming. Buruji walked straight to the barrel and he started exhorting;

`Fear oh citizens! Have the seal being drawn on your hearts?'

`Now keep away from this Buruji. I'm warning you' Lamiri warned.

Buruji undauntedly went to the boiling barrel and kicked it to the ground spilling its content. In a swift reaction, Lamiri punched him hard on the face and the old dervish fell to the ground clutching his face. The crowd became silent as Tugga rushed to the fallen dervish who stood up using his turban to cover his swollen eye. For the first time people saw that he was bald-headed.

People stood in distress for nobody was expecting that any one in Barduvai would strike Buruji. Many were filled with pity as the dervish sullenly walked away. Tugga picked the staff he left behind and followed him to the mosque.

He entered the mosque but didn't see Buruji. He found him in the inner recess, standing mysteriously close to the bier carriage. Tugga stood distress in front of the dervish. He notice pain has disappeared from the face of the dervish and was looking rather too sober and mysterious. Tugga felt anguish as to why he didn't strike Lamiri. He wished he had the impulse and personality of Dabalo Ceddo, who wouldn't have hesitated to slap Lamiri, was he around when the incident had happened.

'Forgive me sir' Tugga said sweating and holding his metal flute on the left and Buruji's staff on the right.

'What have you done my Tugga you can't be responsible for what is happening in Barduvai, hmm' The Dervish sighed deeply

'I'm sad sir'

'Yes life is full of sadness Tugga'

'What can I do sir?' asked Tugga in a serious voice.

'Fight your sorrow, why do you let them disorient you?'

'How do I do that sir?' Tugga asked with a concerned voice.

'Don't be unmindful even for a moment. Now leave me alone. Go', he said collecting his staff from Tugga's hands

Tugga walked out, he wondered about life in Barduvai and how to escape its sorrow and pain. 'Don't be unmindful even once' He recalled how Buruji's method always insisted he ploughed ridges in the orchard or work in his workshop while remembering the fire of Gehenna. The aim is to escape the eternal fire, Buruji had always insisted, all other things were secondary he had said.

He remembered very well when he told the dervish that continuous remembrance of Gehenna rather contradicts the Hime method, and Sheikh Marduka's insistence that the scale is always closer to the people than to posterity. 'Don't be unmindful for a moment' be mindful of what then? Was Rando Cartoza after all right that to be mindful of self is after all the beginning of freedom? Mindful of what, Gehenna, self, what? He recalled vividly how the dervish had once pulled a red-hot iron from the furnace in his workshop and holding it inches away from the twitching eyes of Tugga, had said 'Behold!' watching Tugga intently. That day Tugga had sighed resuming his work but the impression made on him by this dramatic display lingered on for many days.

At the clinic many students of the Kudras confronted Lamiri who kept shouting 'I am! I am! What do you mean by restraint? He provoked me physically!' Citizens were not convinced. Dabalo was away from the city then. Some people said it would have been different was Dabalo around when the incident happened. The situation was as if everybody was waiting for someone or something to happen in retaliation for the incident. Was Burtune going to say 'enough is enough' and dismiss Lamiri? Was a divine retribution coming on the city?

The following day Buruji disappeared from the city without any trace. Before he left, he cleaned the mosque perfectly and filled all the jars with water. Many thought he had retreated to the cave and was to return very soon, but alas! Buruji never turned up again. Many people were angry at the way Buruji was treated but Lamiri too appeared to have fled from the city for he was not seen the following day either. A group of citizens climbed the cave to see if Buruji was there, but they didn't find him. Lamiri was neither in the Kudras, nor in his clinic nor at the palace.

Some people suggested Buruji might have gone to a neighbouring village and would soon return. Soon rumours started to circulate, that some traders have seen him in Walata, others said in Poli among some nomads. They said it was unthinkable for Buruji to leave Barduvai. Who would ever thought of Barduvai without Buruji or Buruji without Barduvai?

A group of concerned market traders led by Halabutu and Jari Daniro combed the surrounding villages and bushes but no news of the dervish was heard. So they returned to Barduvai after three days tired and sad. People never realised how Buruji's Horrifier had become part of them until he left.

Traders felt a certain hollowness which they couldn't explain as they transacted their businesses daily without Buruji hovering over their heads and singing the Horrifier. They agreed they never gave much thought to the Horrifier, and yet they missed it.

Citizens were overwhelmed; things were getting beyond their comprehension. The Tibesti sundered, a comet appeared, Gaulojo's provocation, Lamiri's assault and now Buruji of all had left the city. Everywhere citizens gathered lamenting and sighing, especially at their frustration of not being able to remove the dread in their minds using the Rando Cartoza principle.

A rumour about Lamiri began to circulate that he had travelled to apologise to Buruji and bring back the old dervish. Others said he had travelled to Kudulantis.

In desperation people tried to find a person who could remember the Horrifier by heart. Many students were called upon and old teachers were asked; yet no one could recite a single stanza of the Horrifier. It became horrifying! And the whole city nearly panicked when they realised no one can remember even a single stanza of the song. A brief rumour began to circulate that Tugga Bukele had some years ago started transcribing the song in Kalfuuje script.

Askia Burtune who sensed trouble was brewing in the city ordered Barmaki to bring out the Kalfuuje slates hoping to assuage the anger of citizens. To the dismay of all he brought out the slates that was as clean as mirrors. 'Who washed the slates?' Barmaki swore it wasn't him.

In a frantic effort, a meeting of prominent traders was called in the market square in a session that resembled Hime. They decided on the thema of *restoring the Horrifier*. In that meeting a large sum of cowries was allocated as a prize to anyone who can restore at least seven stanzas of the Horrifier so that they could recite them as they sell their goods. A second meeting was to be convened again after three days.

Habarana reported the meeting to Babbadajaka who knowing the Askia will be bewildered in the absence of Lamiri went to his palace to counsel him.

It was while the traders were having a second meeting that Apiru Daragal, a salt trader, arrived in the meeting and started yelling `May the comet land on our heads this afternoon, yeeeoh hoh!' which he kept screaming repeatedly. It was said somebody in the palace bribed him, but most traders saw it as a punishment for not protecting Hajji Buruji. They reported the case to the market warden, Makawuya.

`I'm surprised; you brought such a case to me. Are you suggesting Apiru Daragal is not worthy of self-realisation?'

Babbadajaka who was among the crowd that day added by saying, `If he had kept silent that would be more sinister of him. Apiru Daragal is, therefore he yelled, because he is'.

After that the traders had no doubt in their mind that Babbadajaka was bribing Apiru Daragal to be yelling. Thereafter the question of his freedom to yell whatever he wanted was only in accordance with Rando Cartoza's philosophy. The traders knew Makawuya hated them for exposing his embezzlement of market funds. He never forgave Halabutu and Jari Daniro for their roles in the affair.

With that, fear of the comet increased and people became more worried about their fates but unsure of what to make of Rando Cartoza's approach. Most people were at pain on how to significantly relate personally to the unfolding events in Barduvai. In bewilderment some people preferred to revert back to older more indigenous beliefs. A new group of citizens vowed to restore the Horrifier in Barduvai. Their creed was based on the belief that all problems in Barduvai was caused by citizen's inability to have listened to Buruji and imitated his Horrifier.

Dabalo Ceddo by then feeling his opinion about Lamiri publicly has been vindicated felt confident enough to denounce Lamiri for what he did and called the Rando Cartoza philosophy a corruption of the soul. He said there was no method to salvation for the people of Barduvai other than the Bazadi incantation, which he claimed he had got hold of.

Bazadi was reputed to have walked over water and had flown like a bird. Dabalo promised to fly and travel along with the comet through the instrumentality of the Bazadi incantations. Thereafter he formed a group called the Sama Jannati Movement. His method was based totally on the Bazadi incantation, an incantory prayer sang by a lead and an elaborate chorus. Citizens who recalled the Bazadi legend said Dabalo had added a lot of salt and pepper in the legend.

First Dabalo sew special gowns for his followers. It

appeared the design was an imitation of the white-crested crow, which became a sacred bird to the movement. He said the colour of the crow signified the aerial and ground exploits of the bird. The crow he said is the only bird that has exploited both the air and the ground. Half of the large gown was dyed black; from bottom up to the breast, the breast up remains white in imitation of the crow.

The gown which was large from the bottom seemed to taper towards the neck and a few flaps were added to the shoulders to aerodynamically aid the Jannati members in taking off whenever they succeed in their prayers. It was a wonder in Barduvai that Dabalo got an extant copy of the Bazadi prayers. Members based the creed on the persistent recital of the prayers. The recital actually sounded like a dirge. One of the members usually starts the recital in a melancholy tune and the other members join in a melodious chorus. It sounded like a dirge:

Lead: *Aye the unseen unseen!*
Chorus: *Aye*
Lead: *Aye the share of the frog is never above water*
Chorus: *aye, aye*
Lead: *Aye the crow that doesn't lay eggs*
Chorus: *aye the crow doesn't lay eggs; all the eggs she comes across are hers. Oh the crow turns other*

> *bird's chick into yours.*
> **Lead**:   *Aye we barrow your wings oh crow!*
> **Chorus**: *we barrow your wing and fly*
> *We never have any wing oh crow just like you never have any eggs oh crow!*
> **Lead**:   *aye the world is a twisting white- crested crow*
> **Chorus**: *aye, aye, whoever sees the black must see the white, aye, aye the world is a twisting white-crested crow*

After that they spring into a take-off with high speed chanting 'Up Jannati, Up Jannati!' The Jannati followers on a take-off sprint were a real spectacle. From a distance, they actually appeared like a horde of white-crested crows trying to take off. Quite often they frightened citizens when they stormed from behind raising a lot of dust in the process.

Dabalo had insisted that with the impending disaster, every human activity is futile. That whatever citizens were doing was nothing and meaningless since the comet will continue to move westward and probably collide with the Tibesti mountain. The members therefore abhor settling down to satisfying the basic appetites and shelter. Most of them sleep in the market square in tents and under trees.

That was a period when various forces contented. Paha became the dumpiest onion seller ever to be seen in Barduvai. In fact for fear that he may burst out with torrents of abuses, he refused to learn the dumb signs further. Customers who bought onions from him remembered Paha as a grocer who quite inexplicably burst into tears frequently. When there was a market lull, the grocers would hear a grunt and they would turn to see Paha crying.

'He has started again! He has started again!' they would lament turning their faces away. Paha was at lost on what to do. Several times he wanted to remove his mask and big hat but the thought of the murderous hostility he was to face made him changed his mind. He knew upon the removal of his mask, all the frustrations citizens felt with the departure of Buruji would be heaped on him. Even if Lamiri's hypocrisy was to be revealed, he knew he was not to escape the wrath of the people especially a new group of people who were staunchly supporting the restoration of the Horrifier whose lost they claimed was a calamity to Barduvai.

Majority of citizens were still adherents to the Rando Cartoza principle. The Kudras, then under the control of Babbadajaka after Lamiri disappeared, was still popular. From a distance the pupils of Kudumaria could be heard singing and in the evening Kudras lessons Babbadajaka spent most of the time lampooning Tugga Bukele and Dabalo Ceddo. He told citizens that if their methods didn't help the city before, reverting back to them wouldn't help any way.

Some citizens started to copy Sharok's manner of speech including his frequent chuckles and askant eyes. Some even started to wrap themselves in white garments to complete what they believe was the epitome of Rando Cartoza principle. It was in this period that Babbadajaka was appointed the mayor of Barduvai in a big fanfare and ceremony. In front of the Askia's palace he was turbaned by Burtune and he later rode on a beautiful horse that was given to him as a present by the Askia. Babbadajaka had always wanted a day when he can imitate Atamin historic ride across the canals of Bazahu. As he rode inside Barduvai in imitation of Atamin, he kept saying `If only we have canals, if only we have canals'.

19

Tugga woke up stretching his torso and yawning. He turned and lit the oil lamp beside his cornstalk bed. Tataraktu was asleep as usual. He picked his large metal compass and walked to the market square. Not a single soul was in sight as Tugga rubbed his eyes walking towards the baobab tree. The sky was clear and the object, as he called it, was shining brightly.

Tugga stood exactly opposite the tree as usual and stretched his giant compass, until the needlepoint fell exactly on the shining object. He stood looking at the bright object. The light from the object still flickers intermittently, and as he drew the position of the object on the wooden board with charcoal, he noticed it was moving faster than a heavenly body.

His heart started to pump fast, as his belief that the interpretation of the rock anagram, and the appearance of the so-called comet underlined a major conspiracy against Barduvai. But who might have sundered the rock? Or was it a natural phenomenon hijacked to enslave the citizens of Barduvai?

Some weeks ago the idea of building an observatory germinated in his mind. He felt it was the best way of achieving the urgent need to prove to the people that the object they see in the sky was man-made not a natural comet prophesying a disaster. The realisation that the cost of the project is high slowed down his design.

It took Tugga two weeks to finish designing the observatory on a wooden slate which he named the *Burankewaal* While doing that the question of finance came to his mind but the idea that Akilu may support his application for cowries from the treasury calmed him.

The night he finished plotting the Burankewaal, he took the wooden slate to Akilu's house. He meets the judge counting treasury cowries beside an oil lamp. Akilu greeted him and asked the purpose of his visit. Tugga produced the wooden slate and placed it in front of the judge.

`What is this Tugga?'

`Sir, do you believe the object is a comet?'

`Have you come to document my view?'

`I'm sorry sir. I come with a plan'

`I see. What plotting is this?' he asked pulling the oil lamp closer.

`Sir this is a design for the making of an observatory that would enable people to see the object in the sky clearly. We need to restore faith sir. Lamiri is destroying the city.'

`Well I don't know anything about designing observatories. If you are soliciting my encouragement then I would tell you to go ahead.'

`Sir building such an observatory would require a huge sum of cowries which I don't possess, I intend to apply for funds from the treasury.'

`Tugga I'm not directing the finances of this city. Burtune does. I know you came to me hoping to receive sympathy for your project.'

`Sir you know the palace is averse to us'

`Still present your proposal. You have a right to do that, then it would be on record what you did and posterity shall judge the decisions taken on that'

After two days Tugga appeared holding the wooden slate under his armpit and his sledgehammer on the right hand. He placed the slate in front of the court and as he expected, Babbadajaka chuckled as he was making the presentation and in the end Burtune said he would think over the proposal.

Babbadajaka broke into a loud laughter after Tugga left the palace, 'unblessed iron monger!'

'People amaze me.' Said Burtune.

'They are mere slaves. The best is to use them and throw

them away!' Babbadajaka said amidst giggles.

Tugga regretted presenting his proposal to the Askia. In desperation Tugga went to Jari Daniro to seek the patronage of the traders in allowing him use the funds reserved for the *Restoration of the Horrifier* in building the Burankeewal. He told them that the building of the Burankeewal might as well serve the same purpose in venerating the dervish.

Unfortunately the traders were not sold to the Burankeewal idea.

'Tugga we know you are inventive. If you can figure out how to shield us from the voice of Apiru Daragal, it would be better to us, than an observatory. Our present problem is Apiru Daragal, he is worse than the comet in distressing us. We don't know anything about observatories'

Tugga pleaded, 'But what is the use of treating just elements of a major treachery, instead of getting to the roots of that treachery an uprooting it. The traders failed to see the point Tugga was trying to make. To them, the restoration of Buruji's Horrifier was supreme in their plans. They failed to see any point in going back to the Hime method.

'The exit of Buruji is connected with the appearance of the comet. It is part of the plot against this city. Don't you see it was when you started reverting back to Hime that Apiru Started yelling?'

'Who will plot against this city?' Halabutu interrupted, 'what is in Barduvai that would merit a plot. Whoever is plotting must be an idle person.'

The traders burst out laughing and were surprised Tugga didn't join them in their orgy.

'Tugga for a plot to move a rock, write on it and give a right interpretation of it...'

'A natural phenomenon can be hijacked to bewilder us' Tugga replied sharply

' Tugga we know how much pain the loss of Kalfuuje project has caused you. We are concerned just with the disappearance of Buruji...'

'That is why I said all this events started when the rock splintered. What caused the rock to tear asunder that Friday? There was no Hime on that and since then can you remember any Hime being held on anything in this city?'

'This is the Askia's business, all the times Himes were held on affairs of Barduvai were they not by the Askia'.

'No. How can you say that? The palace was the venue for the Hime, but it wasn't a palace affair. Who said the Askia must initiate the Hime. We can hold it without the presence of the Askia or anyone for that matter'.

Tugga walked away sad that all those years that passed many citizens came to associate the Hime with the palace and the Kalfuuje group. He knew that the observatory was the only hope for the restoration of faith in the city. He realised that he must quickly make a model of the observatory, a small attractive model that can reveal at least the Peak of Tibesti Mountain. He concluded that when the citizens view the peak of the mountain, a point where nobody had ever climbed to, the community might be convinced about the Burankeewal project.

On the way home he called at the milkmaids section of the market where he told Tataraktu his wife to meet him at home for a meeting. She immediately delegated one of the milkmaids to look after her bowl of millet balls. Whenever Tugga come to their section under the tamarind tree, she knew it was a serious affair that he wanted to discuss with her.

At home he called her aside and told her what he intended to do and how the palace and the traders reacted to it.

'Then if you believe it is the right project, why not build the model', Tataraktu was not very sure about all the facts but she didn't want to disappoint her husband.

They sat silent for a while. Tataraktu feeling uneasy that she was called to contribute to a subject her husband knew better and Tugga in turn not knowing how to approach the matter of borrowing some cowries from his wife.

'Instead of giving up I would comply Tataraktu', Tugga said, 'I sense Lamiri is planning a treachery yet I couldn't bring myself to abandon the Burankeewal project. Anything is better than the pain of watching the city submerge into an ocean of bewilderment and lack of self-dignity that this recalcitrant is bringing on the city. Therefore I want to barrow some cowries from you', he said turning his head aside, for he felt he was unfair in bringing his wife into the matter

`Anything that can protect our dignity is good'

`I'm sorry Tataraktu this has to be so, I know you will be disappointed with me'.

As Tataraktu leaned to bring out her cowries gourd from under the cornstalk bed, Tugga felt a deep pity that nearly made him stop her. Tataraktu broke her cowries gourd and gave Tugga all that was inside the gourd

`Use as much as you need' she told him, `I don't like what is happening in Barduvai as well.'

20

Askia Burtune had to be patient with Babbadajaka's continuous spitting of kolanuts in his court. Babbadajaka was full of his position as the Mayor of Barduvai, at any given chance he tried to prove that he was advanced in Rando Cartoza's principle. He spent most afternoons in the court criticising Tugga and rebellious students like Dabalo Ceddo and Fargarjaji and the young traders, led by Jari Daniro. They had vowed to restore the Horrifier in Barduvai by all means.

'If they couldn't recall a single stanza' Babbadajaka told Burtune, 'then why bother themselves and claim it is important. This is mere troublesomeness'.

Barmaki walked in and announced that Damolishi had come to the palace wishing to speak to the Askia. Burtune became worried. Damolishi had never ventured into the city except on the day of sobriety or when Ba'ashi had called him for a secret meeting of elders. A few days ago when he was visiting the Temple of Light, his eyes met the unflinching eyes of the warrior. Suddenly he felt guilty. He didn't know why, as the eyes of the warrior was not particularly searching, he felt guilty and incompetent. All the memories of the day the rock fell returned to his mind. He felt the prospect of meeting the Warrior again was too much for him, so he delegated Babbadajaka to do that.

Damolishi walked into the palace dressed in his warrior attire. His quiver hanging on his left shoulders and the bow on the right.

'Why has the exercise of sobriety stopped?' he asked.

'Well this is a complex situation sir,' Babbadajaka's heart was pumping furiously, 'now people are entitled to find their own ways of achieving sobriety. I know...'

Damolishi flanged his left arm adjusting the quiver on his back before turning around and walking out of the palace. On his way back to the gizzard rock, he followed through the market where he found a number of speakers were giving fiery lamentations on the loss of the Horrifier. None of them can sing a single verse of it but people were contented to listen as long as the speakers point out the importance of the Horrifier. Some of the speakers like Samba Kundi and Atare Suma wept during their lectures, all in memory of a poem they couldn't recollect.

'Where is the mortal who can save us from a void? Where is the mortal who can save us from disaster?'

The speakers were known for their clean-shaven heads and fiery speeches.

'Buruji had stayed with us for more than fifty years singing the Horrifier' Samba Kundi gesticulated as he spoke, 'yet we never took any heed. We preferred scrambling for our trades, seeking for profit. What a shame we couldn't even protect him. Now that he is gone, we are scrambling for a strange principle to fight an imminent disaster! We are confused because we failed to listen to the Horrifier, thinking it was permanently with us, our appendage, just like the air we breathe. Now we have lost it forever. Where is a mortal who can recall just one golden stanza?'

Samba Kundi started to weep

Kundi and another popular speaker Jibril Nakurna continue to urge the citizens to remember Buruji much so that the void and apprehension they felt could be banished and the comet will not harm them. Halabutu and Jari Daniro suggested that citizens return to the weekly exercise of sobriety since they couldn't find Buruji or restore his Horrifier.

'Who is going to sing for us while we repair the graves? The moment we return to the exercise, Apiru will be there in the absence of Buruji to yell about the comet falling on our heads'

Majority of traders therefore vehemently objected to the return of the weekly exercise in sobriety for fear Apiru will turn it into an exercise in flippancy.

At the Kudras, Babbadajaka deputising for Lamiri emphasised the need to close the gaps between the 'I' through self-remembrance. This is the only way to freedom and the guard against fear of anything.

'Not by the Hime or the Horrifier or the Bazadi incantation but by closing the gaps between the 'Is'. One must be to be free

Disciples lamented that the eschatology of the Rando Cartoza's principle was complex. How would self-remembrance protect a person from a real thing like a disaster?

'Do you know what the disaster will be like? So unless you know how the disaster would be like then how can you argue against any possible solution' Babbadajaka shouted.

It was a particularly contentious period in Barduvai. Sumanguru stopped attending the Kudras and joined the Jannati group of Dabalo Ceddo, where he found the role of a lead singer satisfying. He found the Jannati philosophy enticing especially its belief that if the imminent disaster is true then every activity in the city is mere folly. Most citizens failed to assure themselves on what actually to remember to ensure personal peace of heart and to be protected from the coming disaster. The Kudras emphasised the remembrance of the self as the beginning of freedom, Buruji had said when you remember the fire there was no doubt or speculation, the Hime had said the kernel of existence is beyond the personal level.

And so apprehension increased in Barduvai, assuaged only by Tugga's Almanac, which showed that the comet was still far from the Tibesti Mountain. Citizens daily trooped to watch the Almanac before going on to their affairs or meeting in groups to lament. Many vowed that before the comet is directly over the baobab tree, they would find a way of protection.

21

One day after three years following the appearance of the comet, in the afternoon, the sun was particularly bright and hot. Most citizens were sitting in groups under shades and in market stalls, discussing about the imminent disaster. From the north, they saw a red camel approaching, its rider flexed in a white linen from head to toe. Leading the camel was a tall, stout person who was naked except the skin shorts he wore and a large amulet he wore on his neck. The strange figure was holding a scroll of papyrus. That was the first time a red camel rode into Barduvai. People rose in anticipation. Was it another person from Kudulantis? As the rider approached and was seen clearly, Habarana shouted, `Son of Knowledge!' followed by expression of surprise and clamour among citizens, as Lamiri's camel strutted to the Temple of Light.

Hundreds of people, regardless of what they were feeling, flocked to the Temple. There, Lamiri dismounted his camel chuckling. Babbadajaka and members of the Kudras welcomed him profusely as he entered the Temple to rest. Soon news spread that Lamiri had returned with the solution to the imminent disaster. That after he left Barduvai, he retreated to Egypt where he meditated on the problem of Barduvai in one of the pyramids.

Lamiri went to the palace in the late afternoon accompanied by the tall strange person.

`Have you got a body guard?' Burtune asked him unable to hide his excitement in seeing Lamiri back to Barduvai.

`His name is Nabal Jengeldo; I stayed in their village along the southern Nile for some weeks. Congratulations my lord!'

`On what?' Burtune asked curiously.

`On being the first ruler on earth to be immortal!'

Burtune looked at Lamiri curiously wondering what kind of joke it was.

`I have brought a Pyramid plan for you' said Lamiri collecting the papyrus from Jengeldo.

`What is that?'

`Pyramid my lord. It is an amalgamation of a tomb, a pyramid and a bunker in one. It is supposed to solve the problem of mortality. My lord I have brought to you the most precious of all secrets in the world.

Lamiri unfolded the papyrus, ` this plan you see was drawn by an ancient Egyptian architect, Artifersisis. The plan was written for the young Tuntunkhamen who died before realising his dream of building the Pyramid. The edifice not only protects a king from calamities but solve for a ruler the problem of transition and death. You are given the opportunity to defy death. The king does not die but pass from one chamber to the other. Tuntunkhamen saw the continuum when he joined the solar disk cult at Aton. General Horemheb asked Artifersisis to design the plan before Tuntunkhamen marriage to the daughter of Akhenaton. The young king dreamt of his premature death at Thebes and thereafter complained to General Horemhep who instructed the solar architect Artifersisis to design the Pyramid for the young king

Burtune confessed he didn't understand.

`My lord see it this way', Lamiri eyed Akilu who was looking at him with a cynical eye, `Death is a termination isn't it?'

Burtune nodded.

`So is the end of leadership. Both are painful because they are terminations. It is just like we say here in Barduvai that *the undesirable aspect of pleasure is that it ends too soon*. The ancient Egyptians, my lord, were masters of observation. Something we lack nowadays. They observe nature and see cycles but when they observe the heavenly bodies they see continuum. They see ceaseless continuation in heavenly movements. They deduced therefore that the cycles in life, seasons, creatures and so forth have certain gabs in them, which we perceive as terminal, like death for instance, or birth, to talk about happiness and beginning. So they deduce this beginning and ending is a perceptual fixation, which is causing us a lot of suffering. It is not actually so'

'Remember my lord Tuntunkhamen wrote, `he who disturbs the slumber of the kings*...he didn't say death; it was a siesta you take before and after a court session. He saw the continuum when he joined the cult of the Solar Disk.

Burtune looked at the plan again, `An army general drew this?'

`No, General Horemhep actually instructed the Solar Cult architect, Artifersisis I said, to design the Pyramid for the young king who died before it was started. This plan my lord was confiscated and hidden by General Horemhep. The great pyramids of Egypt are not funerary structures as supposed by naive scholars. These were transition chambers. In short my lord the Pyramid has no beginning and no end. The beginning is the end and the end is the beginning. The building transverses the surface and the bottom of the earth. Some chambers are above the ground while others are below the ground. The riddle of transition is solved my lord'

`Oh son of knowledge!'

`My lord knowledge is there for the seeker'

`Please let me see this unbelievable plan'. Burtune reached out and collected the Pyramid plan. Lamiri moved closer to the Askia to explain the plan, `these my lord are the chambers and here are... the pavilion, then the temples, and here is the bunker proper.'

`Where does the building start?'

`My lord I know it is difficult for you, but imagine the building has no beginning and no end. I want you to stop thinking of beginnings and ends now my lord. Just imagine, try to imagine that your leadership has no beginning and no end'.

`Isn't that difficult Lamiri, you seem to have brought a lot of difficult philosophies for us. Rando Cartoza and now this Pyramid that has no entry and exit. What Lamiri!'

`It is because you think of a beginning and an end. The Pyramid is designed in chambers that are connected in a circle each chamber is the beginning and end my lord. Each chamber is the entrance and exit of the edifice my lord. When it is ready you will understand yourself. My lord when you walk through the chambers after its completion you will understand why the seers of ancient Egypt called the Pyramid the blotter of transition. But first my lord I want you to stop thinking about beginning and end of your leadership or the beginning and end of your life. The protection against the imminent disaster is perfected.'

'What do you think Akilu?' Burtune asked the judge

'My lord there is a present feeling that we go back to the Hime method. This affair is too heavy for my humble opinion'

Lamiri erupted.

'My lord don't be bewildered by the cynicism of a revisionist who is frightened of coming out of his shell! My lord remember you are!'

'Yes I'm' Burtune sighed.

'The comet is moving to the west we either move with it or it moves any way regardless!' Lamiri emphasised.

'Lamiri you heard how some people started to think of our past institutions. They have already paid to recall the Horrifier of Hajji Buruji. Whenever I think of the revivification of that dreadful dervish, sleep flees from my eyes in the night. Then these Jannati followers. You allowed Dabalo to know so much and that is a problem'. Burtune spoke with fear.

Akilu sensing an opportunity, pressed further his point, 'My lord the more you let Barduvai harbour more complicated affairs, the more difficulties we shall have in reverting back. My lord I urge you to have a Hime session. Don't forget too that Tugga demanded for cowries to build an observatory.

'What are you and what is the community? The

protection of the head is the protection of the body. What goes to the head goes to the body... I hate to keep reiterating that my lord.'

`Even then'

`Remember Atamin my lord...'

`Oh please don't remind me of this rascal'. Burtune burst into laughter and glanced at Akilu before using his gown to wipe off tears from his eyes, `Oh Atamin rascal, rascal'

Lamiri continued, `If you remember very well my lord, Atamin said to his people if he hide his promiscuity, it becomes a real weakness, if he doesn't feed well he would be sick, if he doesn't live very well he would be a wretched king'

`Yes, yes and the rascal said would they like a weak king, a wretched king and a sick king, ho, ho, the rascal. Real shameless'

`That is life my lord, those were daring kings. The people understood Atamin, which was why they shouted, `hail! All good to the king' and that was wise because they were protecting their head. All injuries to the body can be cured when the head is healthy'.

Lamiri left the palace contented and proud, and Burtune stayed behind relieved, but he wasn't sure if it was the return of Lamiri or the talk about the Pyramid that was the source of this relieve.

The Kudras was full that day as citizens waited to hear more from Lamiri about the Pyramid and about the mysteries of the solar Cult. Lamiri walked into the class with a new air of confidence, chuckling as often as Sharok

Waladus did when he came to Barduvai.

'I know you heard about the Egyptian pyramids as funeral buildings. This is only part of the truth. Nothing is ever said about the accessories to the pyramids such as the arch complexes, temples, causeways, pavilions and most importantly connection of all that with the Nile river.

If you have a problem like we do look at others who have perfected a solution. Not just to cling to an indigenous method refusing to explore ways. The theory of immortality was perfected and at the same corrupted in Egypt due to sectional selfish interests! Just like we have divisions here. People learning little and believing they had known all. See Dabalo and Fargarjaji, real ingrates! They acquired a little Kudulantic knowledge and they are all over the city bragging about their views. What do they know, as to even challenge me! So this Egypt like I was saying, what was recorded in history is the ritual embalming of corpses and the ritual magic carried out to prevent corpses from decaying, maintaining faculties until resurrection time. But in truth these elaborate and tortuous mortuary preparations are the results of a confusion and mistake in building the Pyramid. They created a spiritual and procedural gap that was not necessary.

The Pyramid is supposed to be a well-equipped

structure that solves the mystery of transition but it was somewhat corrupted by interest groups in the solar disk cult in order to promote mortuary embalming which gave some measure of personal power to them. Mortuarists were the culprits, just like the revisionists that we have in this city!

How blessed we are my people to have the opportunity to build the first and most authentic Pyramid on earth. I have brought the original plan. No people on earth have this plan but us. We must build the corridors, chambers, temples, causeways, gates, pavilions and most important of all to connect all these to the Daula orchard."

22

Damolishi sitting on the gizzard rock and gazing on the rooftops of Barduvai almost looked like part of the geographic features of Barduvai. No one can remember looking up to the foot of the mountain without seeing Damolishi atop the gizzard rock. Citizens spoke a lot about him but rarely spoke to him even though they passed by the rock and had made the flat bottom of the rock a popular meeting point for lamentations and arguments after Kudras classes or in the evenings when the sun was setting.

It was only Tugga who continuously pestered the old warrior whenever he passed by the rock or visits the old man on purpose. Damolishi spoke little and does not feel obliged to reply a question or whatever in a conversation. He usually reacted to questions and statements with a distinct clack of the tongue. But Tugga didn't mind that attitude of the old warrior. Many times when he visited the old man he ended up speaking to himself.

That evening Tugga pestered the old warrior with the question, *'What is the right road for us?'* to which Damolishi kept answering with a clack.

From afar Tugga saw Dabalo Ceddo, accompanied by Sumanguru, coming in their crow gowns, breathing heavily, 'Did you hear about the Pyramid?'

Tugga nodded dejectedly.

'This man has turned us into his slaves'.

'The Askia said he is our son of knowledge'

'That worthless person!' Dabalo glanced at the Temple of light with hostile eyes, when we muster enough arial power the temple will be our first target for demolition'

'What, if a people surrender a method they know for something they don't then these are the consequences. It is sad that even people like you Dabalo has fallen trap to this debacle'

'Don't talk like that Tugga, as much as you believe in the Hime method I also believe in the Bazadi prayers. I'm entitled to my belief'

`Your idea is still influence by the Rando Cartoza philosophy'

`God forbid', shouted Dabalo, `I have since abandoned this corrupt ideology'

`I think you are pursuing this Bazadi prayers because you want to be different, you want to have your own back at Lamiri, Isn't it?'

`This is hardly the reason for my reviving the Bazadi prayers'

`Put aside the Bazadi prayers, what do you think we could do?'

`You are forcing a Hime on me. I'm not ready for that'

`Okay lets us invent a solution and discard it away'

'What solution other than for us to return to our old ways. The ones we know. If it were during the reign of Bazadi, how can a comet hang inexplicably in the sky? Bazadi would have flown to intercept the object. Was anything mysterious in that era?'

'But remember the Hime method also carried on with the spirit, Dabalo. We must go back to where we stopped to find our bearings.'

'Where we stopped was the Bazadi period. Then we had power and methods all our own. Nothing foreign. The Rando Cartoza principle and Kudulantic knowledge is nothing but the sorcery of others which we are imitating. We have our sorceries too, why waste our time learning the sorceries of others.'

'How many months have you been chanting the Bazadi prayer? To what avail. My question is, what is the right road for Barduvai now hence?'

Dabalo adjusted his Jannati gown, 'the song we sing is purgative as well. How many years have we been piling dirt on our souls, corrupt beliefs. It will take time to wash our souls to the extent of being free to respond to the Bazadi prayer. The good news is that whenever we are clean, we shall take off. You will be alive to witness that Tugga! This is the right road Tugga; don't get preoccupied with what is not going to help you in the end. Move with the comet'

From the temple emerged Babbadajaka, Seibu, Habarana and the other remaining disciples of the Kudras. They were holding their leather books and talking excitedly about the Pyramid project.

'See the deluded ones' shouted Dabalo, 'Hear, hear Babbadajaka your height, age, knowledge are to no avail. You don't realise you are deluded by Lamiri'.

'What would you not say Dabalo, a recalcitrant like you! What will you not say, one who rebelled against his teacher!'

'Do you honestly think he is a teacher? This worthless person!' retorted Dabalo.

'Do you have more knowledge than him? The son of knowledge of this city, you, when have you even started to acquire knowledge that you even started talking about flying to intercept a comet! This man has deciphered a mystery for us and has brought a solution for it. Any slave who is not satisfied can die of chagrin!' Babbadajaka spat kolanut, put aside his skin plate and sat on his favourite spot.

'Babbadajaka the eucalyptus tree, the slippery pole, master of Rando Cartoza's principle! Tell them the truth, the sole exporter of vitaspinach' Habarana laughed after singing the praise.

Dabalo moved closer to them, 'what do you know. I escorted Waladus to the temple when he came. Didn't I? Do you know what I saw of your teacher that day?'

'Tell us, not that we shall believe' said Babbadajaka.

'Well upon the arrival of Waladus Lamiri was visibly frightened; I tell you I saw him. What man of knowledge is that, and then worst of all, he washed the feet of Waladus in a bowl while the visitor was reigning abuses on him. Teacher! You said teacher. How can I follow such a worthless person?'

'Because he is' Babbadajaka said swaying and smiling to see if the others felt he made a strong answer.

'Thank you, Babbadajaka. You have answered right' Seibu cheered in appreciation of the short answer.

'Until now no one has answered my simple question, what is the right road to take?' Tugga asked. But no one paid any attention to him.

Sumanguru who was listening throughout the discussion, sullenly folded in his Jannati gown, and said exasperatingly, 'All this confusion and suffering I don't understand. If we are going to use Kudulantic methods to solve our problems, why not let the Kudulantic people themselves do that for us'

'Your naiveté is outstanding Sumanguru!' Babbadajaka shouted.

'I am not naive Babbadajaka, no matter how learned you are in Kudulantic ways and Rando Cartoza's principle you will never be better than them in their ways. Let us make it easy for ourselves, if their methods can solve our problems then let us leave it to them to solve, but if it is ours that solve those problems, then let us re-invent our selves'.

The argument took a new dimension when Fargarjaji arrived and met Babbadajaka explaining the Pyramid project.

'We don't have a river similar to river Nile and our land is flat and dry. Why in the world then do we need any causeways and underground tunnels?' Fargarjaji asked.

'Use your imagination' retorted Babbadajaka 'If we don't have a river similar to river Nile, we can create a canal. In fact son of knowledge said a canal will be duck to link the palace with the Daula pond'.

'This is a white elephant project!'

'You may think as you like but there is no stopping progress'.

'You are conniving' said Fargarjaji 'to enslave the citizens of Barduvai. How can a project like this protect citizens from an impending disaster?'

'So what is the right road to take?' Tugga interjected.

Durugu was coming back from his farm when he saw Tugga and the others under the gizzard. He decided to stop by, mainly because of Tugga and not for the others.

'Durugu what is the right road for Barduvai to take?' Tugga asked him.

Babbadajaka laughed 'Tugga don't force this one on Durugu. What does Durugu know but ancient masonry? We are not holding any Hime here although you keep repeating a thema as if we are'

People burst out laughing.

Tugga smiled 'my idea of knowledge is different from yours Babbadajaka. And we shall never agree on principles. What makes you feel a mason is not capable of any insight on such a problem like this?'

Durugu remained silent and unassuming.

'Didn't you here of the project?' Tugga asked Durugu

'Yes I heard'

'What do you think about it?'

'Ah, ah' Durugu mumbled looking at the gathered citizens one by one, 'well everybody now believe the predictions are coming out true may be whatever is done is also right. We have got everything we want. If you are planning a sanctuary… well, the Tibesti Mountain too is a fortress in that regard. It just occurred to me and to be honest I have been thinking about it. How the Thamudians have some wisdom in carving out dwellings from the mountain. The mountain is the natural sanctuary for man. It is primordial isn't it? From the caves we dared out and to the caves we could return if we lose our wits!' he said in a sarcastic voice, 'Excuse me I bade you good night fellows' Durugu walked away.

23

Paha was selling some onions to a customer when Seibu came back talking about the amount of cowries collected by Lamiri for the construction of the Pyramid. He nearly tore his mask off when he heard the amount of cowries collected by Lamiri.

People were talking about how the chambers of life were designed to solve the mystery of life and death and the freedom of the spirit that the Pyramid can generate. They said the feeling of freedom one can feel when inside the Pyramid was inexplicable. One had to work for a day to earn two hours in the chambers of life. The fortified sanctuary for the day of disaster.

In the night, Paha couldn't sleep well. He kept tossing on the sack of onions he used as his bed. When he realised sleep was far away from him, he woke up and lit a lamp, pulling a piece of leather from a wooden box. He pulled out his bottle of ink and quill, but he noticed the ink had dried and was in a solid state. There was no time to waste. He loosens his waist string and pissed into the gourd, and without tying back his trouser, he started to write quickly in Kalfuuje

Call our virgins to wail and howl
A raging din of ghoulish lament
Perchance my tormented soul escapes
From this granary of herded okapis

Blame not the Jannati furlong dreams
When our minds are bewildered parrots
Our griot is now a palace announcer
Blowing horns on trotting mules
Our dervish has stopped his whirling dances
Punched to exile by a Cartoza marionette

Our guards have shortened their rusted swords
Looking to feast on orphan ewes

Paha tightened his trouser and walked out in the night to nail the poem below Tugga's almanac. After that he went back to the store where he slept soundly, a sleep assured by discovering a way to wreck vengeance on Lamiri and Barmaki. He realised, in writing the poem in Kalfuuje, he was shooting at them with two arrows. In his sleep he dreamt Barmaki was pursuing him with a bloody sword.

In the morning, the poem drew a large group of the citizens who crowded around the baobab tree. A written poem was a kind of a novelty in Barduvai, especially as it was written in Kalfuuje. They wondered who the poet was who could write a poem instead of chanting it. Some citizens said if the poet could not sing, then he must be dumb. Could it be Paha? They quickly dismissed that option, 'This cousin of Barmaki' they said 'wouldn't do a thing like that'. Could it be Tugga then since the poem was written in Kalfuuje? This ironmonger they said was too practical to write a poem. In fact Tugga himself was surprise to see a poem written in Kalfuuje next to his Almanac.

The citizens called Bango to read the poem for them. He stood for some moments reading the poem silently. His heart beating quickly. When he read the poem at first it was with difficulty because he had to fathom some of the words syllable by syllable. The second rendition was smoother and the third drew cheers from the crowd, which kept increasing. That day Bango read the poem several times for the citizens, some of who memorised some lines and kept repeating in the city.

In the morning the following day people resumed discussing about the Baobab tree Poem. Bango having found a role for himself never got tired of reciting the poem for curious people coming from neighbouring villages. It was during one of such crowded sessions that Barmaki arrived with guards and arrested him on charges of sedition. Later he also sent a guard to bring Paha to the Temple of Light. People thought Barmaki summoned him to find out how an uncle of his was faring.

Paha entered the sitting room. The room has changed since he had last visited the temple to accept to parody Buruji's Horrifier while Barmaki was engrossed in eating a roasted turkey. More carpets were spread and the cushions and pillows have been changed. Different calabashes of various fruits from the Daula Orchard were positioned on the carpet ready for the evening dinner. The walls were adorn with the statuettes of Warum Kudulix and Atamin the king of the first night. Barmaki was standing close to the window overlooking the splintered rock, his expression grim.

`Did you write this poem?'
Paha mumbled something before making some dumb signs.

`I'm not joking with you Gaulojo, don't fool around with me!' Barmaki thundered.

Paha groaned, chuckling while pointing to his ears and making some further dumb signs.

`Don't fool around with me!'
Paha made some funny sounds again pointing to his ears and making some dumb signs.

Barmaki once again thought of murdering the poet in the temple but suddenly remembered Damolishi was sitting on the gizzard rock. It was rather complicated he thought.

`Get out you peasant!' he shouted murderously at him.

Paha walked out of the temple sniggering. For the first time since being forced to become dumb and to change his identity he felt elated at having speared

Barmaki.

24

When Tugga finished making the model Burankewaal, he invited the whole city in order to make his demand momentous. Burtune and his courtiers arrived to witness the unveiling of the model. The Askia rode Fileenge the 'windy horse' that day. Half of the citizens of Barduvai were attracted to the horse arguing about the feats the beast can achieve and paid no attention to Tugga's Burankewaal model. Durugu who was hoping people were going to give Tugga moral support couldn't hide his anger.

'Oh you terrible lot, won't you feel ashamed. A man of your own city is inventing something, can't you pay attention for once and know what it is all about'. People disregarded him and continued to admire the Askia's horse.

Tugga welcomed the court, 'my lord I decided to make a model of the Burankeewal before your highness can approve any cowries for the project. Your father had love for our efforts, if he was here...'

Burtune cleared his throat, 'Tugga explain to us this strange construction, it is more important than talking about my father'

'Yes my lord. Here my lord is a miniature version of the Burankewaal observatory with which I believe you can see the top of the Tibesti mountain, which we had earlier believed is topless'.

'Why do I need an observatory to see the top of a mountain?'

'My lord this is only an example to show you the possibility of making a bigger observatory that can show us clearly what the object in the sky is. Is it man-made or natural?'

'You Tugga be mindful!' Burtune pointed a finger at him, 'how can a mere human being create a comet and paste it on the sky!' Burtune walked to the model and peered through the viewfinder, 'I can see clouds, trees, oh there I can see where the rock fractured', He stood up 'But what? What if we see where the rock fractured from?'

'The possibility my lord! The possibility of making something more powerful to see the object in the sky'

Burtune shook his head pointing at the Burankeewal, 'is this the object in which many hoes and tins perished Tugga. Why Tugga can you be so foolish as to melt precious implement to make this!'

Babbadajaka sniggered as great disappointment registered on the face of Tugga.

Lamiri grunted, 'People abhor counselling. My advice is you join the Pyramid project since you are so interested in metals and designs. A *conaskiat* is coming all the way from Bazahu'

'I didn't ask for a counsel from you!' Tugga was

visibly angry, he cleared his throat and said in a strain voice, `my lord I'm not mad or silly as you may think, if your father...'

`Stop talking about my father. This comet didn't appear during his reign'

`Even then my lord, we have a method of reaching infallible decisions. How do we know we are not walking on a fallible decision now? If we all see what this object is using an observatory. And I am not demanding much for the project'

`I can't authorise public funds on such a wasteful project. Already the Temple of Light is built. It is sufficient for the study of this strange phenomenon. And for our protection we will soon start the Pyramid project, my advice is that you join the Pyramid project. Why worry so much, leave such matters to people who have been given knowledge. We all know your expertise in making hoes and sickles why be too ambitious. Why go into areas not your own. Ho Tugga, be mindful of your position. I will make you a foreman in the Pyramid project.'

`I decline the offer my lord!' Tugga said flatly walking into his workshop dejected. People dispersed talking about how Tugga has refused to move with time. A few citizens ventured to look into the viewfinder to see the top of Tibesti Mountain and the point where the rock fractured. They swore that if it were them they would have used the Burankeewal to make many cowries from curious citizens who will be eager to pay a cowry each to see the top of Tibesti Mountain.

In the evening citizens rushed to the gizzard rock as usual where oblivious of Damolishi's presence they talked about Tugga and his Burankeewal and the Pyramid.

'Tugga is really an unblessed ironmonger' Seibu Albasa said, 'appointed the foreman of the Pyramid and he refused. The idiot, unblessed ironmonger'.

Here comes Babbadajaka

'It is now all clear. It is now all clear. There is no confusion. Trust our Son of Knowledge. He has come with a final protection. Anyone who is so naïve as not to know how to apply the Rando Cartoza's principle? Here is the solution. Acquire hours in the chambers of life. The Son of knowledge said a register will be kept for everyone who works in the project'.

Seibu turned nodding his head, 'I never can understand some people how one can hate blessing coming to him. Fargarjaji and Tugga will never cease to baffle me. See Tugga for instance. Instead of accepting our Askia's offer and making gains to improve his workshop'.

"Not only that" Seibu 'but also use that position as an opportunity to supply iron metals and tins to the project. It takes Rando Cartoza's principle to think in that direction, I tell you. This is a clear example of a slave being always a slave'.

The crowd laughed "Babbadajaka, Babbadajaka!"

"If I were him I will use the position to expand my workshop and marry another wife before the day of disaster". Said Habarana.

"I tell you it takes the principle to realise such. If not, how can you understand the reluctance among citizens to sign up for the Pyramid?" Babbadajaka spat kolanut.

"Here is an imminent disaster, here is a merciful solution, a sanctuary for the day of disaster, who then but a mere slave can waste his time building telescopes to see the top of Tibesti Mountain. How can seeing the clouds and the trees help you on the day of disaster?"

25

In the morning people gathered at Tugga's workshop to demand why he didn't paste his regular almanac. Since the palace snubbed his proposal, Tugga was very worried because he used Tataraktu's savings to build the model Burankewaal. He felt sad that he sank his wife's savings in a failed project. So he was hard at figuring how to earn enough cowries to repay her. As people stood by the workshop Apiru arrived shouting, "May the comet descend on our heads!" He looked like a person who wanted to die but wanted to take somebody along. Holding a short sharp metal his left eye twitched wickedly as yelled repeatedly, 'May the comet descend on our heads today! Yeah hoo!' Tugga heard all this inside the house and the pleadings of citizens calling him to come out. So he decided to come out.

'What do you want?' Tugga asked the citizens coldly.

'We want to see the almanac. Why didn't you paste one today?'

'Have you any moral right to ask me this question?'

The citizens begged him to tell them at least the position of the comet in the sky so that they will know their fate, as many have not signed to work at the Pyramid

'Don't you have eyes? The Askia said your eyes are adequate in seeing the object, well then what?' he said walking into the house purposely.

'Where is it now?' they asked him starry-eyed. Seeing that the master of metals was not attentive to them they begged Durugu feverishly to go in and bring out his friend.

'You will have to pay to see that' Tugga said non-chalantly after being convinced to come out by Durugu.

Many people paid a cowry each to see the almanac. After people crowded inside the workshop, he unveiled the almanac and people rushed in excitement to see the new position of the comet. It occurred to them that they had underestimated the significance of the almanac in their lives. Hence after they came in the mornings to view the almanac of Tugga before going on to their daily businesses.

Income from the almanac was however not adequate

for Tugga to repay the debt he owed his wife. He grew lean and virtually stopped working as hard as before. He spent days walking around the city in his usual leather apparel holding the sledgehammer, picking iron scraps. Tugga yearned for a Hime on his condition but the Kalfuuje group was no more. One day he walked into Durugu's house and met the old mason trying to catch a chicken.

`I must be a daring old man to run after a chicken at this age', Durugu smiled at Tugga. `My dear Tugga you have grown lean', he said running after the hen again. When he finally caught it, he walked to Tugga breathing heavily while shaking his hand muttering something about being the first guest in the house since the comet appeared so he was going to slaughter the chicken for him because it was no use keeping it any way since it wondered a lot in the neighbourhood.

`Are you lean because the Askia had condemned your Burankewaal?'

`I'm now concerned Durugu that I borrowed cowries for the model'

'You did?'

They sat silently for some seconds, then Durugu said, `from my experience Tugga nothing is a waste. Look at nature; everything goes into one form or the other. I tell you there is nothing like waste or weakness or such.

These are mere fixations and the result of anger. One day my dear Tugga, Babbadajaka wanted to hurt me. He called me to erect a wall for him. Just when I finished mixing the mud with water and straws, he walked in and said he has changed his mind because that was how he felt'

'That person' hmm grunted Tugga

'I refused to argue with him because I knew he was itching to argue the Rando Cartoza's principle with me'

'So it was. He believes he is the epitome of the principle. But I refused to get angry. I sat aside as he smiled and moved out of his house. It was getting late in the afternoon, I saw his goat sty had collapsed, so I signalled to my assistant and within an hour we had the sty in shape using the mud we mixed.

We stood watching the goats return to the reconstructed sty. Then we washed our hands and left his house. Since that day Babbadajaka has been avoiding looking into my eyes despite the fact he claims he is. If this is what Rando Cartoza's principle is all about I abhor it.'

For the first time after many months Tugga felt happy and felt like he was in Barduvai of Ba'ashi when there was Hime on everything to decide on the best way to proceed to solve their problems. In tears he ate the roasted chicken brought by the wife of Durugu while thinking of what to do with the model Burankewaal.

After he returned home, he melted the model and the following day started making a multiple horned flute from part of it, which he blew when people were watching the almanac. On market days he went from stall to stall blowing a tune, which the traders found saddening. There was something about the tunes that made citizens feel guilty. So they quickly gave him cowries to stop blowing the flute. Some old traders who lived long after said the tune was unlike anything in melancholy. Many traders were willing to part with whatever cowries they had in order to stop Tugga from blowing the tune. They said Tugga's tunes and Apiru's yells were the tormentors of their souls. Tugga stopped making hoes and ploughs and instead spent most of the afternoon practising tunes and polishing the tall compass he used in measuring the journey of the comet.

26

Finally Habarana announced a date for the formal commencement of the Pyramid project. Three days before the formal opening, many horses were brought into Barduvai. Rumours had it that some citizens witnessed the arrival of seven strange people who were dressed like Sharok Waladus and many mules loaded with sacks heading to the palace. The rumour said it was passed midnight when they witnessed that. Some citizens refuted that, claiming that what the naive citizens saw were Babbadajaka's donkeys carrying marble stones for the preparation of the big occasion.

All citizens were talking about the Pyramid, its secrets and how its chambers ensure safety and happiness for those who merit it. Never since Noah was such a rescue scheme contemplated they said.

A day before the occasion the Front of the palace was redecorated by the workforce of Babbadajaka who throughout the week was busy making preparation to receive guests from far. All Curdled milk coming from surroundings settlements were bought and citizens were promised free drinks during the occasion.

On the day of the formal opening, the large, expensively decorated tent outside the Askia's palace was astounding to visitors and citizens alike. A large platform was built. On it was placed various building implements, some of them never seen in Barduvai before. A group of spinsters were hired to be ululating and Habarana had a busy day as he blared messages through his zebu horn.

Finally the Askia emerged from the palace to make his historic speech. Behind him walked Lamiri followed by Nabal holding the Pyramid papyrus, then followed by the rest of courtiers and Babbadajaka in his long strides.

Habarana started praising the Askia immediately. As he walked to the platform to speak to the gathering.

'Fellow citizens of Barduvai' the Askia started his speech, 'those who can recall our history well know that this is not the first time this city faces a disaster. During my great grandfather's time, the city was attacked by the Almoravids but was held back successfully. Like my great grandfather, today our city is faced with yet another imminent disaster, this time more alarming. I call on you all to put your differences aside and ensure that our only hope of protection, the Pyramid is completed before the day of disaster. This Pyramid is for all.

'This Pyramid is a sanctuary for all the people of Barduvai. There are adequate chambers for all creatures in Barduvai; it is up to us to finish the edifice before the day of disaster. Already the Temple of Light is completed for the continuous contemplation of the anagram while the rest of the Pyramid is being constructed. We must be more conscious of our functions in this society. Everyone should stick to his trade and his trade only. Solving mysteries and coming up with solutions is the sole domain of our Son of Knowledge, Lamiri. Those who want to delve in functions not their own must do so privately.

There are three more edifices to be constructed. These are: the pavilion at the market square where events can be staged and citizens can be addressed from time to time. Two, the pond of realisation. This pond shall be dug in front of my palace and filled with fresh water from the Daula orchard. This is to be achieved through the construction of a canal that will siphon water regularly from the orchard.

Lastly and most significantly are the chambers

proper. This is largely an underground construction with four entrances to be constructed in the North, East, and West and South of the city and conical ventilators shall be constructed above the Bunker at various locations. I must emphasise that all the edifices shall be linked up by underground tunnel-chambers that will be interlinked in a circular fashion. There will also be a causeway linking the palace and the Temple of light. The first phase of the plan, which must start today, is the immediate construction of the pond of realisation and its linking canal with the Daula orchard.

The labour plan is simple enough. A register of work shall be kept. The number of hours put in by any one is recorded and after every month, the number of hours put in by a citizen will be calculated.

Amidst the speech, Dabalo started the Jannati incantation and the group responded. All attention turned to them as they fled raising a lot of dust in the process. Barmaki was looking sharp as he stood guard.

Despite the sudden interruption by the Jannati group, many citizens who wanted to gain hours in the sanctuary of life signed up and started digging the foundation of the Pyramid. Mambo Ulal was beating his drum as the hired spinsters Sang. Many citizens were surprised Jabbi was not among the singing girls. Diggers and Shovels rose and fell in rhythm with the song and the drumming.

Burtune and his court retired inside the palace. The Askia was very excited about the Pyramid project.

'How was my speech?' the Askia asked Lamiri

'You are!' Lamiri said and the Askia became very

happy. He felt relieved that the protection from the comet was finally found. It was exciting for him to imagine how he could also in history be saving Barduvai from another immediate disaster.

"Habarana" he called,

Habarana drew closer.

"What was that famous statement uttered by my late grandfather.... when Barduvai was defended?

"Which of your grandfathers?"

"You are asking me!" Burtune exclaimed.

Habarana quickly collected himself. Anxiety rose up to his throat and his stomach rumbled. All eyes and ears were on him. Habarana was called to play his role as a Griot of Barduvai again! Seeing the fear in Habarana's eyes Lamiri interrupted quickly. "By tomorrow he will be able to tell you that my lord! I am sure we are not in a hurry!"

"Why? Why? Tell me now so that we write it in Kudulect and paste it on slates all over Barduvai to silence on enemies," Burtune looked serious.

Habarana cleared his throat and started the narration

"Samba Tengele the son of Askia Dundari was remembered for his wisdom. Samba Tengele was remembered for his courage. He saw the Almoravids invaders. He gave orders to build a trench around Barduvai... He ... He...

"Continue!" ordered Burtune.

Habarana failed to continue. He couldn't recall even a complete stanza of Barduvai's History. He walked sullenly out of the palace feeling ashamed.

27

Habarana arrived into the Temple of Light parlour feeling very depressed. No griot has ever failed in Barduvai but him, he thought.

"It is your gaps rearing their heads back again. Don't let yourself slip off! Makeru! It is your gaps." Lamiri kept reassuring him, as they took their seats.

'I am like nothing', Habarana said slumping on the carpet.

"You are thinking back, Habarana the griot again! Your inability to recite the history of Barduvai and your opinion about it lingers on your old self. You are Habarana. Weren't you walking on foot before?'

'I did!'

'Don't you own a mule now?'

'I do'

"Don't you have three different sandals?"

"I do"

"Haven't you expanded your services?"

"I have"

"Haven't you employed Mambo Ulal?"

"I have son of Knowledge"

'Don't you have a new instrument, the zebu horn? Oh God what is happening to you Habarana? If my bright students like you...'

"I understand son of knowledge, away with peasant habits!" Shouted Habarana as he reached for a piece of peeled paw-paw on the table.

"That is the spirit," sighed Lamiri "you are Makeru!"

Jabbi burst into the room dressed elegantly. She wore a freshly dyed wrapper and glittering copper bangles. Habarana noticed the neck muscles of Lamiri bulged out of the desire he had for the milkmaid. Habarana cleared his throat and bade goodnight to his mentor. Lamiri didn't even answer as Habarana left the room that was filled with Jabbi's perfume. Lamiri's heart started to pump thunderously; he had never desired to possess a woman like he desired Jabbi. He cursed his weakness for the milkmaid trying hard to figure out how he was going to possess 'this wild gazelle'.

"I sent for you to come and sing the Careless Girl at the occasion but you refused. The Askia would have given you a lot of cowries for that"

Jabbi giggled, walked to the tray of fruit and helped herself to peeled pineapple. She walked to the large window overlooking the anagram,

"How can I sing for people digging a ditch? We sing and clap for people to dance, not to work, you settled folks are amazing! Where is the present you promised me? I want to go now. We have a dance at Poli.'

Lamiri leaned behind a cushion and brought out a bag of gift. Jabbi grabbed the bag and removed beautifully woven wrappers. They were newly made of strong thread. She delightfully spread them on the floor examining them and exclaiming in delight.

"Stay with me. Come every evening!"
Jabbi giggled, 'so with just a few wrappers and you have got a milkmaid. You settled folks are really wicked. Four wrappers and you get a milkmaid'

"Oh you stop talking like that. What is beyond my capacity?"

"I want those coral necklaces I saw in the market and the newly dyed mascara wrappers. Buy them and I will think of your proposal', she giggled walking out.

"Where are you going? Came and sing for me. Just once. You and me. Came Jabbi, sing for me. Just for tonight. Stay with me!"

"I am on my way to Bango, we are going to a dance".

"Came and dance here" Lamiri said desperately, "why do you have to go far. Bring your friends and dance here; I will slaughter rams and turkeys for you. Listen, stop wasting your time selling milk in the city, I will buy all your milk for workers of the Pyramid. Tell all your friends to bring their milk. I will buy all. Then we can have time here and you and your friends can sing for me.'

'In a room, you are weird people, sedentary folks. If we sell all our milk at once then how can we run around and have fun and sing and talk! Where is the enjoyment in that? Dancing in a room! Not me. You want, you came and dance with me in the city."

"You know I can't do that! I am a highly placed person..."

"I don't want a man who can't dance. Bye-bye! She left the room wriggling her buttocks and giggling"

Lamiri felt murderously jealous for the first time. He looked at his potbelly and thought may be the milkmaid was right. What was attractive about him apart from his social position and wealth? He regretted he couldn't bring himself to go to a dance with Jabbi and felt truly handicapped. He thought he must plan a trip with her to a distant land where he can be free to dance with her in the open. He must also plan to get a special tutor to teach him how to dance. If only something can take away Bango from her, he thought, probably she would listen to him. May be. He wanted badly to turn the Temple of light into something like Bero Koron Julmire castle where orgies were held every night.

28

To boost Habarana's confidence, Lamiri gave him the contract of supplying curdled milk to the Pyramid project. Within a week, Habarana was able to buy a horse, which he rode on palace announcements. Although his material position has improved tremendously, Habarana felt he loss something intangible. Was it esteem? Or what he couldn't tell. One thing he felt was as if the Askia was treating him like a beggar or a vulture since that day he failed to narrate a portion of Barduvai's history. Lamiri had told him it was his old self reasserting itself. It was no use for him. What did he care if he was treated like a vulture he thought, hasn't he closed his gaps, he thought. He shouts 'Makearu!' involuntarily.

While people were arguing about the day of disaster and the Pyramid, Habarana galloped into the market on his new horse with Mambo Ulal the drummist running behind him, panting and yelling at him to have pity on him.

`Beat the palace tune and stop complaining, the home of cowries is under the sun and sweat' Habarana dismounted his horse and unstrapped his zebu horn, people watching and wondering what the two were up to.

Mambo beat his drum thrice and Habarana placed the horn in his mouth and started an announcement;

`To tell you oh people of Barduvai, that henceforth the Jannati followers are banned from chanting the Bazadi incantations in the city and also banned from trying to take off. To tell them that henceforth they must practice their flight on the Tibesti Mountain. When the eaglet wanted to fly it didn't practice on the ground, let those with understanding understand'.

People laughed when Habarana added the proverb at the end of the announcement. They also crowded around

Habarana and Mambo as he explains the new teaser he had introduced in making palace announcements. He said it was a special practice by announcers in Kudulantis to condense facts in the beginning of their announcements. But as an experienced griot, he decided to substitute that with a proverb or an adage at the end of his announcements. After that he rode his horse and galloped inside the city to make further announcements. Nobody knew what exactly happened but many people reported to have seen a group of Jannati followers beating up Habarana and Mambo in one of the nooks in the city. After that they tied Habarana and his zebu horn on his new horse and tied the reins round the handcuffed Mambo who was forced to head to Burtune's palace.

Barmaki came inside the city and handcuffed a number of the Jannati followers and took them to the prison. It was reported, Dabalo mobilised the remaining members of his group and had spent the night at the Barduvai prison chanting the Bazadi incantations and scratching the walls of the prison with swords. The following day the members were seen with swords dangling on their shoulders.

Burtune got frightened and ordered the release of the imprisoned members and Barmaki ensured the security of Habarana by assigning a guard to accompany him wherever he was going. In fact Habarana restricted his movement to the Askia's place, the clinic of Lamiri and the Temple of light.

Fargarjaji started to give some fiery lectures against the palace of Burtune, 'Imagine in this era of the comet, a leader wasting the resources of his land in building a pyramid. What kind of protection will a pyramid give the people of Barduvai? Look at the Temple of Light. It is nothing more than the Temple of Orgies. Tell me what it is that is newly pondered by our leaders regarding the anagram. Huge state cowries wasted on a temple just for the pleasure of these Kudulantic surrogates. Meditation has turned into banquets'.

People burst out laughing
'You are laughing but serfdom is coming back to Barduvai!'

People as usual went to call Seibu Albasa at the grocer's section of the market. When Paha saw Seibu standing up he followed him as he was worn to. Behind him he heard the other traders talking about how weird he was going to a lecture when he was a dumb. Paha shook his head and followed Seibu who he grew to like and trust. There was expedient sincerity that Seibu displayed which he found so affable.

At the lecture, people started to laugh immediately they saw Seibu coming. They knew a standoff was imminent between Fargarjaji and Seibu who was critical of Fargarjaji whom he regarded as a lazy person; 'Fargarjaji when would you stop shouting and face your personal poverty squarely. Come to my shed I would give you four sacks of onions to start trading'

People burst out laughing and clapping. They knew they were in for another verbal fighting between the two.

'It is people like you who are compromising the destiny of Barduvai. You make thousands of cowries from selling catabeans to the detriment of our local farming.' Fargarjaji fuming shouted pointing at Seibu.

Seibu on the other hand looked calm and composed as he spoke, 'You Fargarjaji, you are a wicked one. After being taught by Lamiri, you now turn against him. Ingrate you are and a wicked one. This is lack of blessing'.

Fargarjaji started to sneeze as he tried to reply Seibu. He sneezed violently, a feature of his speeches, which people came to be familiar with. They waited patiently as he sneezed.

Seibu chuckled, 'See how you sneeze. You are allergic, come to my stall and get some garlic lobes and take to your wife to prepare some pepper soup for you. Please stop shouting'

People burst in to laughter clapping.

'I would rather die than to eat the garlic of a reactionary like you! You are a reactionary Seibu!' Fargarjaji cried amidst sneezes and a running nose.

'Even then I advise you to get some work and fight your poverty before the day of disaster'

'Seibu I'm warning you!'

'I swear you better get a job; your anger is caused by

poverty. If you will sell onions plenty I got. There is the Pyramid project, I'm sure Burtune would gladly give you a position there. Please stop pestering our ears with your criticisms'

Fargarjaji rushed and held Seibu by the gown collar, but citizens rushed and intervened, separating them. Seibu smiling went back to his shed while Fargarjaji sneezing and fuming went his way, swearing and abusing Burtune in the market to the delight of young traders who saw a mouthpiece in him.

Habarana changed the tactics of his reports. Usually if incidences happened in the city, he walked around chatting with people and telling them the stories. Now instead of mongering, he makes formal announcements like the palace announcements.

'To tell you oh people of Barduvai, the needs of the monitor lizard is different from the needs of the monkey. Today at the market, Fargarjaji said Seibu Albasa is a reactionary while Seibu said Fargarjaji should stop fighting his penury by shouting at people. He urges him to find a job and stop yelling, for the day of disaster is waiting for nobody. So said Seibu Albasa, our master grocer!'

Fargarjaji followed Habarana to his house insulting him, 'Sink your head into the ground for the shame you had brought to the profession of the griot. You are the only griot who had turned into a praise singer and a palace announcer. Shame on you Habarana! You have betrayed our people.'

'I'm neither the creator of values nor the custodian of

our history. What is happening is happening Fargarjaji. I have four children and a wife to feed. The Kora cannot feed those but the zebu horn does. For you I know you don't mind seeing me dressed in jute bags. I'm still a griot Fargarjaji; I'm a master of speech. Don't beseech a griot. Yesterday I held the Kora, today the Zebu horn. I am a bard Fargarjaji, allow me to choose my instrument and how I say my words.'

'Even then why did you have to be biased in your announcement?'

'What is the benefit of my self-realisation Fargarjaji? What is an old garment worth but throwing away?'

29

Ardo Husseini, the father Jabbi and the leader of the Toorodbe clan of the nomads migrated to Barduvai about thirty years ago and decided to settle, enticed by the water and the evergreen pasture of the Daula orchard, which ensured that his cattle got pasture throughout the year. With the availability of salt and additional cottonseeds in the dry season, Husseini was contented to stay behind in Barduvai without migrating to river valleys in search of pastures.

Ardo Husseini was greatly troubled by the appearance of the comet and the interpretation of the rock anagram. Especially as in the past two years, nomads never had it good. There weren't adequate pastures and ponds had dried of. He was surprised when the Askia send for him.

`Ardo we want you to revive the soroo game for the formal opening of the market pavilion', Burtune told the nomadic leader.

Hussein sat silent for some seconds wondering how a person knowledgeable in culture of the nomads will call for soroo at that time. If not for the absence of Hime how could he call in like that, he reflected. When he finally spoke, he told the Askia that it was extremely difficult to do that at that time because Soroo is a culmination of a series of events organised to celebrate a good rainy season and pasturage.

`You don't have to make it elaborate. Just a reminder of our old traditions'

`This games are of the spirit sir they are not something to organise; their success come from the feelings of the herders about the season and their conditions of life sir. That is why I said it is difficult my lord because from the news I have been gathering from our various encampments, herders are not satisfied with the seasons my lord. Moreover these lads nowadays are not strong enough to participate in a soroo.'

'You can delegate responsibility to Bango, he is our renown soroo hero', Lamiri said.

Husseini couldn't understand why Lamiri or the Askia could bring his son-in-law in his presence. He heard a lot about how Burtune and Lamiri had become unconcerned with social ethics. He realised the whole plan emanated from Lamiri and no one else. He realised also that Akilu the judge was absent in the court. He would have supported his views he knew. Bango was called to the palace. On his way coming to the palace, he wondered for what reason the Askia was calling him.

He was very surprised when he saw Ardo Husseini in the court. When Burtune told him what he wanted, the immediate thought that came to his mind was a plot. But he didn't dwell on that very much he thought if the Askia and Lamiri were shameless enough to call him in the presence of his father-in-law hoping he will not disappoint them, then they are wrong, 'My lord I have retired from the sport, if you desire I can organise some dedicated youth like Koneri and others for the dance'

'What is such event like without you Bango? I can help you with some medicine if you want. There is nothing to fear.' Lamiri said.

Bango looked at the face of Lamiri and said he was sorry he couldn't participate.

'What Bango are you frightened of a sport that made you?' Lamiri said chuckling. He was bend on making sure Bango agree on the festival and there was no best method than challenging him. The comment was so uncalled for that Husseini and Burtune both kept quiet before resuming their discussion that the ceremony can be held on a low key. Husseini left the palace promising to do whatever he could. In his heart he pondered how the Askia and Lamiri had become real rascally and he also knew the nomadic elders were going to heap all the blames on him. At the same time he was not ready to disappoint the Askia whom he noticed has surrendered all thinking to Lamiri. On his way back to the ranch he thought of calling a meeting of the elders of the nomads but changed his mind knowing what the Askia might think if he did.

Bango on the other hand knew he was in trouble in the sense that he committed himself to something out of desire to protect his pride and that of his father-in-law. It occurred to him that he could have asked for a day or two to decide. How rusty his thinking had become he thought. How he missed the Kalfuuje group who could have helped in taking a decision. Deep in thought he didn't realised he was heading to Tugga's workshop until he reached the door. The figure of Tugga blowing his trumpet filled him with pity. He waited until the blacksmith finished practising his tune, he told him the Askia wanted to revive soroo

`What do you think?'

`Don't participate'

`They would say I'm a coward'

`Let them say so, what is the relationship between what they say and what you are'

Tugga resumed blowing his horn reading scores written on a wooden slate. Bango regretted ever coming to Tugga. He knew it was useless because the Kalfuuje circle broke painfully and trying nifty sessions like the one he wanted was not going to help, nor would it revive the spirit in any of the members. He missed the Kalfuuje group badly.

He arrived in his room depressed and unsure of what to do next. Hanging on the wall of the room were the leather waist and armbands, which he used when he was a soroo star. The day he arrived in Barduvai came back freshly in his mind. His first place of call was Mamman's grain store where he saw from a distant, herders jostling to buy salt.

'Is this the end of the world, is this the end of the world!' he shouted involuntarily.

The herders turned around to see a medium height herder standing at the door. Mamman who was pressed to his sacks by the jostling nomads sighed a breath of relieve and took to liking Bango. Shortly a soroo festival was held and Bango's name was to be known in and around Barduvai. His height and body build made him adept to soroo contest. A group of herders would swoop on him with sticks in pre-bout games and dexterously he would fence their blows, twisting, turning and even rolling on the ground in the process.

While he sat on the bed contemplating, Jabbi came inside the room

'What are you thinking of, didn't you enjoy the dance

at Poli?'

'The Askia called me today and said he wanted a soroo'

'Soroo in this year. Who are those so satisfied with life that they want a festival?'

'Do they know the hardship people are facing. This Lamiri is the main goader of the Askia. Whatever he says is accepted by the Askia.'

Jabbi urged him to forget about the soroo and to migrate with her to Poli the haven of nomads where they can dance and sing without being bothered by the sedentary folks who are too obsessed with the comet, 'Every day they troop to that blacksmith's workshop to see the position of the comet. Today they said it is approaching the baobab tree. I'm fed up with this city. If you are not going away I would. The settled folks are wicked. You know. Daily I urge my father to abandon settlement. It is no good to the spirit. It turns you into a wicked person. You know Lamiri told me to marry him'

'What people say is true then, you visit him'

'Curdled milk I take to him what do I need him for?'

'You yourself said they are wicked, why then, why visiting a wicked man'.

'What of you! You stopped herding. You even refused to attend *Geeroowol* last year!'

'How can I go to Walata just for a dance?'

'Hear you, if it were before would you complain of the distance. Let's leave this city'.

Bango thought for a while and realised Jabbi was right. He wants to participate in the soroo out of pride and nothing else. Bango felt so mixed up and bewildered that he didn't know what to do despite knowing that a nomadic proverb that says, *'running is the medicine'*

30

Leaning on his staff as he watched his son work, Ardo Husseini was greatly troubled. He didn't want to displease the Askia anymore because the last thing he wanted to do was to migrate. He knew if he was to migrate to Poli, the same problem of finding supplementary feeds for the cattle would arise again.

'Wound the ropes more tightly wouldn't you', he shouted at his son Mogoggo who together with a younger brother was erecting two tents in readiness for the arrival of nomadic leaders, 'The sun will go down without you finishing the tents!'

Mogoggo knew the moods of Ardo Husseini. He was one to have different moods for different people. He hoped his sisters were doing their portions well in the house; otherwise Ardo's mood was bound to persist throughout the day.

The declining sun made the surrounding trees and shrubs to look orange. Using his right palm as a shade, Ardo saw Habarana coming on his horse, his long zebu horn hanging on his shoulder.

`Any news?'

`My dear Ardo I have commercialised my services, you will have to pay'

`How much is it?'

`Thirty cowries sir'

Ardo reached inside his pocket and gave him the thirty cowries. Habarana thanked him.

'Many nomads are on their way here. The son of knowledge will be your special guest, the Askia can't come himself. There will be a great prize for the winner of the soroo contest. Do you want me to make jigul jaguls for you in the city, it is the new name for announcement Ardo'

'Have you ever heard us announcing there will be a festival?'

'Whatever you like my dear Ardo' Habarana said riding his horse back to Barduvai.

Inside the house, Jabbi and Adama were frying some meat while their mother Kobi was watching them. She was particularly concern about Jabbi who after the appearance of the comet kept saying she wouldn't get married with an impending disaster fast approaching.

Shefu came into the house and collected some large mats for the guests of Ardo who started to arrive. Ardo knew it was going to be difficult to convince the other clan leaders about the rationale of organising a festival in such a period. He heard a horse neighing from afar, and using his palm again he tried to guess who was coming. It was Jauro Karim of the Uba'en clan who arrived with his two attendants. After the formal greetings, Jauro went and sat down on the mat, 'Well Ardo you are lucky you have settled, we keep roaming until the day of disaster. It isn't long is it?'

'Today I heard it has passed over the baobab tree'

'It is drawing closer to the mountain'

Ardo Husseini ordered Shefu to bring some porridge from the house as he continued to discuss matters with the guest. Shortly Hudahuda the leader of the Uda'en clan arrived on his spotted horse. As he dismounted, he started to tease Husseini. Hudahuda had the habit of wearing the traditional danciki instead of a flowing gown much to the annoyance of the other clan leaders who believed as a clan leader he should be wearing something larger than a herders' outfit.

'I was told Daddo is to be held', he said laughing as he sat on the mat, 'Habarana told me, so I said Ardo does it mean you have been having different rainy seasons than the ones we have been having'.

'Not me, I was called and ordered'

'Well, I understand. I said before, when have nomads gotten so satisfied as to organise a festival of joy. Now I understand'.

'What of the comet?'

'Well what to say? On the way I heard people talking about the comet over the baobab tree'

'Daily my daughters return from the city with the

news about the comet. I say Jauro what are our minions in the matter, us old men. Are you a young person?'

They both laughed.

`Hear me Husseini, does death know a young person from an old person. Oh don't speak like that. Who is gracing the occasion'

`Lamiri is coming. I'm sure he is on the way now. From him I swear you can hear more details'.

Habarana returned with Mambo the drummist. The elders laughed when he explained the teasers he was introducing for palace announcements, for news and for praise singing. This he said was to reduce monotony. The elders laughed when he demonstrated the elephant tune for Askia Burtune, the Pyramid tune and the various tunes for praises and announcements.

When Shefu brought out a bowl of porridge, Hudahuda asked if Ardo had allowed his sons to participate in the Pyramid project. Ardo said they were matured enough to decide their fates and the question of life and death. Lamido Boneri of the Degereeji arrived with his entourage. Mogoggo who had finished constructing the hut ushered him in.

`Oh oh so Daddo is on my dear Ardo', he said sitting on the mat clenching his teeth and muttering something about age.

`Wait, wait...' Ardo protested realising the sarcasm in Boneri's voice.

`My dear Lamido it is not only Daddo but Soroo as well' Hudahuda chuckled.

`Soroo! Aren't we in trouble then? Wouldn't the

youngsters die before the comet crosses over the mountain'

They all burst out laughing

`You know very well I'm not in a position to organise a Daddo or a soroo festival' Ardo Husseini said.

`Who said you are not capable. Who said you are not capable'

`It is Burtune who called for it, not me'

`Oh so it is the Askia, it is an order then. Is he coming for the festival then?' Boneri asked.

Ardo told him Lamiri was coming instead of the Askia. Karim asked them if they had drunk the portion from Sharok's mat. Ardo said he was in no need for any elixir as an old man. They all burst out laughing.

`My dear Ardo death knocks on the door of both the young and the old'.

Lamiri arrived in Askia's chariot and was welcomed by the group of nomadic elders. They called him 'son of sheikh' disregarding his new title. He told them the Pyramid project was the best ever project to come to Barduvai. It was a blessing for people with sense not people like Dabalo Ceddo and Tugga Bukele.

`We still don't understand the building. This is so because we don't attend your school. This Pyramid is it a new palace for our Askia? We never can imagine a building so vast'

`No never' Lamiri said quickly, `When you see a thunderstorm afar, then what remains but to think of where you are going and where to take cover'

The old men nodded in approval

`This Pyramid is an old plan, since the days of the pharaoh I tell you'

`The wicked pharaohs, we must be in trouble' said Boneri

`The Pyramid will solve the mystery of death and the unknown. My dear elders it solves the fear of transition. Oh Ardo the fact that the pharaohs were considered wicked is not an important point. It was their priests who for selfish reasons corrupted a plan that would have saved mankind forever from the fear of death and the unknown.'

'That the temple was built, isn't that enough'

'Not at all, many more structures are to come. You will understand when the Pyramid is finished. Our predicament is caused by fear. Fear of death, fear of the comet. When the project is finished and you are assured of places there, you will understand everything.'

31

At the temple of Light, the splintered rock was fully guarded; nomads and people from various cities came to see the anagram that prophesied an imminent disaster in the land. Nabal stood collecting a cowry each from the visitors, while Apiru was yelling 'May the comet land on our heads. The harbinger of disaster, the bright mistress of death!' Apiru had since stopped selling salt and was carving statutes of Atamin and Warum Kudulix, which he sold five cowries each to the visitors. In between yells and selling of statuettes, he recited the history of Kudulantic kings as he heard narrated by citizens. His fiendish appearance added horror to his pidgin recitations.

Herders who only heard of the fallen rock and the moving comet stood watching the anagram while listening to the pidgin recital by Apiru and wondering of what value was that recital to the life of people. Many said probably that festival could be the last festival to be organised. That day Barmaki was very busy telling the arriving people that the only solution was for them to abandon everything and join the building of the Pyramid. He told them that in the chambers of live people would gather after the disaster has passed to relax for some days before they decide what they want to do next with their lives.

Many visitors signed to work on the Pyramid project and vowed to arrive before the comet moved over the Tibesti Mountain so that they would be among the safe ones. They were particularly frightened by the invocations of Apiru.

Tugga watched the arriving citizens under the

gizzard rock. He blew his flute for some times but that day few people paid any attention to him as they hurried passed to the Temple of Light.

'I have not even stocked an hour at the Pyramid, oldman' Tugga said.

Damolishi only clacked.

'I see it as a waste of time. Yet sometimes I can't keep my mind from worrying that probably the comet is true and a great disaster is coming. But I feel that if I join the project I will plunge into an unfathomable mistake. I feel as if I will experience a great loss and dejection'

Damolishi clacked again and didn't reply Tugga.
'I feel as if there is a spark, a light far away which if I reach can revoke my doubts and eliminate the noise in my mind. But again at times I feel as if I am just a fool in deep imagination'.

'How far is the spark?' asked Damolishi clacking again.

'I know that illusive lamp can guide me. But it is illusive and Barduvai is true'

Damolishi clacked.

32

When Shefu was returning with an empty tray to bring more meat from the house, he met with his sister Jabbi at the door, 'what are you peeping at? Go out if you dare', he said while passing by her.

'Pass by you urchin!' Jabbi shouted.

'Come in and serve some meat for me'

'I'm not your slave, meet Adama she is inside', Jabbi told him without turning her face. She wanted to go out and have fun with the milkmaids who were trooping in the encampment, but she wouldn't dare pass the elders sitting outside. 'Have you seen Bango among the herders?' she asked Shefu when he was passing with a try full of meat.

'Go out and find out!' he shouted at her.

'May the comet land on your ugly head' she said to him.

Shefu giggled saying, 'May a leopard undress you!'

'Why are you treating me like this', Jabbi implored in a feminine voice, 'I hope in the evening you will ask for fried kidneys'

'Oh Bango is around who said he isn't. I didn't know you aren't aware', he said moving out quickly to serve the arriving guest.

Outside youth have gathered in groups talking excitedly and looking forward to participating in their first soroo game. Bango too arrived and was discussing with the elders. In their presence he thought he finally had a chance to say whatever he felt in his mind, 'If it is death or whatever, I'm less concern but this festival is for the Askia'

'Why are you saying that' Lamiri interrupted.

'I will say it in this period of hardship and draught

how people with any sense can stage a soroo festival!' Bango was in no mood to be cordial. Even the elders present were surprised at the tone of his voice.

Lamiri realised Bango was spoiling for a fight, so he decided to play it quietly without letting him know even slightly the intentions in his mind, 'I told you to come and get a portion that can restore your strength but you seem to be unimpressed'

'What I find unacceptable is what our heritage has been turned into. What is the good reason? You our elders are supposed to pose this question'.

To diffuse the atmosphere Ardo Husseini immediately told Bango to go and organise a dance without further argument. Bango left the assembly of elders and called the youngsters who were generally singing and mixing together, chatting noisily. They wore copper bangles on their legs and the girls too wore bangles on their legs and hair.

Bango ordered them to form a circle and instructed Koneri to lead them in dancing and singing. The respect shown to him by the young herders overwhelmed Bango who began to think that what he was doing was treacherous. The youth formed a circle and started to sing. As they danced, they open and close the circle raising their bodies on their toes. Bango was delighted Koneri started a sarcastic song:

> *Bonno oh the foreign song*
> *Short you blame me*
> *Tall you blame me*

The Pyramid of Askia Burtune

What of the hunchback!

Bonno oh the mysterious comet
Take me to Barduvai
To lay some maidens
Under the comet
Mercy and frying
Frying with care

Bonno oh the youngsters in the wild
What is left of a herder?
But staff and tentacles
Mercy and frying

Let seek for mercy
Let's go to Barduvai
Let us sleep with housemaids

Oh heraye
Let us try and see
You sons of nomads
Descendants of soroo

Let's lit the fire
Let's watch the comet
Let's see the laggard

The sun has eclipsed
The comet has appeared
Let's sing with care
Let's push the metal rods
Let's beat the metal rods
Let's mine the hearts
The hearts of enemies

As they dance, Ardo Husseini who realised Lamiri was uneasy tried to banish the atmosphere, 'They think they are dancing'

'May the comet land on their backs!' Karim joked and all present laughed.

After the dance, the elders escorted Lamiri who kept saying they must revive their traditions. The elders agreed out of cordiality and knowing the song hurt Lamiri. As Lamiri entered the chariot, Karim said, 'Your highness this is better to you than a horse then'

'What Karim, this is the closest thing to flying. A horse feed on grass and water. This feeds on nothing and float with a speed of the wind'

Lamiri bid them bye as the chariot started for Barduvai thinking bitterly about the sarcastic songs by the herders. If he was feeling any remorse for planning to rid off Bango, now he was going to do it with a vengeful pleasure.

Meanwhile at the encampment Jabbi was eagerly waiting for her father to return inside the house so that she could go out to meet Bango. She was peeping throughout out the evening carrying some fried offal. She saw her father finally returning home and she ran and hid behind a granary until he passed.

Outside she met Bango who was also anxiously trying to find a way of contacting her. They went behind the compound and squatted aside.

`Are you ready for soroo then?' she asked him as she gave him the fried offal and squatted aside.

`It would come to pass. There is nothing to worry about especially with this inexperienced lads'

You shouldn't participate in this soroo. I dreamt badly last night. You must stop. Let's run away to Poli. I am fed up with this city.

'When it is over we shall leave. Be patient.'

33

When the pavilion at the market was completed. It looked beautiful with its new cloisters. People came from far to see the edifice. The Eastern side of the pavilion wall passed behind the baobab tree. Beautiful columns and arches decorated the outer instead of the inner walls that surrounded the pavilion. It was Friday, the day of the Soroo. People arrived from distant places to witness Bango their hero stage a comeback. They recalled their prominent days with excitement. People who just returned from Tugga`s workshop were saying the day of disaster was coming closer and closer. They recalled when the rock fractured and thundered down the Tibesti Mountain as if it was just yesterday.

Mambo Ulal hit his drum with a vigour long not heard. He arrived at the pavilion with Habarana who was carrying a shorter horn, the one he used for praise singing. Gaulojo had disappeared and Habarana commercialised his services. People found his methods fascinating and tried to guess which service he was offering by listening attentively to the tunes and drumbeats he adopted. For praise singing and sales he used the *Algaita* and the short horn. Most palace announcements were started by drumbeat by Mambo followed by the announcement. He called the palace tune `the elephant tune'. There was another tune for the prominent people and `the volunteer tune' for lesser people. Many nomads found the idea of paying before been praised another chance to play a champion, so nomads tried to outshine each other to the delight of Habarana and Mambo who were making a lot of cowries.

Habarana blasted his horn with a new tune, a tune never heard before, Mambo answered with some drumbeats, and Habarana dancing some few steps started to sing.

Paha stood aside, tears filling his eyes. He adjusted his straw hat, thinking of how he was easily cheated by Lamiri. Now Habarana a griot had taken his role as a praise singer collecting huge amounts of cowries.

Later Askia Burtune arrived together with Lamiri,

Akilu and Barmaki. They took their seats and the praise by Habarana change to the royal presence. Nomads started arriving in numbers dressed for the festival. Holding their staff, they joked and teased each other.

Meanwhile in his room, Bango was pestered by Jabbi not to attend the soroo contest, 'say you are not ready for the contest?'

'Then we stay in shame together. How can I refuse to participate now'

'You know they use charms and even poison, are you sure you are not set up Bango, your enemies abound, you know that'

Bango strapped his waist leather and amulets and walked to the pavilion. Many participants had already assembled; majority of herders just wanting to know what soroo is really like. It was certain however that the appearance of Bango was greeted with a tumultuous ovation that day. He walked into the arena and managed to display a few soroo steps, which was well received by the spectators. To his surprise he saw Nabal standing among the nomads fully dressed for the soroo. He stood shaking one of his legs and watching the assembled nomads coolly.

When the royal presence was ready, Askia Burtune called Habarana and asked to him to announce that the winner of the contest would be awarded the Commander of the Order of the Pyramid (COT) and that he would be granted eternal sanctuary in the Pyramid. Habarana immediately signalled Mambo and he started the Elephant tune:

`Ahoy, ahoy, whoever comes to this world is the only one he will ever see. The creator of disasters is also the creator of sanctuaries. Where are you descendants of Hubaluba gazers of the ominous comet? To tell you oh herders of the west that whoever wins today's soroo shall be named the Commander of the Order of the Pyramid. An everlasting sanctuary in the Pyramid! So said Askia Burtune great grandson of Samba Tengele torso of an elephant.

People murmured in excitement wishing they were in a position to gain an everlasting place in the Pyramid. Bango hissed thinking whom but a fool needed life in the Pyramid anyway. To him, his reputation was at stake that was his main reason for participating in the event. He looked at Nabal Jengeldo again and wondered how in the world a bodyguard could join in a *soroo* event that was meant for herders. A person who just walked in one afternoon with Lamiri. Bango not convinced, walked to Ardo Husseini and asked 'And this man, is he part of the bouts?'

'I don't know I didn't organise the soroo'

'How can you say you don't know Ardo? You are our elders, the custodians of soroo.'

'It was the Askia and Lamiri who wanted this soroo. It is only what they want isn't it?'

'I am surprise with you elders' Bango said walking away without drawing the attention of the other nomadic elders.

Hudahuda who was close to Ardo Husseini cleared his throat, 'What he said is true Ardo'

'What can I do now? The occasion has started already'

When the bouts started, it was apparent that herders had turned soft and the young ones were only in the tournament just for experience shake. Many young lads were crying in pain. What was the benefit of all such pains Bango thought? The herders weren't particularly happy because basically life wasn't like before. There were fewer rains and there were frequent fights with farmers. Most of them were planning to migrate and were really afraid of the day of disaster.

From the start Bango knew he was going to be paired with Nabal. He was worried with his physical state more than he was worried with Nabal. His joints were weak and he felt terribly dizzy. He tried to imagine the best way to beat Nabal when they are paired together, but his mind was muddled and his physical state was terrible. He didn't train very well before the festival, but he was confident he could wield his staff efficiently.

But he forgot the prospect of Nabal taking the first chance to beat him. A few bouts were arranged and it became apparent after the third pairing that Bango was going to be paired with Nabal. When the toss came, the stringed cowries favoured Nabal. Bango was suddenly faced with the prospect of receiving the blows first. With the way he was feeling it was a frightening prospect. Habarana started the customary praise song before the bout, his baritone voice thundered and citizens murmured among themselves, some saying his voice was good, while others saying they missed the voice of Gaulojo:

> *Aiyee, I said Ayiee*
> *Whoever wants some blood*
> *Should follow a wolf with a basket*
> *Warden of the forest son of Manu Toudo*
> *Whoever stays late in the forest*
> *Is the servant of your house*
> *Whoever eats in the same bowl with you*
> *Can only lick the bones*
> *The moon shines in the absence of the sun*
> *Whoever sees you has only seen your shadow*
> *Ancient warriors kindred of the rocks*
> *Son of Manu Toudo herders of Futa Toro.*

Despite his condition, Bango's emotions stirred and his whole body shook. He pushed his right leg forward and took a perfect soroo stance. The move was graceful and the crowd cheered talking about how Bango has not forgotten the soroo game. Images of his youth conquest returned, the crowd drifted into oblivion and his head started to whirl. But he couldn't dare look down. He began to sweat feeling as if he was going to lose consciousness. Habarana's voice praising Nabal in turn come to him from a distance as if he was in a well listening to the world.

Suddenly he felt Nabal's staff on his ribs. The impact reverberated throughout his body. He felt he was losing his body! Even the cheers that greeted his resistance to the first blow came to him faintly. He felt the blue sky touching his face and withdrawing quickly. The second blow was on his stomach and he felt he had stopped breathing.

`Oh God what has entered me!' Bango cried. The silence that followed the second blow told him he had faltered. After the third blow Bango felt detached from his body. Everything appeared to be swimming around him and he felt he was hovering over the arena, but an orange glow prevented him from seeing properly. He felt free and weightless, and voices came to him from a distance and seemed to be diminishing in reverberating echoes.

Tugga was watching the whole affair with some dread. He was standing close to Jabbi when she started to wail after Bango fell down. He looked at the section where the dignitaries were sitting and he saw the glee on Lamiri's face. Something dry seemed to have mounted to his throat and he left the pavilion running toward the mountain waving his hammer.

Citizens rushed to revive the hero, but shortly after, he died. Some citizens were openly weeping while others stood aside in disbelieve. The nomadic elders walked sullenly to their horses, Jauro Karim in particular was saying something about, `today we have killed Bango! Oh we are disgraced!'

`Ardo stop talking like this now' Ardo Husseini was saying full of remorse. Hudahuda walked to his horse quickly without bidding bye to anyone.

'We have killed him' Jauro Karim nearly in tears mounted his horse.

As they left, Lamiri was announcing something about sadness and how rules demanded that the victor still receive the prize despite the tragedy. As he was saying that people started to disperse.

Tugga feeling dejected reached the foot of the mountain shouting, `they have killed Bango, old man, they have killed Bango!' Tugga stood below the rock panting and gazing at the rooftops of Barduvai city, a feeling of frustration overwhelming him, a kind of frustration that left his throat dry. He regretted refusing to hold a Hime when Bango demanded for it. Ardo Husseini returned to his encampment full of remorse, muttering `Eh I am in trouble, eh I am in trouble'. As he dismounted his horse upon arrival home, he nearly shed tears as wailings emanated from his house. Jabbi, Adama her sister and Kobi their mother were all wailing; "Oh Jabbi disaster has befallen you!"

"Was he immortal? Was he immortal! Woe unto you

wouldn't you stop wailing woman!" Shouted Ardo Husseini in a strained voice as he quickly walked to his hut to personally face his remorse.

34

Kumbo was aggrieved. For twenty-five years she had been patient with Lamiri because she never knew anyone else or where to go to for solace. She knew sooner or later she was to leave Lamiri's house. She had experienced nothing but bitterness and oppression.

She was brought to Barduvai when she was barely four year old in company of her nephew Ladi who was married to a trader in Barduvai. The only thing she could remember was that she rode a donkey and they passed many trees on the way. She was told she had some parents in Jara but repeated attempts to visit them was always frustrated by Lamiri who had never forgiven his father for arranging their marriage. Her nephew Ladi had since left Barduvai.

Kumbo has been saving and buying some provisions which she gave Lamiri to send to her mother. She wondered if he ever did. One day she could remember, he came home with a limping herder who was chewing and spitting kolanuts and told her he was her uncle. Kumbo squatted aside and was surprised the herder kept referring to her mother. From their short conversation she gathered her father had died many years ago and her mother was blind. She wondered why Lamiri refused to tell her. Afterward she gave some cowries and grounded baobab leaves to Lamiri to hand on to the herder to take to her mother. Lamiri had never shown her any love, and had spent all his time either in his clinic or the Temple of Light

Kumbo felt she had no reason to stay in Lamiri's house any longer. She collected some few wrappers tied them up in a bundle and locked her room. She didn't know what to do, until she thought of the milkmaids and how by following them, they may lead her to Jara. She thought some of the milkmaids perhaps might have their encampments close to Barduvai.

Under the tall tamarind tree she met the milkmaids chatting noisily about the death of Bango. None of them paid any attention when she arrived because they were looking at a group of nomads further ahead who crowded round something that must have been fascinating. She sat on one of the protruding roots of the giant tree. Tataraktu saw her and tried to recollect where she knew face. She mixed a bowl of sour milk with millet balls and asked one of the milkmaids to pass it to Kumbo. At first she was tempted to refuse but Tataraktu urged her and she accepted the bowl

Frequent ovation came from the crowd of nomads standing close to the pavilion

`What is it that is remaining now?' Tataraktu asked a nomad who was passing by, `Haven't you finish beating yourselves?' she asked him as he passed by.

The herder told her there was a bet between the market warden Makawuya and Nabal Jengeldo, who claimed he could eat a roasted goat at one sitting including its intestines and brain. The crowd of nomads he told the milkmaids are watching Nabal devour a roasted goat on one sitting.

`What is the bet?

`Fifty cowries' the herder told Tataraktu.

When there was lull around Kumbo asked one of the milkmaids around if she knew the way to Jara

`Jara, I don't think those days we have encampments in Jara. Anyone going to Jara today?' she raised her voice.

The milkmaids turned looking at Kumbo curiously, `Jara since the appearance of the comet most of our people have left Jara.'

Kumbo felt sad because she was at lost unto what to do. She knew going back to Lamiri's house was going to be a painful option, but she couldn't figure where to go to. They was no home she could walk into that day to spend the night. Jara she knew was East of Barduvai but that was the only technical detail she knew about her home village.

The sun had already set behind the Tibesti Mountain and the crowd watching Nabal Jengeldo devour the roasted goat burst out in excitement and people began to disperse. For the first time Kumbo saw the killer of

Bango. He was wearing a thin red turban on his head, which they said was the mark of the Order of the Pyramid (OTD). He was tall and strongly build, the muscles of his forearms showing prominently. As he walked, he was followed by some nomadic youth who saw in him a new hero. Ahead of the crowd was Babbadajaka who was explaining excitedly to people, that when one imbibes Rando Cartoza's principle, then everything of his increases, including his appetites. He said Nabal devoured a whole goat not because he has a big tummy but because he was *maekeru*! Since that day Nabal popular praise became 'Nabal the manducator of goats'!

Kumbo stood up bidding Tataraktu farewell. Tataraktu apologised for her inability to help. Kumbo shook her head thanking her walking eastward towards the cattle market where she hoped to ask for the limping herder who Lamiri described as her uncle. There she asked a young herder she saw if he ever saw a herder who walked with a limp.

'With a limp? 'The herder turned looking at her with curious eyes.

'He is supposed to be my uncle', Kumbo said uneasily.

'Can say I saw any limping herder around here, Hey Bonno'; he called his friend, 'Have you seen a limping herder of recent?'

His friend shook his head, 'I don't think, there is any limping herder that we saw here'.

Kumbo realised it was late to try finding the way to

Jara. She dejectedly decided to return home until she could work out a plan. As she walked back home, another mind told her to walk eastward, she may be lucky to find her village, but she was so discouraged she walked back to her lonely room in tears.

35

With the completion of the Temple of Light and the Pavilion, the Pyramid project assumed an undeniable dimension in the existence of Barduvai as a city-state. The canal that was to link the Daula Orchard and the pond of Realisation was still being constructed, but Lamiri wanted the construction of the causeways to start immediately. One was to link the Palace with the Temple of light; another to link the Temple of light with the Market pavilion and the third was to link the Palace with the Market pavilion. The construction of the causeways was to hopefully enable Askia Burtune to ride his chariot more freely in Barduvai. Since receiving a chariot as a gift from Kudulantis, he rode it only once. Many citizens signed up for the construction, but some as well felt not pressed to join the project, especially as Tugga's Almanac still showed the comet far away from Tibesti. It was a dusty affair in Barduvai, as hundreds of donkeys and mules carted red soil for the construction of the causeways. The signed badges that were given out after every day's work were nicknamed 'the stamps of life'. In the evenings after work citizens as usual crowd under the gizzard rock bragging of the number badges they have accumulated. Babbadajaka was given most of the contracts of carting red soil and buying implements for the project. Although Tugga was the renowned blacksmith in the city capable of fashioning any construction implement, he was not given any contract to supply implements. Babbadajaka imported carts, diggers and shovels at exorbitant prices. Several times Akilu drew the attention of the Askia to the need to stop importing implement as Tugga was in a perfect position to fashion them locally for the project. "Oh you Akilu, we are not talking about hoes and sickles".

"What is it he can't fashion out my Lord? One who can fashion a hoe can also fashion a shovel and build a cart, besides my Lord, the profit he can make can help him build the observatory he so much desires"

"I offered him the position of a foreman, but he refused. What else, can you do with such worthless people?'

Babbadajaka mumbled some few sentences to Lamiri and they both broke into giggles. Akilu felt his time as a judge and a courtier was coming to an end. His promise to Askia Ba'ashi notwithstanding, he felt enough was enough. Ba'ashi's heir was anything but an Askia. In most occasions in the court when a tense atmosphere builds up, he took his leave. This time as he walked home, he thought deeply how to repair his cassava farmhouse and if possible how to tame Lamiri and Babbadajaka. Their self-centred arrogance and hypocrisy has to be tamed he felt.

Conscription of citizens to build the Pyramid became intense. Discussions in the city centred on how many stamps of life a person has amassed. Although many citizens were conscripted, equally many did not join the project, preferring to read Tugga's Almanac daily before going to their trades. The Jannati followers in particular were full of scorn for the project, which they see, as futile. Daily they chanted their chorugal song raising dust as they ran in an attempt to fly.

"You have attempted several times to fly to no avail. Who but a mad man will continue in this...? "Babbadajaka told Citizens in the Kudras.

But despite the promissory budges collected by the citizens and the daily announcement by Habarana encouraging workers to exert their labour in the Pyramid project, the labour force was not adequate. In one meeting at the palace, Lamiri presented a plan of action to the Askia. It was a heated conversation between Lamiri and Akilu that day. Prominent item in the plan of action was the introduction of new taxes and the revision of poor dues, and the building of what is called Pyramid Annex at the Daula Orchard. The Annex was to consist of new houses to be built with marbles to house the

Pyramid Committee Members - Lamiri, Babbadajaka, Habarana, Nabal, Seibu Albasa, and a Conaskiate from Kudulantis was to supervise the project.

"We can't just tax people because they are alive!" Akilu lamented. "My Lord you have already exhausted the poor dues in the treasury..."

"How do we complete this project Akilu, you baffle me...."

"All these difficulties wouldn't arise if you have heeded my advice to return to our Hime. If this project was a result of Hime, would it have been facing difficulties?"

"Something we have already gone far in." Lamiri hissed.

"Further into perdition I suppose. You are building new houses for people who don't need houses. Why do the committee members have to live away from the people? I don't understand. Are you planning segregation in this city?" Akilu was particularly sharp that day to the surprise of Lamiri and Burtune. For the first time Akilu left the Palace without bidding the Askia farewell. He only muttered, "I leave you in peace".

They went ahead with the Pyramid Annex construction. When the foundation was laid, the Daula Orchard was fenced and people were prevented from getting into it. Citizens became even unhappier when fruits from the Orchard were later sold in the market by Nabal "The manducator of goats". People lamented that a taboo has been broken. It was extremely absurd that fruits from Daula Orchard could be on sale in Barduvai market. After some weeks, a greater proportion of the fruits were carted away to Lamiri's Clinic. Later gourds containing a cocktail juice of all the fruits from Daula was on sale. *Daulalier* starting appearing in some stalls for sale. The juice was too sweet and expensive, only few people could afford to buy a gourd. Most citizens moreover lamented that the sweetness of a fruit is in plucking it straight from a tree and chewing or sucking it raw and throwing the stones away. That was what they said as their children started developing beriberi.

Most people began to feel something was terribly wrong with the way they existed, but it was like a general pain. They couldn't poke a figure to the exact location of the pain least of all fathom it cause, except to allude it to the impending disaster. Daily in Barduvai it was just mules carting away red soil, dust raised from the causeways under construction, the blaring Zebu horn of Habarana Choodal making various announcements. Yet it meant nothing to the existence of people. Fewer traders came to Barduvai now as tax collectors harass them on the way to the market.

When labour became scarce, The Pyramid Committee concentrated resources on the Pyramid Annex. Babbadajaka imported a lot of implements and tools. Seibu was given the contract of supplying the marbles required for the Pyramid Annex. People found out that contract and supply to the Pyramid was more profitable that working at the Pyramid. The Temple of light, Babbadajaka's Castle and the houses of the Pyramid Committee Members became congregation centres, where people beg and beg for contracts to supply either implements, cart red soil or import marbles from Kudulantis.

36

Babbadajaka's castle was the most prominent feature of Eastern Barduvai. Situated near the Daula Orchard, the edifice was a structural amalgam of the Temple of Light and Bero Koron Julmire Castle. Those who attended the Kudras after Babbadajaka was turbaned the Mayor of Barduvai remembered Lamiri speaking about hybrids, or amalgamation or something about the beauty of mixing.

Daily, feasts were held either at the Temple of Light or Babbadajaka's castle. By then, the canal linking the Daula Orchard and the Pond of Realisation at the palace were completed. In the evenings members of the Pyramid Committee gathered to watch their reflections in the Pond. They do this in imitation of Rando Cartoza, who upon his realisation of truth, Lamiri had taught them, sat by one of the canals in Bazahu.

Babbadajaka particularly enjoyed watching his image in the Pond, as Habarana sang his praise;

"Babbadajaka the eucalyptus tree, the slippery pole, master of Rando Cartoza's principle. Whoever climbs you, slips down to disaster!" Babbadajaka takes a deep breath, sighing as he watches his still image in the Pond. A crowd of people usually gather to watch them in their indulgence, some hoping that one day they will reach such a social position where they can sit watching their reflections in the Pond of Realisation.

After they finish watching their reflections, they normally disperse to their homes feeling more like they had wanted to be. One can see visibly on their faces, pride and contentment. It soon become apparent that whoever desires change in his material existence must pay homage to them.

"By your grace Babbadajaka, by your grace." bewildered citizens seeking for favours flock into Babbadajaka's castle or the Temple of Light in the evenings. There was nothing sweeter to Babbadajaka's ears than to hear a citizen less advanced in Rando Cartoza's principle seeking for his grace. It reminds him of the time when people were seeking for the grace of Sharok Waladus. This habit gained in fervour especially after those working at the Pyramid woke up mysteriously one day to collect seashells instead of signed badges as their wages. Those who had collected many badges returned them in exchange for the seashells.

Sumanguru swore to workers that he was awaken in the middle of the night by the sound of carts drawn by horses heading to the Askia's Palace before the seashells appeared. When he followed them out of curiosity, he saw a lot of sacks unloaded from the carts, and the drivers of the carts were all looking like Waladus, all wrapped up in a white linen from head to toe.

"I saw them. I saw them with my eyes." Sumanguru narrated. No one could doubt Sumanguru, a staunch Jannati who slept in the market square. At first citizens refused to use the seashells which were called Comeria, but wages for workers at the Pyramid and products coming from the Orchard and Daulalier products from Lamiri's clinic were sold in the seashells. At the instigation of Babbadajaka, Seibu Albasa and some few traders accepted no cowries but Comeria for the products they sold.

Some citizens were happy they now have many Comerias in exchange of their Pyramid badges but majority lamented the introduction of seashells as currency in Barduvai.

"How can the Askia force us to use seashells instead of cowries, we don't live close to a sea - we never know seashells."

More people now flocked to the Palace to watch Barduvai leaders stare at their reflections in the pond of realisation as Habarana Choodal praise them in turns.

"Guardoral Barmaki, basket of medals, imitator of Warum Kudulix, the one with the horn helmet, butcher of Barduvai's enemies, whoever set his eyes on you has seen awesomeness!'

Barmaki sighs deeply, his broad shoulders shaking the numerous medals dangling on his chest. The clunky sounds the medals make are sweeter to his ears than Habarana's voice.

"Look at Barmaki." Sumanguru shouted from the crowd as he adjusted his Jannati toga "He is anything but an African warrior, fat neck, bulgy stomach, no charisma, and no wisdom, only good at eating roasted turkey and watching his image in a pond." On-lookers burst out laughing as Sumanguru joined his Jannati comrades in a take-off spring. "Up Jannati! Up Jannati!"

The following morning, another poem appeared on the baobab tree while Tugga was blowing his flute. In the absence of Bango, Halabutu took over the role of reading the poems. Paha stood aside with his straw hat pulled over his forehead, loving every moment of Halabutu's recitation.

We heard the flute of a ghost
And cut our journey short
Host to tunes of our melodies lost
True to our words
We threw our swords
And called on the ghost
To show us a coast
Naked to the toes
We awoke from a dream
Asking each other

Our garment lost
We couldn't recall
We couldn't decide
We were zealous host
Who became stranded guest
Our sagehood shaved
We were beyond care
Heirs of a tune
We couldn't recollect.

It was while people were listening to the poem that Habarana arrived on his horse followed by Mambo Ulal who wisely changed the size of his drum to a small one in order to cope up with running behind the horse of Habarana on assignments. Mambo beat his drum thrice and Habarana started singing. It was unusual, so people stood listening to the two. Habarana on his new horse and Mambo dwarfed, standing aside.

`The slave of the rainy season is the king of the dry season, hasten to gain hours of protection in the Pyramid'.*

Habarana kept repeating the sentence in his old griot voice, which people have long not heard of. When people asked him what type of announcement that was he said it was a *jigul-jagul* from the palace. It was neither a town cry nor a praise song. In his baritone voice, Habarana galloped around the city as he repeated his strange *jigul-jagul.*

`The slave of the rainy season is the king of the dry season, hasten to gain hours of protection in the Pyramid'.*

Meanwhile Halabutu continued reading the baobab tree poem reading the poem over and over to the citizens, Fargarjaji also arrived to deliver his popular lectures. More people came to listen to his tirades.

'How can you work for twenty four hours and only get two hours recorded for you in the Pyramid. Remember each Comeria equals to two hours in the Pyramid. These seashells are brought from Kudulantis. We have never known seashells. How can Burtune and his surrogates force us to use seashells instead of cowries to buy and sell? You are being cheated, you are being exploited. How can you save enough hours in the Pyramid when a bunch of vitaspinach from the Daula Orchard costs two Comerias and a bottle of *Daulalier* cost twice that amount? The idea of saving for the day of disaster is an illusion. It is a mirage that you are forced to accept. Most of you are working at the project because you are forced to not because you want to' Fargarjaji started to sneeze violently.

'Look at them!' He pointed to the stall where Nabal and some guards stood glaring at the crowd. These bouncers of the palace are supposed to take you and me back to the ancient serfdom. You will soon become serfs in Barduvai! We are in a neo-feudal period in Barduvai!'

One of the guards hurriedly took off to the Temple of Light and upon his return; Nabal drew out his sword and arrested Fargarjaji amidst an uproar among the citizens, including even Seibu Albasa who promised to see Babbadajaka on the matter.

Many citizens rushed to the house of Akilu and informed him about the arrest of Fargarjaji. He quickly summoned Barmaki.

'Who ordered the arrest of Fargarjaji?'

'It was an order'

'Well I didn't order you to arrest him. Where is he?'

'In the prison'

'Go an unlock him!'

'I cannot'.

Akilu stood up and walked to the palace and asked Burtune if he ordered the arrest of Fargarjaji.

'I suppose Lamiri did'

'My lord how can you be so lackadaisical. We can't erode our institutions with such impunity. When did you add such powers to his portfolio?'

'We started something and he is against it. What has Kudulantic knowledge benefited Fargarjaji? How can people like Fargarjaji and Dabalo do this to us in the face of an imminent disaster? If it is positions they want at the Pyramid, I will give them, why the sabotage!"

37

Akilu closed early at the court and headed straight to his farmhouse where he left Tugga and Durugu working in the morning. He met Tugga blowing his flute while Durugu was still plastering the outer wall of the house.

Tugga, leaving piles of the weeds to dry, weeded the cassava farm neatly.

"Welcome back sir" Tugga placed aside his flute.

"I greet you all" Akilu saluted tethering his horse, surveying the fresh look the farm and the house had taken. He felt a sense of personal relief that at least he has a farm and a house to fall onto. He thanked God that his first salary went into buying the farm as if in anticipation of how the government of Barduvai will decline. Not a single cowry was remaining in the treasure. He had never imagined such recklessness would arise in Barduvai. He had already concluded his plan when the last cowry was taken out. He planned to audit the treasury, balance up his books and hand it over to the Askia. If they are thoughtless and reckless enough to squander public cowries derived from poor dues, he will have no part of it. But as a trustee of the poor dues, he will ensure that every cowry is accounted for in the treasury. He is not prepared to let some worldlings drag him into an inferno, he swore.

He gave Tugga and Durugu the gourds of curdled milk he bought for them on his way coming to the farm.

"I will check back to pay you up", Akilu mounted his horse again, "please Tugga, in the afternoon Ardo Hudahuda will bring two donkeys for me. Tie them in an appropriate place..."

At the courtroom in Barduvai he started balancing up the treasury records and the fines he collected from cases. He felt sad that he was preparing to hand over an empty treasury, depleted by scoundrels. After sorting out the records, he dispatched his messenger to call Lamiri to the court.

Lamiri had been worried about the witnesses Akilu called and the formal documents he had to sign whenever he collected cowries from the treasury. On the way coming he began thinking of a way to convince Burtune to dismiss the judge. He found the audacity of Akilu to summon him to court as disrespectful.

"I need all the financial report regarding the cowries you collected" Akilu told him when he entered the court.

"Wouldn't that be after the project in completed."

"Were you not keeping record of the expenditure? I am amazed," Akilu said shuffling through treasury slates. Lamiri quickly collected himself "they are in bits and pieces..."

"I give you until tomorrow noon to bring a full report which you will sign in front of witnesses"

Lamiri walked out of court without uttering a word. Afterwards Barmaki arrived telling Akilu the Askia wanted to see him in the palace. There, Burtune asked him to rescind his decision. Akilu refused telling the Askia that he was performing his duty. The next day at Noon when Lamiri didn't turn up with a report, Akilu sent for Barmaki, whom he ordered to arrest Lamiri, Barmaki refused to obey the warrant and for the first time Akilu got openly angry, swearing to show Lamiri that he was not above the laws of Barduvai. He sent for Dabalo Ceddo and ordered him to use some of his members to arrest Lamiri. Dabalo Ceddo swung his Jannati Toga and proceeded with a glee to arrest Lamiri. The Kudras was full when he arrived. To make it dramatic, he handcuffed Lamiri hands behind his back and walked him through the market. It was a disgrace, as hundreds of citizens followed behind to the court.

"I gave you until noon today. But you refused to come. Where is the report?" Akilu asked laconically.

"You have done your heart's desire" Lamiri spoke showing lack of concern but inwardly in turmoil and shock.

"I have done the law, not my heart's desire. Take him to the prison"

In the commotion that ensured, Habarana arrived to tell Akilu that the Askia wanted to speak to him in the palace immediately.

"What is the use of what you did, Akilu?" Burtune asked looking seriously apprehensive. Akilu handed him the treasury record on a slim slate. "Here are the treasury records. You have the power over the treasury of Barduvai, but you don't have power over my soul. I cannot accompany you on the route you have taken. I mean no malice. I wish you all the good. I wish to relinquish my duties as the Judge and the Treasurer of this city. With that Akilu walked out of the palace and rode home to pack out his family and belongings to his farmhouse.

He left Burtune in a terrified state. The Askia paced up and down his court wondering if he shouldn't go and apologise personally to Akilu. Akilu, though critical of his policies acted as a brake on Lamiri, he thought. Deep inside his mind he was afraid of Lamiri and his reckless drives.

"Askia Burtune torso of an elephant,"
Habarana bust in followed by Babbadajaka breathing heavily. "Grandson of Tengele, power is in your blood, don't let sons of slaves derail you, reach up and hit the head of rascals"

"My lord I am surprised you allowed this affair to end into this disgrace. If you had listen to Son of Knowledge you wouldn't have allowed Akilu to hold two portfolios."

"Mayor Babbadajaka Akilu worked with my father and I don't know why he conferred both portfolios on him.... There must be a reason" Burtune slumped into his throne, as he was wont to do when he got emotionally exhausted.

"My lord", Babbadajaka moved closer "When Atamin inherited the throne from Warum Kudulix, did he wear a horn helmet like his father, was hunting his hobby like his father, did he live in the castle left behind by his father?"

Burtune smiled, "please don't remind me of this rascal."

"My lord law is fear, fear and law go together. You must be afraid to obey a law. Give Barmaki that portfolio. He will inspire fear in people. That is law."

"A guard!" Burtune exclaimed, "No no, what will the citizens say"

"When last did the citizens speak?" There was silence in the court. "As for the Treasurer, give someone who can count. Duna Kahuna for instance. Who can count better than him in Barduvai?

Habarana cleared in throat "Don't forget Son of Knowledge is still in prison"

"Tell Barmaki to release him" Burtune ordered. In the evening of that day Burtune gave Lamiri his chariot to ride around Barduvai for all his enemies to see. As they rode on the only completed causeway between the palace and the pavilion in the market, Habarana was on the driver's seat of the chariot, shouting in his baritone voice for all to hear.

"Son of knowledge mentors of Kudulantic knowledge, son of the venerable, master of 1000 minus one medicine, seer into the intestines! Whoever wants to see your downfall son of Marduka, can only see your elevation, Ahoy! Ahoy!"

Citizens emerged lining the causeway, more out of curiosity than sympathy for Lamiri.

"You see how they adore you!" Habarana exclaimed.

"Who will work in the Pyramid and not support me

apart from revisionists!" Lamiri grunted waving to the people who wave back laughing.

The following day in a public ceremony at the market pavilion, Barmaki was promoted from Guardoral to Guardodier and named the new judge of Barduvai by Burtune amidst blaring *algaita* and drums. Later in the evening of the same day, Barmaki and Lamiri rode in the Askia's chariot along the causeway linking the palace and the market pavilion. People stood watching Barmaki smiling in his new uniform and the dangling Guardodier medal.

Changes in Barduvai were so fascinating for people who savoured the newfound habit of rumour mongering and lamentation. "Burtune swore to silent his enemies", "Lamiri and Barmaki were given thousands of Comeria by the Askia" "More Comeria expected from Kudulantis" "Beri Beri and Kwashiorkor to be cured" and so on and so forth.

38

At sunset Tugga walked haggardly to the gizzard rock, he felt so miserable, a spectator of a heedless orgy. On the way he met with Seibu Albasa returning to Barduvai with donkeys' load of vegetables, he pulled aside and smiled at Tugga.

"You amaze me master of metals. Don't you like yourself?" he asked, "See Lamiri and Babbadajaka are your peers. See their position in the society today. See the castles they have built. Everyone in the city is calling you a latrine rat. Stop worrying yourself. Visit Babbadajaka, don't feel shy plead with him to ask the Askia to reappoint you the foreman of the Pyramid".

Tugga shook his head as he passed on. Upon reaching the rock he didn't even bother to look at Damolishi, he just tapped the rock thrice and sighed. He brought out a black bag of cowries and counted them again.

"If only I had one hundred and fifty cowries, oldman. I will pay back Tataraktu her debt and leave Barduvai forever." He sighed again and sat down crossed-legged. He raised his flute and started to blow a sad tune, tears rolling down his cheeks. After some times, he stood up and spoke to Damolishi without looking at him 'I am going to work in Walata oldman, I am going to work to repay back Tataraktu her debt'

"You are bewildered" Damolishi replied him.

'Nothing can make me return to Barduvai'

'You are bewildered' Damolishi told him again 'what is taking you to Walata?'.

'I would stay there. Anywhere is better than Barduvai. Until we meet again old man. For you are tethered in Barduvai.'

'Stop! We are all tethered. Stop don't go now it is already late, it will soon be dark. Walata is not going to run away. Tell me what comes to your mind about leaving Barduvai'. He clacked, "Have you ever slept in a graveyard?'

'No'

'Come with me tonight'

At first Tugga was afraid but he finally accepted the proposal out of curiosity, although he had lost hope that any experience can have any meaning in his existence again. Damolishi brought out his bow and quiver and the black bag he carried daily to the cemetery. Tugga collected the bow and quiver from him and walked behind him to the cemetery thinking about the prospect of spending a night there.

`What do you expect to feel at the cemetery tonight?'

`I don't know, spooky things ... just be frightened for a night perhaps'

`Why are you not afraid to spend the night there now?'

`You will be there'

How can I come between you and the spooky images?'

'I don't know, I just feel'

`I don't know I just feel' Damolishi repeated the statement and clacked. As they passed through Barduvai, they saw Nabal walking around proudly displaying his OTBY turban followed by some youth who were admiring him. Tugga showed Damolishi the man telling him it was he who killed Bango. Damolishi clacked walking without posing even for a moment. At the cemetery, Damolishi spread his mat under the tamarind tree. It was still not dark. He said to Tugga `I want you to stop thinking and to listen and see things. Don't think about them just see'

`Not to think?'

`Yes, just imagine you don't have a mind, just eyes and ears. Listen and look'

`Listen and look at what?'

`Listen and look at the cemetery'

As if it was timed, the bier of a dead citizen was brought to the cemetery, `who is it?'' asked Tugga

`I told you not to think, see and hear'

Tugga tried to stop thinking about whose bier was brought in and concentrated on watching the crowd of people. They appeared like a white mass, a fleet of cattle egret to him. They walked to the farthest end of the cemetery and started to dig a grave. Tugga tried not to think concentrating on watching the crowd.

Finally the crowd began to leave in silence. Damolishi walked to the fresh grave followed by Tugga. They stood watching the fresh grave, he refused to think turning to see the dispersing crowd, and he saw a white mass moving away. He could smell the freshly dug grave as the crickets started to chirp. When darkness fell, they walked to the tamarind tree and sat on the mat.

`So this is how you spend all your nights?' Tugga asked.

`See and hear'

`But it is dark, I can't see anything'

'Then see darkness and listen to darkness'

Tugga knew the prospect of chatting with the ancient warrior in the cemetery that night was over. After looking intently into the darkness he began to see some shapes but dismissed those as phantoms. But he checked himself for thinking they were phantoms. He realised it was difficult to stop thinking and to listen and see only.

When he started to feel sleepy his vision and hearing changed unlike when fully awake, only the sound of the crickets chirping and owls tooting, but when he was half way between sleep and wakefulness there were sounds that tended to draw him into a realm. He was not sure if he heard wailing and crying but the realm was gripping so much so that he had to shake himself free to wake up. When he was fully awake, there was nothing that could be heard but the chirping crickets, hooting owls and barking dogs from a distance.

After a while he called Damolishi but there was no reply from where the old man was last sitting. Tugga wondered why he didn't answer him. His heart started to throb and he started to sweat under his armpit, but he recalled Damolishi's instruction to see and hear only. He switched his attention to looking and hearing again and ceased to resist the gripping tendency of the second realm of sound. When he stopped resisting the second realm, he was carried along as if he was freely floating on the sound. Now and then he returned to the first realm but he didn't do that intentionally until he felt he was spending more time in the second realm than the first one.

When he ceased to interfere in the process, he began to feel that the second realm was actually an expansion of the first realm, and his aural capacity seemed to have expanded with the shift to the second realm. At the break of down when his seeing became more acute, he gradually returned to the first realm. His vision seemed to have affected his capacity to transcend the first level. Tugga looked around but didn't see Damolishi, he was not bothered however.

Later Damolishi arrived laughing at Tugga, 'I had forgotten how nice a bed is for a long time' the warrior said laughing.

Tugga felt the sound of Damolishi's voice differently as if his ears were serviced or their powers increased. He felt and understood every sound with a different level of significance than before. Damolishi removed his bow and quiver from the tamarind tree looking at Tugga intently, 'There is something I want you to learn, if you agree then I show you or if you want to go to Walata then...' he gestured with his finger.

Tugga thought about his experience the previous night and thought any experience is better than going back to his old feeling in Barduvai. He still felt he contributed to the death of Bango and he felt a sense of remorse and anger, 'Not here in the cemetery again?' he asked the old warrior.

`Here or in the forest or on the mountain, why should it matter to the learner', Damolishi replied, `in ancient Gudur where I came from you are either a warrior or bewildered. This bewilderment I will explain to you when you are ready. In Gudur every boy had to undergo the eighteen days of *Waratake*. In fact a man was considered incomplete without undergoing the waratake training. It will be good for you. Yesterday you must have strange experience here. You assumed I was sitting close to you but I left when it was dark'

`I felt there were two realms of sound...'

`*Hain*, many more.' He clacked. 'Many things you may know already, many things the same, many different, so be true to your inclinations and you will be all right. You have the heart but you lack an unbending intent. If you agree to undergo the eighteen days of Waratake then come and tell Damolishi'. The Warrior turned, shifted his quivers on his shoulders and started walking in long strides to the Tibesti to sit on the gizzard rock.

Tugga walked back to Barduvai thinking hard about the training. If the old warrior was suddenly interested in training him, then it must be more important than leaving Barduvai. But if the Hime and Buruji's Gehenna training didn't help what was going to help? His main concern was the repayment of the debt he collected from his wife to build the ill-fated Burankewaal. He considered if he was not a fool after all not to have signed for the Pyramid. Why has it been always his inclination to learn about the meaning of life? What is his business but to save himself and his family? What is more important these days in Barduvai but acquiring more Comerias to buy the products of the Daula Orchard? He recalled Damolishi saying he had the heart but lacked an unbending intent. His fear is not poverty, he had learned a lot from Buruji regarding that. His fear was his aversion with the social milieu in Barduvai so much that citizens have started to deride him as a pretender. Why should he care he wondered.

That night, Tugga didn't sleep he brought out a mat and tried to replicate the experience of the previous night by looking at the comet intently without thinking.

39

One Friday, people trooped to Tugga's workshop as usual to know the position of the comet. That day the almanac showed the comet had crossed the baobab tree and it was a remarkable observation, for in Barduvai they said when someone has passed his prime then he must prepare for his death and now that the comet had passed the baobab tree the preparation for the day of disaster should be foremost in the minds of the citizens.

Tugga was blowing a particularly sad tune that day but most people were not apprehensive, being sold to the idea that the Pyramid was the only solution to the imminent disaster. 'Getting the stamps of life' 'Partake in the Pyramid or you will be a victim'. Life was hard, as everything required Comeria. The Kudras disciples were elevated. Some of them frequently dress like Sharok Waladus. Even Babbadajaka tried the regalia once, but even his admirers advised him never to dress like Sharok Waladus again.

It was on that day Friday that Akilu arrived in the market with a donkey loaded with two sacks of cassava. People were amazed. Many citizens rushed to help him unload the donkey. Akilu told them not to bother, but they still went ahead bowing at him. Akilu smiled at them. If they were surprised he arrived with a donkey they were speechless when he unloaded the two sacks of cassava and started to divide them into piles.

Soon words spread that judge Akilu had come to the market to sell cassava. People rushed to see for themselves. Upon arrival they bow down greeting him and mumbling to each other. Akilu invariably smiled at them a smile that was unaffected and aloof.

A moment later Fargarjaji arrived and resumed his lecture. 'Wake up citizens, don't let the Pyramid members return you to serfdom. We are returning to serfdom oh people. Stop it! You are losing your franchise without knowing. You may one day wake up and find that those wolves have gone with your freedom. You have lost it. What is it you can do here or possess without the approval of one of those? You are mere serfs and peasants under their control...'

Later in the afternoon, Habarana arrived with Mambo

Ulal to make a palace announcement. He announced the appointment of Duna Kahuna as the new treasurer of the city. People were extremely happy that day; even Fargarjaji stopped his lectures to congratulate the kolanut trader. Duna was a short trader with a baldhead, fond of wearing long caftans but never wore a cap on his head. People said he couldn't wear a cap because his head would boil due to his profuse arithmetical talents. He was an unusual kolanut trader who can tell the exact number of kolanuts in a sack. A number of times people disputed this ability and they foolishly betted and lost to Duna Kahuna

But he was best known for developing a system of monetary calculation called *gotilloro*, it was a system the traders in the market couldn't understand although Duna adopted it from a local draft game. First using his hands he collected a heap of sand, then using his right hand he levels it into a plateau, then he brought out some coloured sticks which he assigned numbers. With his forefingers he plucked in grid of holes into which he placed the sticks.

To most traders it looked like a draft game. It was only when Duna started to move the sticks that it appeared complex. Traders threw in sums and figures and Duna shifting the sticks told them the answers. It was miraculous to them. Duna tried to make them learn the *gotilloro* but they refused saying this is a talent not knowledge. He told them it was neither magic nor a game, but they refused to learn saying knowledge can be learned but talent is a limp of the talented. Whoever tries to dance the steps of a talented dancer would lack the tunes to match his steps! They were contented to bring sums and figures for him to calculate for them and they called him 'Duna the owner of a reckoner head'.

It was believed that with the appointment of Duna, the financial problems of Barduvai would soon be a thing of the past.

40

After Tugga returned from Akilu's farm in the afternoon, he began to pack the hoes, tins and trinkets he had displayed outside his workshop. Since the Pyramid project started, he sold only few hoes, tins and trinkets, most work implements were brought from Kudulantis. He stopped the habit of picking pieces of abandoned metals in the city, preferring to work on Akilu's cassava farm after opening his almanac to the public in the mornings, playing his flute in the afternoons and teaching the Kalfuuje scripts to Akilu's children in the evenings, thrice weekly.

When Tataraktu returned from the market smiling and joking with the milkmaids who followed her home. She stood apprehensive looking sweepingly in the workshop, before putting down the calabash of millet balls.

"Where are the implements?" She asked
Tugga told her he wanted to speak to her in private. In
the room he told her he was to be away for some days.

"All is well?"

"Ah nothing, everything is well", Tugga was
determined not to reveal his mission. It was personal and
it was to remain so. Since the decline of Hime, he had felt
that his personal suffering must be really private and he
really felt guilty whenever, he felt his countenance or
experiences were either a source of embarrassment or
pain to others. How he had wished that everyone but
himself be shielded from his personal suffering; all his
fears, sufferings and shortcomings be cocooned on him.

When he tucked the last tin away in his room, he felt a
sudden feeling of relief as he placed his flute and hammer
under his cornstalk bed and walked out of his house with
only his leather apparel on.

At the Gizzard Rock he met Damolishi dressed in a
warrior attire his bow and quiver hanging on his
shoulders. He descended from the rock upon seeing
Tugga; he turned and started to climb the mountain,
followed closely by Tugga. They climbed the mountain
until they reached a sharp cliff overlooking the setting
sun. Damolishi sat on the edge of the cliff, Tugga walked
and sat beside him in trepidation.

Until then not a word was uttered by the warrior,

they just sat watching the setting sun, its orange glow so enticing and mysterious. It appeared so close to Tugga, as if it was an arm length, so comforting, something to reach out and touch. It was only when his attention turns to the cavern below that a fear of falling pervaded his mind.

Damolishi clacked.

`Last night you spent a night at the cemetery. You must have some unusual experience, based on what I told you to do. I told you to concentrate on looking and hearing...'

`It was difficult. At first when they were bringing a bier it was difficult for me to concentrate on looking and hearing only without thinking. But when I checked myself I saw a white mass moving. Then in the night, I at first dismiss whatever I was seeing as illusory'

`You shouldn't have', Damolishi clacked.

`But I realised that after listening deeply, the sounds of the surroundings changed into a different realm. I felt there were two levels. The second one felt like gripping me but at first I had preferred the first until I got used to the second realm'

`Well your experience is more important to you than to me. I only intentionally chose seeing and hearing as a booster for you because many methods place too much emphasis on feeling and thinking. The booster is the first stage of waratake. It can come in three ways", Damolishi raise three fingers, "naturally, circumstances or on purpose. This booster is the stage in which a person's thinking about life becomes deficient. Important, person must experience this stage. This experience through any sense can come".

'When I was visiting Hajji Buruji he used to make me plough ridges at the orchard thinking of Gehenna'

'Well this is another way, many ways exist. I want to tell you that there are many who were lucky to experience it naturally. Like through extreme difficulties, diseases or most importantly, sorrow. I was lucky mine was sorrow". Damolishi clacked. "The heart is important in waratake. No heart" Damolishi pointed to his heart, "just bewilderment!"

'What is this bewilderment?'

'This bewilderment is what is happening in Barduvai for instance. On a larger scale. But on the personal level it is when one's devising fails in life, your attempt to rationalise life fails, but instead of realising the insufficiency of your parameters you devise some more. Later you will understand the meaning of devising, *darkun* and folly. Be patient. My father was a bewildered one. He said he was a prince, I don't know but it appeared to me my grandfather must have been a chief somewhere and after his death there must have been a leadership tussle in which my father lost'

'It must have pained him' said Tugga

'He took the decision of the *darkun*, the type you were about to take. He migrated to Gudur and settled there marrying my mother. Then he started beer drinking and chattering with his equally idle friends. From afar you could hear my father's voice shouting and bragging about his pedigree and how important his family was in their village. How he had denigrated himself by coming to Gudur.

I loved my mother Janada and I believe that love was my source of sorrow. She was strongly built, tall and immeasurably resilient. Her height, I took but her strength I didn't. She had the largest number of granaries among women in Gudur. She cared for my father but he was a bewildered one and that depressed her very much. I sensed that because at first she thought she could change him but later realised he was a loafer and there was nothing she could do. She regretted marrying him I noticed.

She stopped brewing beer hoping that would make him stop drinking too much beer, but it didn't help. As she went to the farm, he went out with his friends drinking beer and they returned late in the night. The argument would start, he would be boasting and my mother would be rebuking him. He would be shouting until in the morning.

`Why didn't he get at least a small work to do?'

`Bewilderment! He started to sell my mother's goats and chickens to satisfy his hedonistic life. One thing about him though was his attitude to me I would never forget. He couldn't look into my eyes'

`Strange'

`Yes. He avoided my eyes whenever he was talking to me. Even in bewilderment people feel they could do better. Man is supposed to hate bewilderment. My father resented his bewilderment but he was helpless'

'Later I noticed Janada was getting listless, something that derive from disappointment'

'Your father's behaviour'

Clack. 'She gradually got sick. Something with her joints. There was this pain in her eyes that I saw whenever I had walked into the room. She wanted to work but couldn't'

'Couldn't your father change even a bit?'

Clack, 'He grew worse, in fact he got into affairs not his own. He began to stay long outside and used to return with a bruised face and swollen eyes. He must have been getting into fights. My mother's condition continued to deteriorate. Her joints swell and my father began to take advantage of her sickness. Together with his friend they would come and break into mother's granary or steal her goats. In the night when they returned drunk they would kill a chicken and roast it outside. In her room she could hear the chickens squeaking and she would call out complaining and my father would begin to shout, ` Does she want him to die of hunger?' I can remember his voice like that.

Damolishi clacked, pausing in his narration while gazing at the Eastern horizon hanging over the east like a blue drape.

`Whenever he came with his drunken friends to remove mother's grains or kill a goat, then my mother would ask with a sick voice, `Damo, Damo who is it?'

`It is him', I replied. Then from her sick bed she would be imploring in a sick voice. It is that voice that made me sad' Damolishi sighed deeply. I did my best to take care of her. A friend of her usually brought some food to her. She hadn't many friends because she was mostly engaged in farming and other trades during the dry season. One day I followed her friend and pleaded to her to let me bring the remaining animals and chicken to her house. At first she was afraid but I persisted and she agreed. In the night when my father was not around we transferred the animals and the chickens and that night as usual coincidentally his friends wanted to roast a chicken and there was none. That day he was hollering all over the house telling my mother that she was lucky he descended so low as to marry her, a daughter of a crocodile hunter, wasn't she lucky he, a prince descended so low as to marry her.

Subsequent days were terrible. One afternoon I returned with some cassava, my mother's favourite food intending to boil them for her. I heard voices of men inside the room. It was strange because usually at that period father would be out drinking beer. I rushed to the room and was trying hard to adjust my eyes to the darkness. They saw me and one of his friends Damagan immediately grabbed me. I struggled hard to get loose but his grip was tough and I wasn't strong enough. As he dragged me out I caught a glimpse of the others including my father tying my mother. I started to scream. Damagan held me down tightly. His goatee beard was brushing my face and his breath smelt alcohol strongly. Hai, Hai! No pain pass the one on that day, no pain equal the one of that moment!

'The whole world changed to me. My heart sensed something sinister and started to wail on its own. They brought out her body on a mat tied up with strong ropes. I jumped up but was forced down by Damagan.'

'Why didn't you scream loudly, were there no neighbours around?'

Clack 'they timed their sinister operation. People had gone to their farms only goats bleating and birds chirping'

'What actually happened?'

'Premature burial'

'Oh my God' Tugga sighed looking at the setting sun, as it loses it bright orange glow, he didn't see its attraction any more.

Both of them remained silent for a long time.

'It was a calculated premature burial', Damolishi sighed. 'When they returned from their sinister operation their eyes were fiery red. They had to drink a lot to do a thing like that. I wailed and wailed, when our neighbours returned from their farms my father told them Janada had died and he had buried her with his friends. The more I told them it was a lie the more they tried to comfort me saying I was only a miserable boy who couldn't comprehend death.

My father abandoned me after five days when he was pestered by the villagers to show her grave so that some rites could be carried out. He realised it was getting dangerously to disclosure. I am sure he found where she kept her cowries and up till today I don't know what they did with her body.

I had nightmares. Before falling asleep I would see the body of Janada struggling to get free from strong ropes. I would wake sweating profusely. In desperation I went around the entire burial sites but couldn't see any fresh grave. Then I started to climb the mountain and sit by a cliff where I thought they might have thrown her body. There I would sit crying in anguish.

Like I said the booster can come to you naturally. It is up to you to decide on how you want to get the booster, you might have gotten it already'.

Tugga heaved a sigh, he never heard of such a terrible story before, 'I told you about the tutorials I have been having under Hajji Buruji'

'It is good, but you need to catch a kernel from a booster'

'But I like to explore the visual and the aural dimension further'

Tugga carefully dragged himself away from the cliff, by then the sun has disappeared in the west leaving a receding orange glow.

41

Rahila the wife of Duna Kahuna leaned out of the window of their new house at the Pyramid Annex. Built on an elevated ground, the Pyramid Annex overlooks the Daula Orchard, a greenery stretching far into the East. It was like a dream to her. In the past few days troupes of women from the city came to visit her to share her joy in their new home and the happiness of her husband's new position. She showed them around the new house sharing in their exclamations and awe.

Inside his room, Duna was preparing to deliver the budget speech on behalf of the Askia. He wore a long Kaftan dyed in blue. He stood before the mirror reading the speech and adjudging himself. When he finished he hesitantly reached out for his calabash facial mask, which he wore. Wearing such a mask was then a novelty among leaders in Barduvai whenever they attended occasions. Sitting in the front row, it gave them an enigmatic aura among the public. Barmaki was the forerunner of such a habit, which was quickly copied by the Askia, Mayor Babbadajaka, and the rest of the Pyramid Committee. Barmaki in his full Guardodier regalia and the calabash facial mask instilled fear in the mind of whoever had set an eye on him. This was so especially as Habarana Choodal kept saying about him in praise singing that whoever has seen him has seen awesomeness. Standing erect in his grim countenance, he was a monument of dread.

After rehearsing his budget speech several times, Duna walked out of the room. Upon seeing him in the facial mask, Rahila was taken aback. She didn't know if he looked ridiculous, loathsome or sinister.

In his way out of the house, he met his parlour full of citizens waiting for him. The uproar of greetings that erupted embarrassed him. Before then the only people he had met in his mornings were one or two kolanut traders who had come to count kolanuts. As he walked out of his parlour, people were stumbling over themselves to draw his attention to their problems. He walked quickly to the parked chariot given to every member of the Pyramid Committee. He nearly run, as he felt uneasy and he kept repeating in a desperate voice; "Wouldn't I be back! Wouldn't I be back?" He wondered as the chariot pulled out, how Babbadajaka enjoyed such an atmosphere and had looked unable to do without being surrounded by an enormous number of people in his sitting room.

Most citizens were in wretched conditions; many having given up their trades but were unable to relate to the Pyramid effectively. This was so because how to benefit from the Pyramid was not a clearly cut affair. It sure was nothing to do with spending your energy on it. That day in protest to the situation in Barduvai, Fargarjaji wore a gown made of hastily sewn jute bags. Despite their conditions, people were very amused when he stated to sneeze violently due to his allergy to the fibres of the jute dress. They wondered why Fargarjaji wore a jute dress knowing fully well he was allergic to fibres.

If people were amused by Fargarjaji's behaviour, they were speechless when Habarana appeared in a herder's *danciki* dress accompanied by beautifully dressed milkmaids carrying gourds of *Daulalier* juice on their heads singing

'Daulalier, Daulalier, you and beriberi never meet'

'I say away with beriberi and kwashiorkor!' Habarana kept adding in his baritone voice waving his arms and swaying his torso.

'Daulalier, Daulalier, you and beriberi never meet'

'I say away with beriberi and kwashiorkor!'

When the crowd swelled to the maximum, Duna arrived. People murmured that the dress Duna wore was supposed to symbolise the opposite of the Jannati philosophy. If they wanted to fly, Duna wanted everything on the ground. But people were still not impressed by Duna's dress. They said there was nothing more ugly and sinister than the sight of Duna Kahuna wearing a calabash mask in addition to his baldhead and long caftans.

'Citizens of Barduvai' he started in a voice that sounded as if he was trying to imitate Sharok's husky voice, 'I address you from the palace of the Askia. He asks me to tell you that there is absolutely no need for the despair currently in the city. From the glitter of the ominous comet we can also discern the glitter of hope. From the rays of the ominous comet we can also see the rays of a bright future. Hasten to work at the Pyramid and secure a future for you and for your children. That is why today we shall call the measures we are going to take to restore hope in the city as *the glittering plan for a wealthy Barduvai.*

This is a unique budget as it is the first in the history of Barduvai and the first since the appearance of the comet. Our macro achievements since the appearance of the comet are the building of the Temple of Light, the Pyramid Project, the change of our currency from cowries to Comeria, the Pyramid Annex and the fencing of the Daula Orchard. You will agree that the building of the Temple of Light is a crucial project in Barduvai, our existence as a city-state derived enormously from the Temple where our eminent personalities contemplate the problems facing Barduvai and the solutions to it. No enemy of this city-state can scuttle the Pyramid Project. Its recognition as the only solution to the imminent disaster is indisputable. Extremist can go their ways. So also is the change in our currency and the loan we received from Kudulantis to the tune of 2 million Comeria.

But due to citizens not working in the Pyramid, most of our macro-economic gains are lost. At the end of last year a deficit of 520,000 Comeria was incurred.

Our revenue outlook is gloomy. Our dependence on the Daula Orchard is not helping economic matters in our city-state. 3000 fruits and nuts per day estimated at 2 Comeria per fruit/nut. Consequently our total collectable revenue for the coming 10 months is 1.8 million Comeria. Out of this, a provision of 250,000 Comeria has been made as recurrent expenditure to make up for the observed under funding of the Pyramid Annex and the Temple of Light.

The main thrust of this budget shall be: the completion of the Pyramid and the encouragement of laradish and vitaspinach farming. The Pyramid will be pursued with greater dedication so that the linking tunnels of the West and South will be completed at a total cost of 1.05 million Comeria. The causeway between the palace and the Temple of Light will be completed at a cost of 250,000 Comeria

In addition to the Pyramid project, citizens are urged to farm and export vitaspinach and catabeans. To this end Seibu Albasa and Babbadajaka are given a total of 250,000 Comeria to farm the crops for export to Kudulantis..."

After the speech, citizens dispersed sullenly, not one of them understood what deficit, recurrent and revolving meant. This Pyramid they accepted must be a weird project. Anything that is recurrent, revolving and deficiting must be weird!

Fargarjaji resumed his tirades against the palace analysing the speech by Duna Kahuna as the beginning of the enslavement of the people of Barduvai.

'This is the beginning of neo-feudalism in Barduvai!' He shouted swaying in his jute gown, 'Why do you suppose they wear calabash masks whenever they want to speak to us. Deceit, I tell you!'

Dabalo on the other hand began speaking about the whole of the city turning into a buffer zone due to their obsession with sedentary activities like farming and building, especially a useless edifice like the Pyramid. Dabalo especially was highly critical of the Pyramid, which he regarded as a useless edifice. "Why not fly and join the comet and move with it. That was the surest way of protection". They grew to hate the citizens who they believe are supporting the Askia and the Pyramid committee members who create a milieu that was preventing them from taking off.

Desperate citizens as usual flocked to the houses of the Pyramid Committee members especially the recipients of the 250,000 Comeria grants. Those were the successful they said. They were relieved of labour and an everlasting protection has been bestowed on them. Many youth now figured that working at the Pyramid daily is not the smartest thing to do. Discussions in the city now centred on how many Comeria one has gathered, as most citizens balked from working at the Pyramid, preferring to sit under the shade of trees talking about who and who had amassed enough Comeria to ensure protection from the imminent disaster.

That day Akilu brought his cassava late to the market. While he was unloading the donkey, it got stubborn and started to run in the market. With a display of non-challance and strength he followed the donkey and caught it amidst cheers by the traders who saw an inspiring lack of arrogance in his action. When he tied the donkey to a tree he walked across to the milkmaids and ordered curdled milk from Tataraktu.

42

Ardo Husseini used his palm as a shade to see whose cattle is migrating amidst a huge dust raised. From a far he recognised the horse of Jauro Karim.

`What Jauro, where are you heading?'

`I'm fleeing Ardo. Running away is the medicine, it is said'

`Oh no', Ardo Husseini got apprehensive

Jauro Karim dismounted his horse offering his hand to Husseini, `I'm fed up Ardo. Everything has an end'.

`Let us be patience. The reign of every ruler shall pass. Isn't it?'

`But Ardo I'm a herder not a farmer. What catabeans and Laradish! How can Lamiri be so wicked enough to deny our animals food just for beans?'

`Patience can eat a mountain, Jauro. His reign would come to pass'

Jauro Karim returned to mount his horse shouting,

`How long? How long? I'm not eating any stone. I have gotten enough pebbles in my kidneys. It is said that the heart of an old man is like a junkyard. Well mine is full Jauro. Farewell, may God bless you'

'May God protect you', Ardo raised up his palm

Jauro Karim spurred his horse waving at his men to proceed on the migration. He left Husseini in deep contemplation. How could he migrate after thirty years of sedentation? For the first time he realised the danger of sedentation to the human spirit. The wisdom of transhuman migration filtered into his mind with a sudden clarity. `Koli Tengele was right', he murmured `we are like birds, our spirits are of the wild'.

From a far he saw Mogoggo and Shefu returning from Barduvai. He had never discussed their involvement in the Pyramid, although they daily went to Barduvai purposely to work at the project. Their bodies covered with dust, they argued noisily about the number of chambers in the Pyramid.

`Come this way', he called them. `Do you actually understand this project?'

Mogoggo smiled, `Ardo four doors are already finished, one in the East, one in the West, one in the North and One in the South.'

'This is better for you than grazing then?'

'Ardo we wanted to speak to you.'

Ardo Husseini nodded.

'Ardo you know Lamiri, all you need to do is to go to him and ask him to give you the order for supplying milk and meat to the project. Habarana Choodal Ardo… you need to see the castle he is building. He is the sole supplier of milk and meat to the project. Meet Lamiri Ardo. He respects you'

Ardo Husseini shook his head. Someone who knows next to nothing about livestock being given such a contract. After the death of Bango, he had never again visited either the palace of the Askia or any notable place in Barduvai except the market. He had since banned Jabbi from selling curdled milk in Barduvai. As he walked into his house just to be certain, he cleared his throat and called for Jabbi to bring him water to drink. As he sat on the mat, he felt as heavy as the worries in his mind. So many changes in Barduvai are beyond his comprehension, especially the leadership. He honestly wondered what was preoccupying the minds of Askia Burtune and Lamiri. This Pyramid project of theirs was also an enigma. He quite often felt as he passed by the furious constructions going on, that it was a monument of deceit. Why the deceit or who were they trying to impress was unclear to him. Commodities in the market were getting scarce. Salt the main stay of commerce in Barduvai was in short supply.

Traders were daily harassed by the Jannati members; they have made farming a difficult occupation due to their incessant preaching to recruit members in surrounding villages. He knew it was only a matter of

time before those living in the outskirts of Barduvai
become members of the Jannati group.

43

The footpath that curved round the Tibesti Mountain to
Walata was a busy road especially on market days. It was
one of the remaining routes that were not totally
dominated by the Jannati followers. Although fewer
traders plied the route than before, herders, milkmaids,
and grain sellers still throng to Barduvai on market days
unperturbed by the activities of the Jannati followers.

Tugga had never felt as embarrassed and nervous as
he sat by the path begging for Comeria. On top of a big
tree lurked Damolishi observing everything that was
going on below. As he blew his flute, Tugga prayed
furiously that someone familiar would not pass by the
route. His thoughts centred on what people will think of
him, mad? Desperate? Shameless? The whole of Barduvai
will be pervaded by the story that he was found begging
along Walata route. And then the Pyramid Committee
especially Babbadajaka would be in a state of glee. He
started to sweat under his armpit as he saw Halabutu
coming back from Walata on a donkey full of loads.
Halabutu pulled by his side greeted him, looked down on
the wooden plate before him containing Comeria, and
then threw some few seashells on the plate. He shook his
head as he spurred his donkey toward Barduvai. Tugga
nearly jumped up but for the presence of Damolishi on
top of the tree.

After a while he noticed passers-by reactions were not as alarming as he thought they would be. Most traders cast a surprise glance once but after that only threw some seashells. After they passed he at times heard some of them laughing but wasn't sure if they were laughing at his condition or at something else.

By the time the sun was setting, Tugga felt calmer and had even counted the number of Comeria in the platter. Damolishi descended from the tree he was hiding on, smiling at him.

Tugga stood up eagerly, collected the warrior's bag and followed him as he walked towards the cliff again. Tugga had expected the warrior to immediately start giving him insight into what he went through but Damolishi only kept quiet even when they sat facing the setting sun again.

"When Halabutu reach Barduvai today, the whole city will be full of this story." Tugga said as a prompter.

Damolishi clacked, "You are impatient with the heart. You are too much of the head!"

Tugga kept quiet trying to understand what the warrior said.

"Remember how I told you I experienced great sorrow at the death of my mother." Damolishi started, "I told you I kept on sitting on the edge of a cliff. I nearly jumped off that cliff. I thought about death. I began to realise that during my isolation at the mountain that my sorrow was not the same. At times it was more and at times it disappears and return with a great fury. Our elders say that the reason for our bewilderment which results into feeling like sorrow, fear, worry and so on is *darkun'*

'*Darkun?*' Tugga repeated.

'Yes it is called darkun. We learned early in life that man couldn't bear his position in relation to Geno the irresistible. The main reasons why you felt you wanted to leave Barduvai and your fear of what they will say in Barduvai today is self-importance

'Pride?'

Damolishi clacked, "The self-importance I'm referring to is not the same as pride. I can't find the right word for it. It is something like an imprint on the psyche of man that took a long time to build. Ages man thinking that he is central in the affairs of the universe. Remember this. Creation is a ceaseless mystery, know that man is unimportant in the creation of the universe, so he creates darkun to banish two things that he perceives as threatening-nothingness and Geno's awesomeness.

Man can't bear his position in relation to Geno the irresistible so he creates darkun buffer to give him self-importance, to banish the ceaseless mystery of existence. Man fears Geno's awesomeness, so he cringes, in the process he device a cover called darkun to screen Geno's awesomeness. When there is a screen then you turn to repeating actions, manner and thinking so that nothingness is banished and 'somethingness' is maintained.

Something within us urges us to weave the darkun. When it is lightly weaved, then some of Geno's awe filter in, but when thickly weaved Geno's awe can't come in. When Geno's awesomeness is full, then there is nothingness; we can't indulge to forget our nothingness and his awesomeness. Every situation big and small is supposed to affect our darkun, but mostly we fortify it instead of removing it.

Tugga shook his head, 'I don't understand old man. How can that happen since we don't control our thoughts?'

'Old warriors say if you don't control them, observe them, Damolishi clacked, 'but later on seers say even observing your thoughts lead to indulgence again. There is no substitute to unbending awareness'.

'So Hajji Buruji was right?'

Damolishi clacked.

'Some events or thoughts don't just scratch our darkun they shake them or shatter them. Darkun can be shattered, then you either device another one or do away with it all together. One of such bashers is extreme pain, extreme experience, but death is the ultimate basher, then Geno's awesomeness would be in full', Damolishi open his palms to demonstrate what he was saying.

'You must find your darkun basher. I used the

remembrance of death as my basher. You may like to use Geno's awe or continue with Buruji's Gehenna school. They can all bash you darkun. What makes the waratake teaching different from the other teachings is that the stages are cyclical that you repeat over and over again in life. Some teaching have linear stages so people begin to feel they have graduated from one stage and need no repetition, self-importance back again, darkun, waratake back to darkun!' clack.

'Beware, darkun is a deceptive affair. Elders in Gudur said come to it repeatedly don't come to it confrontationally. Hit the beast and if it is not dead then ran around and pick a fresh club and hit it again, show it your dedication not your courage and it will die.

Both Tugga and Damolishi remained silent for sometimes.

Damolishi clacked; "Would you beg on the road again tomorrow?"

"Yes I would", replied Tugga confidently.

44

Durugu after returning from Poli, heard about how some traders spotted Tugga begging on the route to Walata. The news had troubled him. He had not met his friend for a long time but he still cared. Several times he had advised Tugga not to bother with the fate of the city. Its leaders he told him are beyond the border of recall. Life became difficult for Durugu after the ascension of Askia Burtune to the throne of Barduvai. Burtune had never called him for even minor construction repairs at the palace despite the fact that he built the palace. To buy anything in Barduvai had required the Comeria. To make ends meet, Durugu resorted to selling clay pots in surrounding settlements.

"Is Tataraktu inside, peace be upon this house!" He announced his presence from Tugga's empty workshop. While waiting for a reply, he looked around the empty workshop getting more apprehensive. What has happened to warrant Tugga abandoning his trade?

'Welcome sir', Tataraktu said as she spread a woven mat on the workshop floor. After profuse greetings, Durugu asked if all was well with Tugga. Tataraktu swore her husband didn't tell her where he was going or what was in his mind.

Durugu sighed.

'Please drink water sir'

'No, thanks be to God', Durugu said thinking hard what to do next. Just then, Habarana's zebu horn blared,

> *"To tell you oh citizens of Barduvai! That a new tax is ordered by the Askia. This new tax is called the Cometic tax. Every adult will pay 30 Comeria to the treasury before Friday. If you know you can't pay the tax, the Askia has ordered that you work the equivalent at the Pyramid. When the ear hears, the body is safe"*

'Calamity', Durugu muttered. He sat silently for a while as Habarana continued the announcement in the city.

"This city-state might as well be ruled by the devil. Tataraktu, I was passing by the market pavilion two days ago. I saw a group of youth cheering and clapping, being eager I ventured to see... I swear I saw this vagabonds watching nude girls dancing and what else I was not sure, because I was so unsettled for venturing to look in"

"You have just seen the lighter side of it. We who spent the whole day in the market can tell more that you may never like to hear"

"So I heard. They say the youth are dramatising the Confessions of Atamin"

"More will surely come"

'Who knows? I will set out tomorrow to find him', Durugu promised Tataraktu as he departed.

45

Apiru couldn't sleep well due to his excitement of being appointed a senior tax collector to assist Nabal. He had gained favour with the palace since his famous yells after the appearance of the comet. He can gauge how much Lamiri and Babbadajaka had wanted him around them whenever they were to appear in the public. His rascally behaviour and his fiendish appearance, he finally found, were tremendous assets. A month didn't pass without either Lamiri or Babbadajaka or both of them giving him some Comeria. At daybreak he picked the sharp piece of metal he had always carried and headed to Barmaki's residence.

'Do you have to come as early as this?' Barmaki barked.

'Traders arrive early sir, right time to catch them sir'

'Go to Nabal!' Barmaki shouted closing the door of his Annex house.

Apiru's excitement was not dampened, he heard how tax collectors make cowries from collection and he was determined to buy Habarana's mule, which the griot had not ridden since he bought a horse. Habarana had promised to let him have it at two hundred Comeria.

Hundreds of traders especially those coming from other settlements didn't even hear the tax announcement but were still asked to present their evidence of paying the Cometic tax.

Many traders were herded and taken to the Pyramid Annex to work for equivalent hours. Apiru had a busy day harassing market women who came to sell dried leaves, wild berries and guinea fowls. He set aside one guard who collected whatever he confiscated from them.

'Do you want the comet to land on your heads?' Apiru yelled kicking baskets of squealing fowls.

'Please my son, please my son', some of the elderly women pleaded, some of them old enough to be his mother.

At noon when the market was full, Nabal appeared in the market with some five other guards. That day he wore both his OTBY turban and the *rigan tsamiya*; a swordproof dress, which was worn only during wars. People were amazed Nabal had access to such ancestral dress.

After harassing some few traders they headed for Akilu, who behind his heaps of cassava was watching them. Nabal asked him to pay his Cometic tax.

`What is Cometic tax?' asked Akilu

`Everyone must pay, there is no exception'

`I want information about the tax, who want an exception. I shall pay if you explain and justify the tax'

`Didn't you hear the announcement made by Habarana don't tell me you didn't hear. The Cometic tax is incumbent on every citizen for his protection against the day of disaster. What you pay is going to use to build the Pyramid'

`I don't believe in the Pyramid'

`You still have to pay the 30 Comeria or work the equivalent at the Pyramid' shouted Nabal.

`This is no taxation but extortion. I don't see how the building of a causeway between the Askia's palace and the Temple of Light can protect us from a disaster if there is going to be any'

Traders crowded the scene astonished at the daring and unrespectable way Nabal was speaking to the retired judge. Irate citizens started shouting, `extortion!' `extortion!' Nabal got jittery and he was unsure of what to do next. He knew if he walked away, he was paving the way for further dissension and if he arrested Akilu... He decided to arrest the retired judge. He ordered the handcuffing of Akilu and they marched him across the market, by then traders were shouting `extortion!' `extortion!' But they had no tradition of protest; in fact they didn't even know how to demonstrate their disaffection.

Way inside the market in one of the stalls, Habarana was cornered by Dabalo Ceddo and Fargarjaji, both of them had felt he was a disgrace to the descendants of Hubaluba by first abandoning the institution of the griot and secondly being the mouth-piece of Lamiri and Burtune.

`What is difficult in being a griot Dabalo? You are shouting so much, I say what is difficult. To cut the matter short, my Kora is still hanging in my bedroom, if you are so concern with the history of Barduvai, very simple. Let us go and I would give you the Kora and I swear I would spend the next three weeks reciting to you the stanzas of Barduvai history. You are learned, you can write it down'

'Look at you, can you even remember a stanza of that history? I say if you father was like you and had thrown away his Kora where would we have been?' Fargarjaji asked him

`During the days of my father, had the comet appeared? Fargarjaji please stop talking like this'

Fargarjaji said, `You ought to be ashamed of yourself Habarana for using the talent you learned from being our griot to enslaving our people'.

`In those days when I was trekking to Poli, Jara and Walata on foot do you know my experiences? Who had ever given a single cowrie to me for chanting the stanzas of Barduvai history? Who? Tell me! The only thing I would say is I'm grateful Burtune has raised my family and me. I would never have ridden a horse or sleep in a concrete house without the goodwill of Burtune and Lamiri. You people have knowledge, you are learned. For me I don't see myself spending the rest of my life chanting the history of Barduvai in village markets for the rest of my life'.

It was then that a Jannati follower arrived shouting, `they have arrested Akilu they have arrested Akilu!'

Dabalo, Fargarjaji and Habarana run out of the stall promptly. Despite their differences, all the three had respect for the judge and no one would have ever expected the arrest of Akilu in Barduvai. Dabalo removed his sword from his shoulder shouting, `Not even their fathers dare! Not even their fathers!' He went ahead waving his sword violently the other two calling for restrain.

Meanwhile at the market people were trying to barricade the five guards who arrested the retired judge, but were at the same time afraid of the swords the guards were holding. Dabalo Ceddo arrived and without thinking confronted Nabal. 'He is wearing the *rigan tsamiya!*' people warned him but it was too late, in a furious battle Nabal cut down Dabalo and two other Jannati followers. The guards departed with the handcuffed judge, people shouting helplessly behind them.

A wounded Jannati follower ran around the city with blood soaking his body calling his comrades, 'they have killed Dabalo! They have killed Dabalo!' When the other Jannati followers run to the market they found the dead bodies of their leader and their comrades lying on the ground. They removed their swords and started threatening the people saying they partook in the killing of their comrades and would pay for it. Within a short time people fled the market more afraid of the Jannati followers than Burtune's guards.

The Jannati followers ran between the market and the Askia's palace, which was securely locked chanting the Bazadi incantation in anguish. Citizens locked themselves in their houses for fear of their lives. After sometimes it was quiet in the city. When people finally came out, they began to ask where the Jannati followers had gone. Some said they had flown away, others said they have migrated but a more reliable source said that Dabalo had predicted he would die a martyr before the successful take off by his followers and had told them to flee to the mountain after his death.

The following day the truth surfaced. It was reported that Burtune received a formal warning from the members who had changed their name to the *Shining Jannati Guerrillas*. According to the report, they had warned that they would wreck vengeance on the city, which had not only killed its leader but also created a buffer zone that was preventing their success in flying up.

Their new leader, Jonkal Awembi was reported to have said Dabalo was not orthodox enough, for the members were not supposed to have stayed in Barduvai. As staying with people who were engrossed in feeding and buildings in the face of an imminent disaster were signs that they were themselves acquiring the thinking and the feelings of those citizens. He said they were supposed to stay in the bush like wild animals and to avoid the exaggerated appetites of the citizens for food, houses, and large farms. The Jannati members therefore started a rigorous regime of fasting and promised to burn all food items and farms. Very soon they became known as the 'beckoners of the desert' for their scorch earth activities.

Some citizens began to say the situation was becoming more dangerous than the comet and the imminent disaster. Some even said they were no longer afraid of the imminent disaster or of the comet.

Burtune ordered the release of Akilu who returned to the market to a tumultuous welcome. Many asked him to lead a revolt against the rule of Burtune, but Akilu refused and resumed his cassava trade and in the evening return to his farmhouse where he spent the evenings.

46

Kumbo had not seen Lamiri for more than a week, she was bewildered; she had nowhere to go to find solace in Barduvai. She tried hard to think of a single household to go but failed to imagine who it was in Barduvai she could go to share her torments. She couldn't figure out if the bitterness she felt was part of marriage. How was she to know? But for sure she wanted a change in her life. She wanted to be with her parents. But who were her parents?

She began to pack her belongings into the woven baskets around. After she finished packing her possessions, she selected some few wrappers, her trinkets, heirlooms, necklaces and brass rings and tied them into a neat small bundle. She was determined to leave Barduvai. She sat on her bed trying hard to figure out how best she was to travel to her home village, Jara. All she knew was that Jara was East of Barduvai. Outside she realised what people said about Barduvai was true. The market square was a shadow of its former self. Fewer people now come to Barduvai from surrounding settlements because of the incessant attacks by the Jannati

Guerrillas, all over the city discussions centre on the Guerrillas and their strange philosophy which abhors building houses, feeding, and other life preoccupations like agriculture. They said the act of building houses is the foundation for supporting self-importance, so as a policy they roamed in the wild, sleeping on trees and eating wild berries. Wherever they come across farms they burnt them and they attacked traders, calling them hypocrites and greedy creatures.

Along the way she passed a group of people discussing about attacks by Jannati Guerrillas. They said the Guerrillas are closing on the city now. Travelling has become hazardous. Jonkal Awembi had threatened to invade the city. Fewer nomads and milkmaids now come to Barduvai to buy or sell. Farmers were afraid of cultivating crops. The Guerrillas attacked the Daula Orchard thrice carting away unripe fruits; Duna has announced how this will seriously affect the building of the Pyramid. Many believe that the new tax was a desperate action by the Pyramid Committee to get funds for their luxury and the Pyramid.

Near the fenced Daula orchard at the outskirts of Barduvai she met some milkmaids who were returning to their encampments. They gave her some mangoes after they greeted her wondering where she was going. She thought of following them to their encampments but she failed to approach them out of shyness.

Towards the evening a heavy rainstorm formed in the east. The sun had set by then. A misty wind was blowing across. Kumbo was at lost at what to do. It was getting dark and yet she hasn't even decided if she was in the right route to Jara, for all she knew was that Jara was east of Barduvai. There were fewer farms around her then and she thought she must have been far from Barduvai. She wanted Barduvai and Lamiri to be a far recess in her mind. When it was dark, she could hardly see where she was going, until the lighting from the pregnant sky showed her the way.

After sometimes the wind grew stronger and the first drops of rain stared to fall. Kumbo stopped walking. She realised she was standing on a farmland, because there were hardly shrubs and bushes around her. In between two flashes of lighting she saw a farm hut on her right. She rushed to the hut holding her only bundle of clothes under her right armpit and the ripe mangoes in the left. The rain started to pound as if it was waiting for her to find a sanctuary.

She found the hut was leaking except at the farthermost end. There she sat facing the entrance. The rain was heavy typical of the beginning of rainy seasons in Barduvai. In between flashes she saw the ground was waterlogged outside, she heaved a sigh and started to suck one of the mangoes. She soon realised the hut was full of mosquitoes which started to swim all over her body. She went ahead eating her mango nevertheless using her left hand to whisk of the flies. Suddenly a black figure barricaded the door of the hut. Kumbo's heart skipped a beat.

The dark figure rushed in and seemingly unsure of himself, squatted in the middle of the hut. From his attire, Kumbo realised he was a Jannati guerrilla. He was oblivious of her presence and he kept hissing and swearing. Kumbo's blood froze. The rain outside continued drumming hard and never seemed like ceasing. She didn't dare whisk the mosquitoes as before. Soon they started to bite the martyr too. His curses increased and he kept slapping his body and swearing.

The rain poured down like a basket of water and the mosquitoes bit Kumbo all over but she didn't dare scratch her body least the martyr realise she was in the hut.

Then something compounded the situation. A solitary hyena on its way to scavenge for food in Barduvai rushed into the hut to shelter from the rain. Typical of the `forest boxer' it was contented to push its rear inside the hut and exposed its head to the rain. The hyena therefore barricaded the door panting noisily. It must have arrived from a far. It was oblivious of the presence of Kumbo and the Jannati martyr in the hut. The martyr froze in his position neither slapping off mosquitoes as before nor cursing. Kumbo watched all these from the rear of the hut. The rain continued to pour, all the creatures in the hut preoccupied with their thoughts. The hyena oblivious of the presence of the two, the martyr aware of the hyena's but oblivious of Kumbo's who cringed at the rear end of the hut, her chest burning from irregular breath.

After what seemed like ages, the rain stooped and the

sky cleared quickly. Soon the new moon was shining brightly outside the hut. Kumbo caught glimpses of the farm outside; water was running along old corn ridges. She waited for the hyena and the martyr to leave the hut so that she can quickly find her way to Jara. Kumbo after seeing the Jannati guerilla reasoned that their group may not be far from the hut, or perhaps they could be far. She thought of changing her mind and returning to Barduvai, but when she recalled that she would have nowhere to go but Lamiri's house she decided to proceed against any consequence. The moonlight gave her some hope and she silently prayed that she meets a nomadic encampment where she can spend the night before tomorrow.

But to her despair neither the guerrilla nor the hyena made any sign of moving out of the hut. The hyena barricaded the door as if it was going to spend the night there or was not certain which direction to go. The guerrilla was more visible then, his dangling sword and Jannati toga made him look like a crouched vampire.

The mosquitoes resumed their flight after the rain. Apart from their drone nothing else could be herd in the hut. The hyena made no move to depart instead it started to flap its ears laughing. As Kumbo got more and more afraid of the situation, an idea occurred to her. She realised she was the only one who was aware of all that were present in the hut because both the hyena and the guerrilla were oblivious of her presence. Stretching her hand therefore, she carefully scratched the neck of the stupefied martyr. It was like lightning. The guerrilla let out a thunderous yell and involuntarily dived on the hyena gripping its rear firmly. The beastly howl the hyena gave, coupled with the screams let out by the martyr nearly made Kumbo to faint. The hyena and the martyr disappeared into the bush as if they were a piece of a dream.

Kumbo heaved a sigh and waited for some minutes before she ventured out of the hut, her heart beating wildly and her throat dry. Outside the hut she realised she forgot her bundle of clothes but she was afraid to go back into the hut. The full moon shone brightly reflecting on run-off water and distant ponds. Kumbo turned to the east and started to run. It was easy for her to find the footpath again. Her heart was pounding wildly. She was afraid the martyr was hiding somewhere so she started to run again amidst the chirping of crickets and croaking toads. When she got tired of running, she started to walk. The crickets and toads were less noisy then, but Kumbo was astounded she didn't yet come across an encampment of the nomads. She hastens her pace and began to pray silently in her mind.

She must have walked for a long time; the trees and the shrubs were more clustered hiding the bright shining moon. She hadn't met a creature on the way nor had she stumbled on any nomadic settlement. The footpath wound round thick bushes and trees, and she had to make her way by fencing of twigs that threatened to scratch her face. Then from a distance she saw a fire and hope returned to her heart, she thought at last she had come across the encampment of some nomads.

Alas she came across four Jannati Guerrillas roasting a lamp. They gave a start upon seeing her and one of them exclaimed he thought it was Sumanguru coming back from Barduvai. 'Where are you from?' the one who appeared like their leader asked her. She imagined he was Jonkal Awembi their leader whom much was talked about in Barduvai. The amulets he wore over his toga made him look like a voodoo priest.

'I'm travelling with my uncle'

'Where is he?' They asked in apprehension

'One of the donkeys got stubborn', she lied to them, 'he is behind, but he will come very soon'

Jonkal Awembi ordered them to quickly clear the fire, 'Another hypocrite is coming' he said, urging the other Guerrillas to hurry and hide behind the bush, 'Go ahead. Go ahead' he whispered to Kumbo behind a thick shrub.

She walked quickly restraining herself from running. Her legs were numbed by fear but she continued walking glad that her lie had fooled them. After walking for a distance, she glanced back over her shoulder, satisfied the Guerrillas could not see her; she started the race of her life. She knew the Guerrillas after waiting for sometimes would know she lied to them and would definitively come after her and what they would do to her was unimaginable. Soon she came across a cleared land with fewer trees, it must have been a farmland she thought. She stopped running realising it was not the best solution to her predicament. There was no doubt the Guerrillas could run faster than her and in no time catch up with her. She surveyed the fallen trees in the farm and noticed a huge tree trunk lying at the north of the farm. She walked to the trunk and found out it was hallow. She made to go into the trunk headfirst but changed her mind and went in legs first.

Her head was hardly inside the trunk when she heard some heavy footsteps approaching. There was a pause and the voice of men shouting. It sounded they were approaching the trunk and were arguing about something. She caught her breath, praying hard. Despite her state she found her pains unbearable. After a while she felt she was beaten by termites all over her body. The voice of the Guerrillas grew louder and she nearly fainted in the tree trunk. She wanted to turn and scratch her body but the trunk allowed her only few inches of space.

`Which way has she gone?'

'If we catch this woman today!'

`She fooled us didn't she?'

The Guerrillas reached the trunk. Kumbo heard them panting and cursing and she thought some of them actually sat on the trunk, `She must be a good runner', she heard Jonkal Awembi saying. `Her uncle she said, her uncle and we all agreed instead of keeping her hostage, ho!' he exclaimed tapping the trunk with his sheathed sword. Each tap sounded like a thunderclap in the ears of Kumbo. After swearing for sometimes the Guerrillas left the trunk and she heard them chattering away. Kumbo heaved a sigh of relieve, but all her bodily pains returned and she thought miserably what was the best thing to do.

She thought of spending the night in the tree trunk but the termites were determined to drive her away. Their bites had swollen her body all over. Without second thoughts she crawled out of the tree trunk and squatted aside the trunk scratching her body all over. She wished she had a hundred hands.

The moon was shining outside, but fewer crickets were chirping. Dogs were howling from a distance, an indication that a settlement was close by. At her right side her attention fell on a rocky outgrowth. She walked to the rocky surface and fall to sleep out of exhaustion and pains.

Kumbo woke up when a crow cawed close by. It was a bright morning, the sunrays warm and refreshing. She stood up and walked down the footpath that went behind the rock. Farmlands and rising smoke from a distance greeted her sight. That must be Jara she thought.

She followed the footpath that went through newly cleared farms wondering how many of the farms would yield any produce with the Jannati Guerrillas roaming around the wood. Shortly Jara came into clear view. The sight of the old cotton silk tree was like lightning. She didn't know how to feel, sadness or happiness. Their house was in shambles, a far cry from what it used to be. Part of the collapsed walls was replaced by a woven grass screen, which was pierced in various spots by erratic goats.

It was clear the previous night rain was also heavy in Jara. There were water paddles all over. Kumbo walked inside the house announcing her presence. But no one replied. Far away among the shambles she saw a solitary hut standing erect, all the others had caved in. With trepidation she walked toward the hut. A thin cloud of smoke was coming out of the room. She called out for her mother. An old woman coughed painfully inside the hut, she pushed the cornstalk door and walked into the room. It was too dark for her to see properly inside the room.

When her eyes adjusted to the darkness of the room, she saw an old shrivelled blind woman curled up on a straw bed behind a dying fire. The room was full of irritating smoke and was filled with broken pots and woven baskets that had turned completely black due to smoke.

'Who may it be' asked a weak, sick voice.

'It is I mother'

'Who?'

Kumbo sat down looking at the old shrivel woman who was supposed to be her mother. Three pieces of burnt sweet potatoes were lying close to the hearth. One of them was bitten on one side, an indication that someone wanted to eat the piece but changed his mind.

Kumbo waited for her mother to respond to her presence but the old woman kept silent, `Mother, mother' she called out loudly this time.

`Umm' her mother grunted

`It is me Kumbo remember me?'

`Kumbo', the old woman muttered, it was neither a question nor recognition. Then she sighed heavily. Kumbo started to shed tears and felt like screaming.

`Help me roast one of the potatoes, I haven't eaten since yesterday' said her mother.

Kumbo stirred the charcoal and pushed one of the potatoes in. With tears flowing from her eyes she looked at her mother's eyeballs which although blind, darted like trapped swallows that wanted to escape from a cage. After some moments her mother sighed heavily again, `Get me some water to drink', she mumbled

Kumbo leaned on one of the pots close to the door and to her shock found it empty. A large Agama lizard was scurrying inside the pot. In terror she exclaimed, `the pot is empty!' She stood up picking a clay jar and rushed out of the hut. She wondered how many days her mother went without water. Outside she couldn't decide which way to go in search of water. She headed west and along the lane, she found an abandoned compound. Two sheep were grazing close to an old well, the side of which was covered by some old logs. There was nothing she could use to fetch the water. She thought of her mother hungry and thirsty, so she untied her wrapper, wrapped it through the semi-circular handles of the jar and threw it into the well. The jar landed with a plop in the water. Kumbo pulled the filled jar quickly rushing back to her mother's hut; afraid the last piece of potato will burn in the charcoal. "Oh my mother, oh my mother", she kept mumbling and shedding tears as she rushed to her mother's hut with the jar filled with water.

47

Lamiri stood by the window overlooking the veiled rock. For a long period, the rock anagram was not revealed to the public. A long table carrying various exotic dishes and fruits stretched along the whole breath of the parlour at the Temple of Light. Surrounded by many invited dignitaries, Lamiri was smiling beside Babbadajaka as people walked up to them bowing down in respect.

When the parlour was full of people, Habarana Choodal who just finished eating a piece of watermelon thundered 'Ahoy ahoy! Lamiri Son of the Venerable Sheik, Decipher of the anagram, master of the pyramid'. Lamiri walked to the middle of the parlour and started to speak; "We are aware of the hardships citizens are facing, but once the pyramid project is completed, life will change in this city state. Remember undoing years of damaged done by the Hime to our psyche is not easy. It takes time, it takes time! The enemies of Barduvai speak only of the difficulties facing Barduvai. These difficulties are temporary compared with the imminent disaster we face. Building the pyramid is the single most important project we can carry out presently...'

Throughout his speech, nothing was mentioned about the Jannati Guerrillas despite the devastation they wreck on Barduvai and surrounding settlements. As Lamiri, Babbadajaka and Duna Kahuna stand aside drinking from gourds of Daulalier, many youths mill around them seeking for favours.

Most people have abandoned their dedication to the pyramid building. A cynical atmosphere was created where people were considered according to their closeness to the Pyramid Committee Members, regardless of productivity and dedication. More chariots as well were imported into Barduvai. Daily, the chariots carrying members of the Pyramid Committee sped along the completed causeway between the palace and the Temple of Light, raising dust in the process.

The completed market pavilion was used for colourful ceremonies, ranging from speeches, to turbannings. People attended such ceremonies out of idleness and boredom. *The turbanning of Habarana as the voice of thunder, the turbanning of Seybou Albasa as the Merchant of Tibesti,* etc. Such occasions draw people from far and near. But after such occasions nothing changed in Barduvai. The state grocery under the management of

Nabal became the only busy part of the city-state. Young people can always be seen milling around seeking for opportunities to be given contracts to cart fruits from the Daula Orchard to the Central Store. Some privileged youth cart Daulalier gourds from Lamiri's Clinic to the store. Large sums of money were paid for such exercises. Now and then new colourful chariots with well-fed horses passed by the bewildered citizens who close their nostrils against the dust the chariots raised.

Citizens who were able to get favours from Babbadajaka and Duna Kahuna were given token signs to bring to Nabal who in turn award such contracts. Barduvai was no longer the commercial centre it used to be. Less people come to the market for fear of their lives and property. As the Daula Orchard was completely taken over by the Palace, few people can afford fresh fruits or buy a gourd of the Daulalier juice for their children.

Few people talked about the imminent disaster anymore. Probably nobody cared as well, for citizens wearing a gloomy outlook pursued the little futile activities left for them to carry out. No visitor could fail to notice that there were only few centres of activities in Barduvai - The Askia's Palace, The Temple of Light, and the State Grocery in the central market and the Pyramid Annex. These were places you find people milling around.

Beautiful chariots and carts were by then imported into Barduvai in greater numbers. Some of the chariots were rumoured to have been ridden by only kings and

the wealthy in Bazahu. The four city gates of the Pyramid were completed. Citizens who had usually nothing to do by the day flocked to the erected gates to marvel at the new structures. On them were inscribed
'To be commissioned by Askia Burtune, The Torso of an Elephant'

Habarana Choodal had by then added amazing innovations to his trade. Instead of carrying a drum, Mambo, his tireless assistant, quite often carried a charcoal drawing of a smiling Askia drawn by Apiru on a wooden slate. Carrying either a drawing or a carving, Mambo followed Habarana on his *Jigul – Jagul* assignments.

> *"Everything will be okay*
> **With Askia Burtune**
> *Support the Pyramid Project*
> *Support Prosperity in Barduvai"*

Habarana bellowed through his Zebu horn while Mambo holding the reins of Habarana's horse by the left waved the charcoal picture of the Askia to the citizens with the right.

The novelty of Habarana's *Jigul – Jagul* was lost on citizens, as they begin to see him as nothing but a surrogate of the palace. Some people actually plug their ears with their fingers whenever they hear his zebu horn blaring either the palace tune or the pyramid tune.

The most difficult part of the Pyramid project, the digging of the tunnels was to start. All the four gates were to be linked by a circular tunnel, decked by thousands of chambers to act as sanctuaries on the day of disaster. Some desperate citizens lamented that disaster has already fallen with the rampant beriberi and the Jannati attacks. The Jannati guerrillas have grown in size as armies of youth jobless, helpless and poor join the group. The group not only waylay travellers, they were bold enough to venture into the city anytime of the day to cause havoc. In the night especially, they descend into the city like swamps of grasshoppers carting away goods and harming citizens. Their tactics were strange, especially their molestation of women and children. This, everybody had believe was alien to the values of Hubaluba people. "Blame it on Atamin Stores!" Elders cried out, all decadence, all evil behaviours spring from these dens of Kudulantic evil. Who but a wretched soul will open his ears listening to the confessions of King Atamin or watch a re-enactment of it by misguided boys and girls?

"Disaster has arrived!" Elders say shaking their heads ruefully, "There can't be any other!"

48

For the past seventeen days, Tugga had followed the mysterious warrior from Gudur. He obeyed whatever Damolishi told him to do and listened attentively to his strange teachings. Tugga began to feel differently. He was feeling exhausted but fresh. His awareness had changed as if his senses were expanded. It was as if an image on a mirror, which was lacking focus before, gradually gained focus. Damolishi had continuously emphasised sobriety and impeccability as the target of learning. For the first time he had a convincing explaining of what education was.

'It is like the food and the air we breathe, each is suppose to affect our darkun', Damolishi had emphasised. During the training, after a day's activity, the warrior led him back to the cliff facing the setting sun or if it is a night activity, they sat facing the rising sun in the morning as he taught Tugga the Waratake. After intensive activities on the seventeenth day, Damolishi had motioned for them to sit under the shade of a tree. Just when Tugga was beginning to relax, the warrior commanded;

'Build a hut for us, we shall rest here tonight'

'I don't know how to build a hut!' Tugga complained before collecting himself.

Damolishi smiled as Tugga stood up not knowing exactly what to do, but having a vague visual idea of how a nomadic kraal looked like. He didn't even have the tools he thought miserably. Was the warrior trying to test him in something he pondered, but as he learned in the past days, plunging himself into activities is the solution. First he climbed a tree and broke a suitable branch using his hammer. He then sharpened it into a suitable wooden digger using the rough suffice of a rock.

It was at dusk that he completed the construction of the hut feeling satisfied for doing so for the first time in his life. But throughout the construction, Damolishi didn't show any kind of expression on his face.

When Tugga sat beside sighing and looking at the fruit of his labour, Damolishi started; 'knowing how to do something perfectly from the beginning to the end is a boon to the warrior, because it frees him to concentrate on his inner world'

They retired inside the hut and Tugga slept off until the warrior awaked him before dawn. He followed the warrior until they reached a rocky kopje facing the rising sun.

Damolishi called him aside, `after independence the warrior must seek for a loop. Never believe the creation of the universe is an accident or meaningless, this is intoxication with folly. Men are the agents of Geno' spark. This spark is the essence of Geno and each man has a specific gap to fill', he saw that Tugga was not understanding him fully.

`Men are agents of Geno's spark. Each man has a specific gab to fill to complete Geno's spark. In the process he is accepted into Geno's unfolding loops. Those who can't find their loops are left out. It is the greatest rejection. Don't be afraid to spend your whole life seeking for that loop. If you spend only a day in your life and complete this loop then you are lucky

Any generation that finds its loop and fulfils it has been a successful generation. Copying this, copying that is folly. To copy the folly of other people is the greatest folly. Because you will be in perpetual disarray. If in Barduvai we can discern our loop then we would be lucky.

Many movements, ideas and religions fail at this stage, so that generation of men spend years in vain. The loop is a fine thread surrounded on both sides by follies. So many old men spend their life on earth and assume they have gathered experience and wisdom but it is all vain because they were follies. The reason why folly is deceptive is because it is sweet and obsessing. Follies are exciting and fulfilling, because darkun comes in to it

It is difficult to discern ones loop because what is ordinarily displayed as occupations are like wares displayed from a creation of folly. I can't tell you how to find your loop. It is beyond my power to tell you. I don't know if I have found mine. It may be in the pass days I have been teaching, could be my loop. I don't know. The secret is to keep it in the mind

Tugga sighed pondering if Hajji Buruji departed Barduvai because he had completed his loop.

'It is not our duty to make guesses.' Damolishi interrupted Tugga thought as if he was reading his mind,

'Know that many people as well find their loops but their darkun remains a clog. This is the worst clog in the realisation of Geno's spark.

49

The parlour of the Temple of Light was redecorated. A thick wall was erected to shield the anagram from view. Most people have already forgotten how the anagram looked like. It was almost like closing a chapter of undeciphered writing in a book.

If people use to gather pondering at the mysteries of the anagram, now it was all state festivities and fanfares. Two days hardly passed without an occasion being held at the Temple of Light. Lamiri spent most of his evenings there meeting members of the Pyramid Committee and some privileged traders.

On that fateful day, Babbadajaka arrived to discuss the award of contracts for digging the Pyramid tunnels. He had with him some names he wanted favoured.

"We have to be cautious with the present mood in the society, we have to be cautious".

Babbadajaka smiled, 'People are less concerned with what we do now. Hime is gone! Have you notice they don't care!"

"If we give this contract to people who know next to nothing about building, people will talk mayor, they will talk"

"The people of Seybou are our strong supporters"

"They are traders not builders, we are talking about people with the knowledge of building", Lamiri grimaced wondering the extend Babbadajaka had taken the Rando Cartoza principle. Yet he was his closest supporter, he knew that.

Habarana entered the parlour beaming with smiles,

"Habarana, you ought to stop making references to the Jannati in your announcements, you are making them look more important than they are!"

Habarana sat down, knowing well that Lamiri was in a sour mood,

"Sir we go around the city, people insult me for not announcing the attacks on their property and lives", Habarana grunted hoping Babbadajaka will start a different topic to take away Lamiri's attention from him so that he can walk to the dining table.

"Apiru has finished making another figure of you sir, you need to see that one!" Habarana tried to enliven the atmosphere.

"Apiru, this Apiru is getting wonderful in drawings and carvings", Babbadajaka added, "And he started by imitating those of Warum Kudulix, you know"

"Ahab," grunted Lamiri, What expertise? This one who cannot even draw an Askia smiling. Look at the carvings he nailed at the gates, these are not pictures of our Askia. They look like old men weeping, Ahab".

Habarana knew there was no end to Lamiri's mood tonight, he stood up heading to the dining table, "This dinner is not prepared for you!" Lamiri shouted.

"Yes sir", answered Habarana as he turned heading to the exit, "Good night sir, God bless the Mayor".

Babbadajaka kept quiet for a while wondering what to do next. He had promised Seybou that he was going to assist his cousin get one of the Tunnel contract, but now wondered if it was wise bringing up the topic again even though he knew Seybou will be waiting for him all night in his house for a feedback.

While he was thinking of what to do, Jabbi walked into the parlour. She was beautifully dressed, her copper bangles making some enticing noise. She looked as charming as before, although she had grown plumy.

"There!" thought Babbadajaka as he watched the face of Lamiri lit up, his neck veins bulging, "It is time to go" he thought to himself. "Son of knowledge good night, blessing of the Lord" he said not bothering whether Lamiri replied or not as he headed to the door.

"You people, do you know what Jannati are doing!" Jabbi said as she sat down, her perfume pervading the whole parlour, "last week they attacked our cattle"

"How much was the lost?" Lamiri asked petulantly.

"How will I know, do I know the cost of cattle"

"Jabbi come close let me tell you … just tell Ardo to abandon cattle rearing, this is not the age of rearing. Tell him I will give him a contract to build one of the tunnels, then he can come into the city to settle" Lamiri walked to sit close to her.

"Building! Ardo! Go and tell him yourself", Jabbi stood up abruptly.

"My proposal Jabbi"

"I am telling you about Jannati, they are coming inside the city!"

"Can they pass beyond the market square and the orchard?"

There was a sudden noise and commotion outside the Temple, Babbadajaka and Habarana rushed into the parlour looking horrified and breathing heavily.

"We are trapped sir!" shouted Habarana bolting the doors.

"They are all over the city son of knowledge! We could not pass through the market!"

"Where is Barmaki?" Lamiri asked visibly frightened as he stands up. Jabbi crouched into her seat muttering something like "You people! You people!"

The distant shouts and wails can be heard distinctly now as dogs howled from a distant.

"We are trapped son of knowledge!" Babbadajaka said in a shaky voice.

"How do we get to the Pyramid Annex, I know it is fortified… We are trapped!"

All four stood up horrified, as the pandemonium outside grew louder. Jabbi sobbing on her seat compounded the atmosphere as wailings and sparks that sounded like fire outbreak increased outside the Temple.

50

From a far, Tugga saw spiralling smoke and a white mass of people fleeing Barduvai. Without being told, he knew it was an attack on the city by the Jannati. By the time he reached the market square, he had passed through an unbelievable carnage. The Temple of Light and the Market Pavilion were smouldering.

There were women sitting aside wailing, and men persistently howling about their lost goods and burnt houses. Their anxiety and desire to migrate reminded him of the day he wanted to leave Barduvai but was stopped by Damolishi. There was not a single guard or member of the Pyramid Committee around.

'Where are people?' Tugga asked a woman sitting beside a basket.

'Some have ran to the Annex. There it is guarded'

A trader was loading his donkey and shouting at his family. His wife rode one of the donkeys and he beat the donkey so strongly that the beast withdrew its tail before starting to move followed by his entire family. Tugga asked him where he was going

'I'm going to Poli what is remaining here now', he replied rudely without turning his face.

Tugga wanted to started running to his house to find out about Tataraktu but he felt like restraining people from migrating, 'stay behind, let's us reassemble'.

'But we have no food, no clothing and our houses are

destroyed', they kept yelling.

`*What do we want*?' asked Tugga earnestly, `you say your houses, your Comerias, your food. What is yours there? Can't you stay behind? Can't you stay behind?' He pleaded

It was then that Paha appeared from one of the market stalls holding a slate. He walked to the Baobab tree pinning a poem. Some curious citizens started to walk to the tree in astonishment

A strange feeling pervaded the mind of Tugga. What was his loop? He asked himself as he walked towards the group of people reading what Paha the dumb had pinned. They were asking him with dumbfounded expressions if it was he all along who was writing the baobab tree poems. He kept silent. Tugga read the poem, which was written in charcoal:

DIVINE MARIONETTES
In a treacherous day of whimpering guerrillas
Only the blank eyes of the slaughtered stared
These speechless effigies of a wanton carnage
These heedless throng of a Cometic fright
The theatre of doom has no day or night
Until the anagram is deciphered to rest
In the market square gathered the remnants
Wailing their losses and shedding tears

Oh you marionettes of the Kudulantic plot
Can't you see the blade I ask?

Tugga bent down and found a piece of charcoal, which he used in adding a line to the pasted poem, *Can't you find your loop I ask?* Paha read the line he added and turned smiling and nodding to him. When he was writing the poem he thought of removing his mask, but he realised then it was Gaulojo that was going to pin the poem not Paha, so he decided to remain Paha the dumb grocer. Who said he wanted to be Gaulojo in Barduvai again anyway.

www.ingramcontent.com/pod-product-compliance
Lightning Source LLC
Chambersburg PA
CBHW070505160726
48003CB00004B/1431